Homecoming

Michael Colin Macpherson

"Michael Macpherson, you've done it again...you've made us cry together in remembering why we came to this planet. A simple but complex, magnificent, modern day fairy tale that expresses all the truths of the 90's."
Earle and Nancie Belle
Publishers of Planetary Connections

"I continue to be in awe of Michael's books. His writings keep me in constant amazement as I realize that his "fiction" is so uncannily close to my "reality". The intricate tapestry of his story propels me on. I have become intimately involved with the characters and their situations."
Sandy Gostel Perkins
Book Reviewer
Awareness Magazine

"With Earth changes and social trauma becoming a daily occurrence, *Homecoming* is a hopeful oasis in a desert of turmoil."
Deborah Wright
Native Communications
Vashon, WA

"I had the feeling I was reading some kind of blueprint; a plan on how to proceed from this point on."
Shalanah/S. Konivov
Editor, Connecting Link

Books by
Michael Colin Macpherson

Remembering
Homecoming

Homecoming

Michael Colin Macpherson

Green Duck Press
Mount Shasta, California

Homecoming

© Common Law Copyright
1996 Michael Colin Macpherson

All Rights Reserved, Without Prejudice,
U.C.C. 1-207, U.C.C. 1-103.6

This is a work of fiction. Characters, corporations and government agencies in this novel are either the product of the author's imagination or, if real, used fictitiously without any intent to describe their actual conduct.

Green Duck Press
Post Office Box 651
Mount Shasta, California 96067

Cover Art, "The Valley," Kay Ekwall, Mount Shasta, CA.

ISBN No. 0-9642136-1-3

Library of Congress Catalog Card Number: 96-75496

Printed in the United States of America

Acknowledgments

My thanks to all the people who read my manuscript and offered encouragement and advice: to Claudia Balassi and Pam Neronha. To Shalanah. To Earle and Nancie Belle. And to Sandy Gostel Perkins and Debbie Wright. My special thanks to Kay Ekwall for her beautiful painting that became the front cover of *Homecoming*; to Yola Kaskey and Mary Ann Uetrecht for their caring and meticulous proofreading. And to Spirit...always.

Prologue

October 1998: One year later:

The intervening year has been difficult for everyone. Despite the huge sums of money pumped into the economy by the Corporation, little has changed—millions are still out of work and thousands of businesses remain closed. The money has gone mostly for the reorganization of the financial institutions—there are now only three huge banks in the country—and for "improvements" in the debit card system. The Corporation has not followed through on its other promises to "mend" the economy. The hungry and the homeless and the unemployed wonder why.

The group of people who met in Alana's living room a few months after the great California earthquake still gather to give each other support, to share news and information, and to discuss plans for their community. Recently, they have talked about finding other New Age communities to correspond with, or perhaps to visit.

Mother Earth continues her transformation. The weather is now so unpredictable that no one is surprised when the South freezes in near zero temperatures while the North swelters in tropic-like humidity. Added to this, the Ring of Fire has come alive. Earthquakes of magnitude 7 are now a common occurrence everywhere around the Pacific rim. Four months after the mighty California quake, Japan's Northern island of Hokkaido was leveled by a tremor measuring 10 on the Richter scale. The Philippines, Australia, and Mexico have also been hard hit.

More than 98 percent of the people have taken the debit card. No one in the group has accepted one, however.

The Corporation continues to occupy Mount Shasta and many other cities and towns across the country; they have no plans to remove their administrators or their troops.

Alana's publishing company did not rehire her. She does freelance writing now. Jeff works part-time at the local hardware store and does consulting for some of the small businesses in the area.

There is great unrest in the country and much talk of revolution. People are beginning to choose sides, and many believe a showdown with the government is inevitable. Incidents of violence against the government and against the Corporation increase daily.

The country sits on top of a volcano.

Chapter One

October 1998:

Alana picked up the small hand mirror and glanced at herself. "Susan Langley, Susan Langley," she repeated softly. "Is this who I am?" She put the mirror down. "No, I am Alana."

The name change still didn't feel quite right, though. She sighed, leaned back in her chair, and closed her eyes.

Why *had* she changed her name? For forty-seven years she had been Susan Langley. Why was she now Alana?

The change had happened so suddenly, or so it seemed. A few short months ago, right after the huge Los Angeles earthquake, a group of people had come into her life. No, that wasn't quite correct, they hadn't simply *come* into her life—Spirit had brought them. Now they were her family, and she knew someday they would live together as a community...for that was their *intention*. Not just any community, however; *this* community would be an example of true brotherhood and true sisterhood, a coming together of people in openness and honesty and love. Something seldom seen on Earth.

During the first joyful gathering of this group of friends, Susan had known she was also Alana.

Alana was another aspect of Susan, an aspect who had lived many thousands of years ago in Lemuria. They were part of the same soul group, so it was fairly easy for Susan to invite Alana into her body to see through her eyes and share her life. They were like sisters, although truly the bond was deeper.

Why had Susan invited Alana into her life? Because it was time for this community to come into manifestation, and Alana was the carrier and the nurturer of this dream. For thousands of years she had carried the dream carefully in her heart, as one might carry a precious ember from one location to another, through the cold night, to the new place called home. Once Susan felt the power of this dream, once she experienced its incredible love, and once she knew it was her destiny to help birth this dream, *this dream whose time was now*, she had welcomed her soul-sister with an open heart.

Although unsettling at times, she could cope with the name change; it was the *other* changes that made her feel confused and wobbly.

When *did* everything start getting turned upside down, anyway? After the earthquake? No...earlier, back in their Mill Valley home on the morning when she and her husband Jeff first noticed the unusually warm weather. Or maybe even before that, maybe long, long ago in other lifetimes events had been set into motion that were only now revealing themselves. She shook her head. She wasn't sure about the other lifetimes part. Best to stick with the facts. So, what *were* the facts.

She and Jeff had led a happy, comfortable life in Mill Valley. She was an illustrator of children's books, and Jeff was the proud, happy owner of a hardware store. Then, for no apparent reason, she'd begun feeling restless and vaguely dissatisfied, as if something inside her was urging her to see beyond her comfortable, middle-class life and into another reality.

Well, she had, she had indeed.

Her transformational journey had begun on that morning, that very *warm* morning, back in Mill Valley. She remembered waking from a dream, not wanting to let it go, wanting to understand what it was telling her. In her dream, she was floating down a river. She heard her mother and father and sister calling to her from a cliff high above. Although she couldn't make out what they were yelling, she knew they were warning her of some impending danger. Taking the dream seriously, she had examined her life and had made some changes: Reviewing her pictures of reality, she found many that were limiting her; these she began changing. Also, she listened more carefully to the voice of her inner wisdom; and, although she didn't exactly understand what it meant, she at least admitted the possibility that she was a multidimensional being who existed simultaneously in other dimensions.

She'd come a long way in the months since her dream, and she silently thanked herself for doing the work that had brought her to this place in her life.

She opened her eyes. Her golden retriever Sam was staring at her expectantly, his bushy tail thumping the floor. "You want to go for a walk, do you?" she asked, knowing he did. Sam's huge, liquid brown eyes signaled yes. "In a minute," she said.

The bright, sunshiny October day beckoned to her; she was eager to revisit the trail she and Jeff had discovered last week. She smiled as she remembered the tiny brook that wound along the trail, keeping it company. She shook her head. First things first. She drifted back inside, reviewing the events of the past few months.

In February of 1997, the abnormally hot, stifling weather had begun suffocating the state. She and Jeff and their Mill Valley friends Glenn and Vicki had braved the searing, summer-like heat of the Sacramento Valley to visit the tiny mountain community of Mount Shasta. There she had met the Mountain, the Mountain that sang to her and filled her heart with joy. Later, Spirit introduced her to the elf-like Evelyn, owner of SHAMBHALLA, Mount Shasta's metaphysical bookstore. And when Evelyn invited them to a channeling given by Veda, she'd met Saint Germain. Remembering that wondrous meeting, her eyes filled with tears, for she knew the meeting was actually a reunion—*a reunion of old friends.*

As quickly as it had begun, the heat had stopped and the rain had started, a warm tropical rain that beat down on the Earth day after day, saturating the ground with water, causing mud slides and floods, permanently scarring the once beautiful state of California.

But none of this, terrible as it was, would have forced her to uproot her comfortable Mill Valley life and move to Mount Shasta. No, it was something else. It was the assassination of President Tipton, for on that rainy morning when Jeff had come into the bedroom to tell her that someone had shot the President, she had known that dark and sinister forces were at work in the world and that for some unknown reason she needed to be in Mount Shasta. Spirit wanted her there. It was her right place and it was *time*.

Jeff had not been as convinced. He held back, unhappy at having to move. But Spirit was speaking to him, too, and when he agreed to go with her, she'd breathed a sigh of relief, knowing that they were a *team*.

The soft chirruping of the phone pulled her out of her reverie.

"Hi, sweetie," Jeff said. "Whatcha up to?"

She laughed. "Oh, just reminiscing. I'll tell you about it later. Have any luck getting what we need?" Jeff and Glenn and Anna had traveled to Medford to get supplies for a greenhouse. With the economy sputtering and with some food shortages beginning to appear, growing a garden now seemed like a *very* good idea. But the frigid Mount Shasta winter required a greenhouse.

"That's why I called," Jeff replied. "They have lots of stuff for greenhouses. Some nice steel frames. Expensive though. And some plastic ones, like PVC pipe. What about the PVC, think it would hold up in the wind?"

Alana's intuition said they would need this greenhouse for quite some time. "Probably, but let's get the steel frames, they'll last longer," she replied.

"Okay. Anything else we need?"

"Nope. How's Anna doing?" Anna was one of the people who'd come into her life a few months ago. Anna was bothered by very painful rheumatism, a condition she

attributed to her years of sleeping outside on the cold ground while serving in the Peace Corps. Alana and the others were working on her, using group healing to see if they could alleviate her distress. She heard Jeff ask Anna something, heard Anna's muffled reply.
"She says to tell you she's feeling better," Jeff reported.
"Great."
"Gotta go. See you in three or four hours. I love you," Jeff said.
"And I love you. See you later." She was about to hang up when she remembered something. "Oh wait! You having any problems paying with our gold?"
"Nope, these guys up here are happy to take it."
"Hmm. I thought they might be. Okay, take care."
Many people in the country were now using gold or silver or barter to obtain what they needed. The reason was a story in itself and began with the huge, devastating earthquake that had nearly obliterated Southern California.

What had triggered this earthquake? Was it the tremendous amount of rain Mother Earth had soaked up? Probably, although Alana knew that other factors—or perhaps other *entities*—had contributed to the 11.4 quake, the mightiest in recorded human history. She vividly remembered sitting with Jeff in the Sunshine Cafe as the jolt traveled through the Earth from Southern California. Even before news of the disaster had reached Mount Shasta, she had known that a monster quake had occurred and that life in the United States would never be the same. She had been correct.

She looked out the kitchen window at the Mountain, almost bare of snow now, but still able to make her heart sing with happiness and joy. Spirit, how long will you let me stay in this beautiful place? she wondered. The thought of moving distressed her and she pushed it from her mind.

The quake and the subsequent Market collapse had triggered the worst depression in the history of the country, closing factories and throwing people out of work. Then, President Storr, who had taken over for the slain President Tipton, delivered the fateful announcement forever changing the course of the country: The government was broke! There were no funds to help ease the crisis in California; no funds to end the depression; no funds to help those who had lost their jobs. Nothing! Washington was paralyzed! From now on, he'd stated, the country's monetary policy was in the hands of a private group of world and domestic bankers—plus the Federal Reserve. In time, this group called itself the Corporation. She and others secretly believed—no, they *knew*—that this group had waited *decades* for the right moment to seize control of the country.

She preferred to call these individuals the Gray Men. It seemed a perfect name.

Like sharks smelling blood in the water, the Corporation moved swiftly. They recalled the currency and outlawed the use of gold and silver as a medium of exchange. Also forbidden were barter and trade. They issued the debit card, which was in reality a national credit card. Alana and others soon realized that the Corporation intended to use this card to control the country and then the world. And again, she'd been correct.

She and Jeff had refused the debit card, as had others in the group. For the past months, they had used their supply of gold and silver, or else they had traded or bartered for what they needed. The Corporation had declared these activities "illegal," but so far they hadn't arrested or even reprimanded anyone. She wondered how long the Corporation would wait before enforcing their own recently enacted laws.

She shook her head. Enough daydreaming, time for a walk. She called to Sam, "Come on sweetie, let's get out of here for awhile."

They ambled down Old Stage Road, walking in the shade of the tall pines, breathing in their fragrant aroma. She found the steep dirt trail leading to the creek. Careful to keep her footing, she scrambled down the incline, grabbing branches or bushes every now and then to keep from slipping. Reaching the bottom, she stood up, brushed herself, and almost immediately felt the coolness of the water. She loved water, loved its sound and feel and smell. She

Homecoming

found a comfortable, moss-covered rock, sat down, and listened to the tiny creek splashing and tumbling over the stones. Sam flopped down beside her, sighing, resigned to waiting, watching her patiently for any clues that she would change her mind and resume their walk.

She breathed deeply of the alder trees and of the moist earth and of the creek vegetation. She telepathed a greeting to the nature spirits she knew had gathered around her. Closing her eyes, she cleared her mind of all thoughts. The soft, musical gurglings of the creek filled her entire being, the sound becoming louder and louder and louder, like the crashing of the ocean waves!

Riding these waves, she traveled inward.

She had a vision: a road, no two roads, about to meet. A being traveled down each road; down one, a reptilian creature—a dragon or a giant lizard; down the other, a human being, whether man or woman she couldn't tell. The two roads became one, so they must walk along together or else...

But the roads had *always* been one. She was confused.

She asked for understanding.

Calling up her vision again, she saw the two beings coming closer and closer together, but no understanding of what this meant.

Opening her eyes, she came back into the now moment, hearing the creek, smelling the pine needles piled at her feet. She felt vaguely frustrated at not being able to comprehend her vision.

The creek widened into a small pool. She sat down on the bank and stared into the almost black water. She thought she saw a tiny silver fish dart shyly behind a rock.

Although she didn't exactly understand her vision, she knew it portended what was to come in the country: two energies—angry and restless—about to clash! And the coming together of these energies would send sparks shooting in every direction. The confrontation would start in the West, but would not stop there, and like a huge, out-of-control forest fire fanned by hundred-mile-an-hour winds, the unrest would engulf the entire nation.

Was there any way to understand what was coming? The media was useless—the skimpy news they doled out was cleaned up, sanitized, and managed. No problem, Alana had other sources. Many people in Mount Shasta had access to information from other parts of the country, and she learned much from listening to stories told over cups of coffee and hot chocolate at the Sunshine Cafe. Stories of farmers and ranchers and others who had "had it" with the government. Stories of people—often average citizens— who were slowly waking up to the lies being fed them.

She sat quietly, watching the spot where she last saw the tiny fish, hoping it would peek out from behind its hiding place.

Her thoughts drifted back to the early nineties, to the time when many Westerners had begun speaking out against the bureaucratic rudeness of government agencies such as the Bureau of Land Management. Some had gone past the talking stage and had taken action. Mostly, she had sympathized with the farmers and the ranchers, although in all honesty some of *their* motives and what *they* wanted to do with the land had also troubled her.

Many of the government critics—those who were troubled or "fed up"—had organized into militias. Alana was uncomfortable with the energy of some of these groups, especially the ones predicting an inevitable armed conflict with the government. Even more troubling were the ones who eagerly *anticipated* it, for she knew that with these pictures of reality the confrontation would surely come, and it was not her way—she was not a radical or a revolutionary.

This had not always been so, however. Raised in a religious household, with a pacifist minister father and an equally pacifist mother, she had done the almost expected thing, had renounced *their* way and had turned into their worst nightmare: a radical, free thinking, sexually unrepressed hippie.

She'd loved the sixties, loved the freedoms and the refreshing winds of change that blew away all the old forms, and she had embraced the counterculture wholeheartedly.

Homecoming

Leaving school at seventeen, after her senior year, she moved out of her family's comfortable home in Hammond, Indiana and, much to her parent's horror, joined a hippie commune. They were sure it was a passing phase—a summer adventure—and that she would be back by the fall to start her classes at Indiana State. She knew otherwise.

Growing her hair long, she threw away her shoes, her bras, and the rest of her underwear, along with most of the inhibitions so patiently instilled in her for seventeen years by her religious, conservative, God-fearing mother, to live with a longhaired aspiring novelist named Frank.

Thanksgiving came and went without even a phone call home. Sensing her seriousness, her parents sent out little feelers of reconciliation, even agreeing to come and visit them in their teepee. She'd read all their letters, most of them written by her mother, then she'd carefully folded them and put them in an empty tin of hot chocolate. She still had the tin stored someplace.

Two years later, on a cold, rainy April day in Berkeley, she was arrested for protesting the Vietnam war, proudly spending a night in jail singing songs of solidarity with her fellow inmates, most of who were in jail for other reasons.

She spent the next few days in Berkeley waiting for her arraignment, missing Frank, wishing the teepee had a phone. Returning to the commune, she discovered that Frank had left her for someone new. No problem she told herself, commune life was beginning to stifle her anyway.

Leaving the commune, she returned to the Bay Area. But protesting the war didn't interest her anymore. It seemed like a game and not a very interesting one at that. Besides, she needed to get on with her life. Turning her attention to art, she enrolled in a fine arts college near Oakland, California.

Then Jeff came along, the sweetest and most loving man she had ever known. They had waited six months before having sex. This had impressed her greatly—Frank was on top of her in less than an hour—and added to her growing conviction that *this* relationship was different. One crisp October day, sitting in a coffeehouse on Telegraph

Avenue drinking café mochas, Jeff had shyly proposed and she had immediately accepted. She liked being married, liked being an illustrator for a children's publisher, liked having enough money to buy a decent car. She knew the world wasn't "right," that the rich were getting richer and the poor, poorer and that nothing had really changed from the sixties. But for awhile she turned away from even thinking about the state of the world, except to get incensed every now and then at some obvious injustice reported in the media. Thinking about it now, she could see that she'd been confused about what to do and how to help. Since violence and confrontation were not her way, and since her parents' rather gentle acceptance didn't work for her either, what *was* her path? She didn't know, and so she focused on *herself*. Perhaps she had been one of the "me" generation...perhaps...except she'd always deeply cared about Mother Earth and about her fellow human beings.

The veils began dropping after Harmonic Convergence. She knew she was on the planet for a reason, that they *all* were. She dreamed interesting dreams, seeing herself in other lifetimes, once on another planet, a place of mile-high crags, huge, languorous lizards and twin red suns. But there was no one to talk to—Jeff scoffed at even the *mention* of the word reincarnation—and so she kept her thoughts to herself.

Her awakening came in the nineties.

In March of 1993, the killings in Waco shocked the world. And her. So many had died! Yes, she knew it was an agreement, that there were no victims, that events were unfolding for a purpose. Yet her heart grieved that it must be so.

Watching the events unfold in Waco, she was sure that the government, or *someone*—she didn't yet call them the Gray Men—had deliberately exterminated this group. Why? For many months this question troubled her, and then she understood: The burning of Waco was a warning to other groups like the Branch Dividians that it was *dangerous to come together as a community*, especially a community that attracted, or had the potential to attract, a

Homecoming

multitude of followers. Why? Because the government — the Gray Men's *secret* government — did not want independent bases of power, especially independent bases of *spiritual* power, to exist in the country.

Now she and her group of friends were contemplating forming their *own* community. Not exactly like Waco, but still...

At the time of the Waco tragedy, she'd felt alone in her views and not very sure of them. She remembered a scene in the living room of their Mill Valley home with their friends Glenn and Vicki. Glenn had been a New York City stockbroker until the pressures of "The Street" began to ruin his health and he and Vicki had moved to the relative calm of Mill Valley.

Watching the terrible burning of the Branch Dividian headquarters, she had felt a sickness in her stomach and in her soul.

"Huh, that's weird," Jeff had commented.

"What's weird?" she had asked.

"That they'd all commit suicide. Reminds me of Jonestown."

Feeling so upset she could hardly speak, she finally managed to say, "They didn't commit suicide. They were *killed*."

Her remark surprised Jeff. "Well, sure...but they provoked it, didn't they?"

She and Vicki had exchanged glances. Vicki had tears in her eyes.

Glenn scratched his balding head. "They gave them lots of chances to surrender. Pretty harsh treatment I guess, but what else could they have done?"

She was afraid to say what she knew, was afraid even to admit it to herself. She shook her head and wiped away her tears. She'd seen a picture of David Koresh in the papers. The media had accused him of child molestation and other disgusting things. She had "read" his picture to get the truth of the man, and what she got was that the paper and the other media accounts were lies. Exactly *why* they were lying she didn't yet understand.

"I feel like there's another side to it, that's all. I don't believe all the rumors," she'd said.

Like many news stories, this one, too, gradually faded away...at least in the media.

Many people, though, did *not* forget. They were convinced that, like the Kennedy assassination and other national tragedies, the truth of the Waco drama had been covered up.

Two years later to the *day*, the federal building in Oklahoma City blew up, killing one hundred sixty-eight apparently innocent people. The majority of Americans believed it to be the act of a single crazed man, or at most a small group. Others believed that the government had blown up their own building to justify tightening the laws in the country, especially laws allowing them to go after the militias and other similar groups. At the time, Alana wasn't sure *whom* she believed, although now she felt she knew the truth.

Tired of waiting, Sam got up, shook himself, gazed longingly down the road, then watched her to see if she'd gotten the message.

"We'll go in a minute," she said.

The Congressional hearings on Waco had pretty much exonerated the government from any wrongdoing. This was the last straw for many Americans and convinced them that the government had to go! But except for lots of angry, disgusted callers on the radio talk shows, a smattering of violence here and there, and more people joining the militias, nothing much happened—no angry crowds marching on Washington and no armed uprising. But the fire was started, and the first small flames of revolt were licking around the edges of the tinder-dry country.

Now, a scant three years later, the unrest threatened to explode into armed revolution. Alana understood why. Millions were out of work...permanently it seemed, for the Corporation's promise of jobs for everyone had not materialized. And, with almost no money being pumped into the infrastructure, the nation's cities were rapidly deteriorating into one huge, stinking slum. Also, the country's civil liber-

Homecoming 13

ties were being whittled away at an alarming rate...under the guise of national security. Had the United States become George Orwell's *1984*? Many thought so.

Alana had heard an interesting rumor that several Western states were thinking of seceding from the Union. She thought they might really do it. Several of the state legislatures and one or two governorships had recently fallen to militia-sponsored candidates. The government was fighting back, claiming voter fraud in many of these elections. Tempers were short, and many in the West saw secession as the only answer.

She got up, brushed the pine needles from her pants, said good-bye to the creek, and continued her walk. Sam joyfully leaped ahead, happy to be on the move again. She walked a mile, then headed back home.

She picked up the mail from their roadside mailbox.

Yes, something was going to happen; she could feel it gathering in a tight knot in the pit of her stomach. Another quake? A volcanic eruption on the Ring of Fire? Mount Shasta or Mount Hood? No, something else, *something involving everyone living in the United States*. Something big. *Big. Very* big.

She fed Sam, then began preparing for the group meeting. They hadn't met for awhile and she missed them — their faces, their sharing, and especially their support. Saint Germain had said they would need each other's support in these turbulent times. He was right.

Would Saint Germain have more to say about their community? She hoped so. But he'd been strangely quiet these past few weeks, almost as if he was leaving them alone on purpose to work out the details of their community for themselves. The rat.

Picking up one of the letters, she saw it was addressed to Susan Langley. "No, I am Alana," she said aloud. It felt right. Even Jeff, conservative Jeff, who liked things to stay the way they were and got upset if she moved even one piece of furniture, had welcomed her new name. "You know something, I can *see* you as Alana," he'd remarked. "It's a beautiful name and it suits you."

Too overwhelmed to say anything, she had simply hugged him.

"So, Alana—you who are also me—what would *you* make of all that is happening? Or is about to happen?" she asked. And she knew that if she was quiet inside, Alana, the Alana from so many thousands of years ago in Lemuria, would answer.

Chapter Two

Monday, October the 16th dawned crisp and clear and cold, with the smell of snow in the air. Graceful saucer shaped clouds—Mount Shasta's famous lenticular clouds—crowded around the Mountain's peak giving it the appearance of a landing port for spaceships.

Alana shivered as she got out of bed; she slipped on her robe and padded into the kitchen to join Jeff for breakfast.

"Hey, sleepyhead. Up late last night playing with your new toy?" Jeff teased.

Alana smiled, careful to hide it from Jeff. Pouring a cup of the strong Mocha Java coffee they had bought at the new coffee house in town, she promised herself—again—that she would seriously consider giving up coffee. One of these days.

The new toy Jeff referred to was her new computer. Two weeks ago, Spirit prompted her to begin chronicling the events of the past few months—to write a kind of diary. *And* to use a computer. The writing she welcomed, the idea of using a computer she did not. For years she'd told everyone who would listen that she would *never, never* own a computer. She loved her fifteen-year-old electronic typewriter—loved the sound of it as it clicked merrily along, loved the feel of the paper as she inserted it into the machine, loved watching her manuscript pile up on her desk. Computers were different: no ribbons to change, no piles of paper...nothing. Besides, computers were, well...there was something she didn't like about them, something she didn't *trust* about them. They had "dark energy." But Spirit's prompting was stronger than her resolve not to own one of the machines, and she bought one, hoping, as she drove away from the computer store, that she would not live to regret her decision. After less than a week she was...well, totally in love. Friendly and effortless to use, it made writing much easier. There it was, another example of what happened when you said the word *never*.

"It's just a tool you know. For writing," she replied, half joking and half serious, knowing that she was simply attempting to save some face.

Grinning, Jeff teased, "Uh-huh, *sure*. That's what Glenn said when he got his a couple of years ago. Now Vicki can't pry him away from it."

"You'll see. It's only for writing," she maintained stubbornly.

Jeff decided not to pursue the matter further. "I'm making scrambled eggs. Want some?"

"Mmm, sure."

As Jeff hummed happily at the stove, Alana got out her phone list. She needed to call Jerry and Karen to tell them about tomorrow's meeting.

The group of sixteen people had met many times in the past few months. Although their intention was to discuss plans for their emerging community, they usually ended up talking about other things: the news, scant as it was, from earthquake-ravaged Southern California; the reports of scattered social unrest; and especially the juicy "gossip" coming through the New Age grapevine. In her opinion, they would need to cease their fascination with the dramas of the outside world and focus on *themselves*, on their *inner* dramas. But for now she kept quiet, hoping, in time, they would see their path more clearly.

Alana counseled herself to be patient. Not the easiest thing for her to do, and therefore very necessary.

Her mouth watered as she smelled the onions and the mushrooms Jeff was slicing.

Homecoming 17

She dialed Jerry's number. He hadn't been at their last meeting and Alana wanted to remind him about tomorrow. Jerry was, well, a lovable, slightly overweight, fifty-year-old ex-hippie who, in his own words, was still a hippie at heart. Although he tended to be a "left brain" person, she loved listening to his interesting, innovative ideas. And she loved his sense of humor. The conversations and the energy in the group got very heavy at times, and it was wonderful—no, *essential*—to have people who could laugh and who could help everyone lighten up.

"Hi Jerry, this is Alana. How are you?"

"Great. Hey, you hear what happened in Montana?"

"No."

"There's a group up there called, uh, something like the Montana Freedom Fighters. Kind of hokey, but heck, what's in a name? Anyhow, they marched into this little Montana town and arrested the sheriff. And the town cops. And anyone else they could get their hands on. Trussed 'em up and took 'em back to their ranch." Not a big fan of the government, Jerry cackled at the thought of this scene.

"Why'd they do that?" Alana asked.

"They're sending the Feds a message. They declared themselves an independent country. Said they'd expel anyone who resisted their authority. I guess that's what they were going to do with the sheriff and the cops, expel them. But it didn't work," Jerry said, sounding disappointed. "The Feds sent in their new mobile antiterrorist team and the Freedom Fighters surrendered. I would have, too. I mean these guys had armored personnel carriers and even a couple of tanks. But here's the trippy part: the cops had UN people with them."

"UN? You mean like in United Nations?"

"One and the same. The guys in the famous blue helmets. I watched the news and these UN dudes were crawling all over the place."

"Hmm. What was the UN doing there?"

"Beats me. But those guys are up to something. I can *feel* it."

Alana agreed, but didn't pursue it with Jerry. She told

him of the meeting, then listened as he brought her up to date on some local gossip.

As she hung up the phone, she sat for a moment, pondering what it might mean to have the United Nations involved in the politics of the country. She was so preoccupied thinking about this she misdialed Karen's number twice before she got it right.

Karen was in her mid twenties and was the quietest member of the group. Quiet and shy and withdrawn. And *very* sad. She attended every meeting, at least her *body* did; but for now her spirit had flown away to some safe place. Karen's brother had been killed in the Southern California earthquake, and she still grieved for him. Everyone in the group knew of her loss and their hearts went out to her, although there was little they could do except send her love and light and be available if she asked for help. In the meantime, no one objected when she sat apart, distracted and silent and sometimes tearful, for on some level they had agreed to offer her the group as a place to rest and to heal, had agreed to demand nothing of her except her presence. *And* she had readily accepted their offer. Later, perhaps, when she finished her grieving, her Spirit would return and they would see her strength. Or perhaps not. No matter, they would love her anyway.

Karen didn't answer; Alana left a message on her answering machine.

Finished with her calling, she sat down at the table to find her plate piled high with steaming mounds of Jeff's scrumptious eggs, along with slices of hot buttered toast, a fresh cup of coffee, and a dish of Evelyn's homemade blackberry jam. Alana grinned at Jeff, blessed her food, and dug in.

"Are they okay?" he asked, knowing they were.

Alana just nodded happily.

After breakfast, they went out into the crisp October air and began unloading the greenhouse supplies Jeff had brought back from Oregon.

Alana let down the tailgate of their truck, slid out a box, and carried it around to the back of the garage to the spot

Homecoming 19

they'd selected for the greenhouse. Jeff followed close behind with some shelving.

Alana talked as she worked, telling him of her conversation with Jerry. "Why do you suppose the UN's getting involved?" she asked.

Jeff stacked some steel framing next to the growing pile of boxes. He thought for a moment, then replied, "Brian was talking about this the other day. Went on and on about it."

Brian was the other quiet, shy one in the group. A bit reclusive Alana thought. She knew little about him except that he was unmarried and in his late forties. A nice man. Kind and compassionate. At the first group meeting, he'd offered Kate and her husband the use of a small cottage at the back of his property. Red-haired Kate was also a charter member of the group and passionate about the idea of community. Not her husband, though—he *hated* the idea and objected to Kate's involvement. Alana wondered how long Kate would be able to stay in the group with her husband pulling on her like that.

Alana noticed the shy but intense way Brian looked at Kate and knew that his heart was open to her. She didn't wish Kate's husband any ill will—she didn't even know him—but if he got tired of Kate coming to the group, or got tired of *her*, or if Kate got tired of *him*, well, maybe Kate and Brian could get together. Alana's intuition told her they were a perfect match.

"So, what did Brian have to say?" Alana asked.

Jeff was glad for the opportunity to stop and rest. "Well," he began, "you know how the UN's been poking its nose into the affairs of every country lately? Brian says the Gray Men own the UN and so *they're* behind all this."

Alana nodded, feeling the rightness of Brian's assessment. The Gray Men, the United Nations and the Corporation, they all had the same energy. "Did he say why the Gray Men want the UN here?"

Jeff plopped down on one of the beautiful, large rocks someone had lovingly and artistically placed around their house. He continued, "Here's his theory. Let's say there's lots of unrest in the country, a lot more things like Waco. But *different* from Waco—no David Koresh, just ordinary citizens mad enough to take to the streets with guns. You know, an uprising of some kind, but bigger than the local police could handle. What could the government do? Send in the national guard or federal troops? Brian says it won't work and I agree. Hey, you tell the troops to shoot. You think they're going to kill ordinary citizens? Maybe even their neighbors? Unh-unh," Jeff said, wiping his face on the sleeve of his shirt. "So, if you can't trust *your* troops to shoot Americans, you bring in someone *else's* troops...like, you know, troops from other countries. They'd be like mercenaries and mercenaries don't have the same loyalties. Tell *them* to fire on a crowd of Americans and they'd probably do it. I agree with Brian, we're going to see more and more of the "blue helmets" in this country."

Listening to Jeff, Alana suddenly realized that the Gray Men and the Corporation were *expecting* trouble; and not just isolated incidents—they were expecting *big* trouble.

Jeff stood up and stretched, ready to return to work. "Oh well, like you always say, that's someone else's drama. Right?"

"Right," she answered. And she believed this, believed that no matter what happened in the country, no matter how much violence or bloodshed, no matter what the government cooked up, they could step aside and let it pass around them. *If* that was their intention. She worried about some people in the group, though; they seemed to relish the thought of a confrontation with the Gray Men. It was old programming, a lot of it from the sixties when it really did seem that they would have to battle "the system" to have a better world. But the truth was, they didn't need to fight the system at all. Built on lies, it would inevitably crumble on its own. *Fighting with it only gave it validity and strength.* Their way was much simpler now—not necessarily *easier*, but simpler: They needed to focus on the inner truth of themselves; they needed to raise their consciousness; and they needed to follow the path of their highest possibility.

Homecoming 21

By so doing, they would dream their dream of Heaven on Earth into manifestation, showing others what could be done.

And if they held onto the old pictures of confrontation, then what? They would surely be sucked into the conflict...and that would be the end of their beautiful dream.

Smiling mischievously, Jeff said, "Hey, guess what else I learned?"

"Sweetie, you're a fountain of information. Where are you getting all this?"

"I dunno. People tell me things now. I don't get it."

Alana did, though. Her husband had changed dramatically in the past few months, had grown more than anyone she knew. He'd relaxed *and* he'd opened up inside. Thirsty—that was the best description of Jeff. Thirsty to know *himself.* Instead of hanging back when they went into Evelyn's bookstore, or to one of Veda's channelings, now he wanted to know *everything.* He bought armloads of books—they were stacked in teetering piles all around his favorite chair—and he *read* them. Alana had heard a wonderful saying: "The Universe rearranges itself to accommodate your pictures of reality." Jeff was proof of this; he'd changed his picture of himself; his new picture said: I want to know the truth of who I am. I *deserve* it. The Universe was accommodating him by dumping information into his lap. *Tons* of information. Last week, for instance, someone loaned him tapes made a few years ago by a group in Sedona, Arizona. Wonderful, incredible tapes! Tapes illuminating the human condition so beautifully and so clearly, Alana wept every time she heard them. She and Jeff spent hours listening; they couldn't get enough of them.

"Okay, what did you hear?" she asked.

"Anna's got a man friend."

"Anna? You sure? How do you know?"

"She told me. Name's Steve. He's from Australia. They met a few years ago at some conference down in the Bay Area. They were together for awhile and then he went back home. Now he's popped up again. She seems happy."

Anna brought something special to the group: a clear thinker who was also in touch with her inner child. To be able to play and think clearly was a rare combination. People listened to her; *Alana* listened to her; but if she was having fun with Steve, maybe...Stop! she told herself. Stop worrying about everyone's commitment! Anna has a right to her private life. If she drifts away from the group, well...so what?

But, telling herself to relax, to let go of caring how the others acted, didn't help. She cared— *deeply*—about everyone's commitment. She wanted them to be as interested and as involved in the group as *she* was. Was she becoming obsessed with this dream of community? Hard to tell. She didn't *want* to; she wanted her journey to be fun, to be easy and effortless and fun. But her constant worry said it was becoming something else—not fun—and *that* wasn't good. She felt confused.

Maybe Jeff could help her. Yes, great idea! But wait, what exactly did she want to know? She wasn't sure. Perhaps she'd best wait for more clarity and *then* ask him. Yes, wait.

She waited until just after dinner.

Jeff had plopped down in his favorite chair and was engrossed in Barbara Marciniak's *Bringers of the Dawn*, a book he'd bought at Evelyn's the day before. He peeked at Alana over the top of the book. "Hey, sweetie, this is *great*. You read it?"

Alana *had* read it, had enjoyed it, and had also read the companion volume, *Earth*. "A few years ago," she replied.

He didn't hear her. "Great stuff. Gives you a feeling of the big picture. You really believe we were created by lizards?" He put the book down. "Did you say a few *years* ago?"

"When it first came out."

Jeff looked slightly hurt. "Why didn't you *tell* me about it?"

Alana laughed in spite of the tenseness she was feeling. "Oh, you're funny," she said and genuinely meant it. She doubled over with laughter. "If I'd told you about the book back then, I mean told you that almost everything you believed wasn't true, and *then* told you about the Lizzies and the Family of Light, you know what you would have done?"

"Nope."

"You would have given me one of *those* looks. You know the look I'm talking about?"

"You mean the self indulgent look with the raised eyebrows?"

"Uh-huh. And?"

"Ah...like I was humoring you until I could get a psychiatrist over here to talk to you?"

"Yep. That one."

"Guess I was pretty obnoxious."

She sat on the arm of his chair and rubbed his shoulders. "You could say that...or you could say you weren't ready to understand about *you*."

"I like the second one better."

"I'm sure you do," she replied absently. She sighed. She got up and walked around the room, stopping now and then to pick up something and then put it down. She went to the window and gazed at the Mountain. With her back to him, she asked, "Sweetie, do you think we're getting anywhere in the group?"

"What do you mean?"

"I'm not sure. Sometimes it seems all we do is *talk*. Words, words, words!" she spat. "And we're not even talking about what we *should* be talking about."

"Which is?"

"Do we really want to *do* this? Build a community I mean."

"Do *you* really want to do this?"

"Yeah, that's a good question. Maybe I do have doubts." Then she asked him something she would not have asked even a few months ago, for fear he wouldn't get it or that he would laugh at her. "Is that it? *Do* I have doubts?"

"I think you want this community very much. I also

think you're taking too much responsibility...like believing you have to work out every single detail by *yourself*."

"I can't seem to let go and let things fall the way they need to."

Jeff put down his book and asked, "What do you think would happen if you relaxed and let the others take over? I don't mean take over the whole project, but..."

"I know, what if I quit trying to motivate them and direct them."

"Exactly. It's lots of work and it isn't necessary. When I read the energy of the group, I get lots of commitment from everyone. They *want* the community to work."

"Why can't *I* see that?" she wailed.

"Want me to say what I think?"

"Sort of," she replied, feeling like Jeff was about to tell her something she wasn't quite ready to hear. "Sure, of course I do. Tell me."

"You're afraid."

Jeff's assessment surprised her. "Me? Afraid?"

"Yep."

She hadn't considered that. She went deep inside to find the fear... *if* that's what it was. "Yeah, okay. You mean afraid the community won't happen?"

"Exactly. You're afraid the others won't share your dream. So...well, you're kind of holding your breath, hoping they will but sort of expecting they won't."

"That's true."

"You've heard this lots of times, but maybe you need to hear it again: Everyone's dream is different. Maybe some people *won't* see things exactly the way you do, or won't do things the way you do. I wouldn't let it bother you."

But it *did* bother her. Sometimes the way people behaved pushed her buttons. Big time! Especially Cassandra. Cassandra was an artist. She was Emil's friend. Emil was writing a book about the sacred places on the planet. Raised in Germany, he had lots to say about the similarities between the Nazis and the Gray Men. Alana enjoyed listening to him. Cassandra was a different matter—she never stayed *focused* on anything. Alana liked her, and she thought her paintings were wonderful; but she was like a beautiful little butterfly, flitting from one idea to the next, never *landing* anywhere, never *definite* about anything. Cassandra was *wishy-washy*. Well, perhaps wishy-washy was too harsh; meandering was a better description. She *meandered*. Yes, that's what Cassandra did, she meandered this way and that way, over here and over there. It drove Alana crazy. Probably a mirror, she admitted to herself, and added it to her growing list of things to work on.

Suddenly, she felt so completely overwhelmed by her fear she almost couldn't speak. "Right now I don't understand...*anything*. How can you see this so *clearly?*" she finally managed to ask.

"Well, I'm not sure. I guess..."

"I feel like I'm not getting it. Like I'm failing somehow."

Jeff ignored her last remark. "I guess I see this because I don't have the same issues you do. I have mine and you have yours."

"Okay," she said, doubt in her voice.

He could see her distress, but he couldn't identify it. "You see what I mean?"

"Sort of," she answered, feeling herself slip deeper into her scared, confused child.

He wanted to reassure her. "There's lots of things about the people in the group that aggravate me. Those are the issues you help *me* with. You can see them because *you* aren't as involved. Got it?"

"Oh, sure, I understand what you mean," she replied, still feeling scared and shaky.

"We take turns helping each other, don't we?"

"Yes," she answered weakly.

He got up and walked over and put his arms around her. "What's the matter?" he asked softly.

"I don't know! I really don't! I just feel crappy!" she sobbed.

He held her for a long time, then whispered into her ear, "It's okay to be scared. And it's okay if you don't always understand what's going on."

She nodded but remained tense.

"I believe this community is going to work. But, we've got some...some *barriers* we need to break through to get to another level," he said. He felt her body shaking and he knew she was silently crying. "It's possible most of us are as scared as you are. Ever consider that?"

Her eyes wet with tears, she said, "Unh-unh. You really think so?"

"I really do," he answered, gently rubbing the back of her neck. "*I'm* afraid... *lots* of the time."

"You are? You never talk about *your* fear."

Jeff shrugged. "So, maybe now's the time. You remember one of the channelings Saint Germain gave last year, when he said that we would all need each other for emotional support? And to help each other figure things out?"

"Sure. That's when he advised us to be clear about our overall intentions for the group. And that's the meeting when I knew I'd be calling myself Alana."

"Uh-huh. Well, with everything going so fast, it feels like we've reached the time Saint Germain was talking about, the time when we're going to *need* each other, *really* need each other. I get scared that we aren't ready to create that kind of loving and supportive community. Yes, *that* scares me."

"What do you do when you get scared?" she asked.

"I have a little heart-to-heart talk with myself; sometimes it works and sometimes it doesn't. I tell myself this community *is* going to happen, because it's our destiny. But let's say it doesn't happen right away? Or with this particular group of people? Or in exactly the way we envision? I mean, so what?"

Alana's face fell. She fought to keep back her tears.

"Sorry sweetie. I didn't mean it quite like that. I didn't mean so what, who *cares*," he said gently. Taking his time, he added, "You've taught me lots of things. One of them is that everything happens the way it's supposed to. Right?"

"Mm."

"I believe that and it helps. When I *don't* believe it, I

Homecoming

get scared and I start feeling like you are now—kind of lost and helpless."

Her heart was beating very fast. "But you do want this to work, don't you?"

"Absolutely."

She picked up a green wooden duck from the table and ran her fingers over its smooth back. "This meeting tomorrow, I don't want to go."

"Oh horse puckey."

"But what are we going to do?" she wailed. "I don't know what to do anymore."

"Why not ask people if they're feeling the way *you* are?"

"Hmm. *Hmm.* Yeah, that's a good idea."

"I have a few every now and then," he said, grinning at her.

"Indeed you do."

"I've had a good teacher."

She smiled and rubbed her eyes and said, "God I'm sleepy. This self awareness business is *tiring.* I've got to get some sleep. See you tomorrow," she said, heading for bed.

"Hey!" he called after her. "You forgetting something?"

"What?"

"Our good night kiss."

"I'm glad one of us is here tonight," she said, putting her arms around him. "Thanks for being who you are. I love you."

He hugged her. "And I love you. See you tomorrow, sweetie."

Before going to sleep, she picked up her copy of *Mylokos of Lemuria,* a book she'd bought at Evelyn's bookstore her first day in Mount Shasta. The book was obviously channeled, although, interestingly enough, the name of the channeler was nowhere to be found.

She felt such a strong affinity with this man Mylokos who had lived thousands of years ago in Lemuria. Had she lived in the same village? She was sure she had. Opening the book at random, she read:

> "I will tell you some things about my village, Anu. Anu has been here longer than anyone can remember and it is beautiful beyond any words I can use. From the trees surrounding each dwelling hang flowers of every hue and fragrance. Water is everywhere; small streams wind their way around most of our houses and the water is fresh and pure; the ocean is near and we go to sleep at night listening to the comforting sounds of the waves as they come ashore onto the beach."

She put the book down for a moment. How her heart yearned to live in such a place! She loved Mount Shasta, but it wasn't...it wasn't quite her *place*. She couldn't explain it. It was a feeling, a feeling deep within her being. She resumed reading:

> "We are about three hundred in my village. Some leave and others come. Many have been here for years, and I am one of these. There are men and women and children here...although not so many children as in other places.
> Of course, as in any gathering of people, tasks need to be accomplished. We have tried many ways of sharing these duties. It is now our custom, as it is in most places in my homeland, to take turns, although this is not a requirement, for we have freedom here as in all other aspects of our living."

She knew that someday she would live in such a community, for that was her intention.

She put the book on the night stand. She heard Jeff puttering quietly in the living room, heard Sam come and lie down outside her door, heard an owl hooting softly outside. She closed her eyes and prayed, "Spirit, I have lots of confusion. Please send me a dream that will give me clarity about this community my heart longs for and about what I can do to be on the path of my highest possibility."

Chapter Three

The sunlight streaming in through Alana's windows crept along her pillow and then onto her face. She blinked, opened her eyes, then shut them immediately, for the dream was already slipping away!
No, wait! Don't go! she called to her dreaming self.
She relaxed and drifted back into a semi-dreamstate, not quite awake, not quite asleep, perfect for returning to work on dreams.
She and Jeff were inside a house; not the house they lived in now; this one was smaller and round, a dome or a yurt. Jeff was in the other room. She was idly looking out the window when the sky suddenly turned a deep blood-red! And then hundreds of birds streamed past the window— *all flying upside down!* She called frantically to Jeff to come and see! She couldn't hear his muffled reply, but she knew he wasn't coming. From across the room, she became aware that a special announcement from Washington—a *very important announcement*—was being broadcast on the radio. She desperately wanted to hear, but she couldn't tear her eyes from the scene outside the window. She tried to move, but her feet felt heavy and leaden. Her eyes still glued to the sky, she strained to hear, but could only catch a few words: "...are here...have been expected for years now...The President will speak to the nation shortly...alarm...keep you informed as events unfold."

Homecoming

She fought to keep the dream from slipping away, but to no avail—it vanished. She opened her eyes and lay in bed for a few minutes wondering what the dream was telling her. Or rather, what she was telling *herself*. Most of her dreams pointed to some inner work she needed to do, but this one felt precognitive, as if she was peering into the future and seeing a possible reality. Yes, that was it, she was seeing something coming. What? She could almost *feel* it, but the understanding eluded her. A huge Earth change? No. Just as big, though.

Oh, of course! The dream portended the social unrest she saw engulfing the country. She'd had a premonition about it yesterday and here it was again.

She sat up and swung one leg over the side of the bed. No, wait, *this* dream was about something else—the sky and the birds and the message from Washington signified a *different* event. She was confused. Was she getting two separate messages about two separate events?

She glanced at her bedside clock. No more time for lollygagging in bed trying to interpret her dreams; the group was coming this afternoon, and she had lots to do.

They arrived in twos and threes, late, a common occurrence for Mount Shasta gatherings. After some small talk, they settled down, some on the chairs and couches, some sprawled out on the floor.

Alana had not been completely able to shake herself free from the energy of her dream; she felt edgy.

The wind suddenly howled around the corner of the house, rattling the windows and stirring up a little flurry of ashes in the fireplace. Alana jumped. The wind picked up in intensity, beating against the house as if it wanted to gain entrance and tipping over one of their empty garbage cans, sending it rolling noisily down the driveway. Now she felt spooked. If she looked outside would she see a blood-red sky filled with upside-down flying birds? She stole a glance out the window: lots of dark clouds, but no birds.

Veda raised her hand. Veda was in her thirties and had lived in Mount Shasta all her life. About ten years ago, right after Harmonic Convergence, Saint Germain suddenly began "talking" to her, asking if she would agree to help him bring his message to the planet. Convinced that she was going crazy—or worse, that she already *was*—she'd told no one of these "conversations," until finally, knowing that she had to tell *someone*, she told Evelyn. Evelyn spent many long nights that winter brewing endless pots of chamomile tea, talking with her, reassuring her that although what was happening to her was certainly unusual, it did not signal the onset of a nervous breakdown. She told Veda—who then called herself Carolyn—that many others were having similar experiences. Perhaps most important, she told Veda it was up to her whether she wanted to be the channel for Saint Germain. A year later, Carolyn—now calling herself Veda—held her first public channeling; not her *first* channeling, however. That one she held in Evelyn's living room with Evelyn as the only member of the audience.

Being a channel and something of a local celebrity was difficult for Veda. Shy and retiring by nature, she seemed almost painfully embarrassed sitting in front of audiences allowing Saint Germain to speak through her. But she did it anyway.

"May I make an announcement?" Veda inquired softly.

"Yes," Alana answered.

Veda turned to face the group and said, "Saint Germain wants to speak to us soon. I'm not sure what he wants to say, but I can feel his sense of urgency. He would like to speak to us today if possible. What do you all think?"

Alana took a deep breath to calm her racing heart. What did Saint Germain want to tell them that was so urgent?

"Sure," someone said. The others nodded.

"Good, how about..." Veda began, then glanced at Alana.

Why do they all look to *me*? Alana wondered, and knew it was because that was how she pictured herself: as the leader and the facilitator. She didn't want this role today. "You folks decide," she said, hearing the testiness in her voice, hoping no one else did.

Homecoming

"Today's great," Anna replied. "Can everyone stay after the meeting?"

Andrew hesitantly raised his hand. Andrew was a "loner" who traveled around the country with his dog "networking the God energy" as he was fond of saying. He'd explained his "mission" once to Alana; it had made perfect sense to her. Tall, with dark, piercing eyes and a sometimes brusque manner, he often intimidated people...until they got to know him and saw that underneath his sometimes gruff demeanor was a gentle soul who meant no harm to anyone. Alana and Jeff had met Andrew at the Sunshine Cafe right after the earthquake. Alana decided that what set Andrew apart, and what bothered so many people, was that he really and truly followed Spirit, and most people weren't ready to gaze into this powerful mirror—it made them nervous. "I have no wish to spoil anybody's plans here, but the thing is I got no light up at my camp, so I might have to miss this here meeting with brother Germain," Andrew said somberly.

"Okay," Anna replied. "Anyone else have a problem with staying for awhile?"

"I don't have a problem; but it's going to make such a long meeting," Cassandra said. "How about tomorrow?"

Glenn agreed. "Maybe tomorrow *would* be better. We're getting our winter wood delivered and we'd like to get it stacked and covered before it rains."

His wife Vicki vehemently shook her head. *"No!* I want to listen to Saint Germain. I vote for tonight."

"I've got some things to do, too," Connie said, scowling.

Why is she so angry? Alana wondered. She liked Connie and wanted to get to know her, but Connie pushed her away, as she did most people. Alana had telephoned her a couple of times, suggesting lunch or a walk on the Mountain, but Connie put her off and Alana hadn't tried again.

"I could stay," Evelyn began, "but my butt can't take all the long sitting anymore, so I guess I'd vote for tomorrow; or maybe we could shorten *this* meeting...or something like that."

Alana's frustration boiled over! Damn! Something was *happening* in the country, something that would impact them all, and Saint Germain could help them figure it out! Didn't they feel the urgency of the situation? Did they actually have such important things to do? Was it really so hard to sit for a couple of more hours?

Brian shared Alana's irritation. "Well, so, where are we?" he asked sharply. When no one responded, he glared at each person. "Are we all here today?" he asked sarcastically. "Sorry, but you seem asleep."

Alana silently thanked him. Maybe she was being selfish, but she was glad there was at least *one* other person who shared her frustration.

Karen nervously glanced around the room. "Is there a problem here I don't know about?"

"Yeah, what's happening here?" Jerry asked. "Feels like the energy's pretty tight. Hey, let's loosen up."

Glaring at Jerry, Connie snapped, "That's your answer for *everything*! Loosen up and kick back."

"Well...I don't see what's wrong..." Jerry began.

Connie didn't give him a chance to continue. "Because that stuff doesn't *work*," she snapped.

"So, what *does* work?" Emil asked.

Ignoring Emil, Connie pressed on angrily, "You're living in the past, Jerry, when you and all those other radical hippies bummed around in your bus and got loaded every night."

"Not *every* night," Jerry answered defensively.

Sighing, Alana rested her head on her knees. What was happening to them and to their beautiful plans for community? Was it only a silly, childish dream of hers, a dream no one else shared? Furtively, she wiped away a tear.

Kate had been listening and watching, and she now spoke up, "You know what you all remind me of? You remind me of a family that's having problems. And I'm part of it. I'm not very happy about what's going on, but I can't quite put my finger on what's wrong."

"What's wrong is we're not *getting* anywhere," Connie said angrily. "We come here and drink our herb tea and talk and talk and talk! Oh God, I get so tired of talking! We haven't done one damn thing, and it doesn't feel like we're going to! Personally, I've had it! I'm about to leave and find a group that wants to *do* something!"

"That's always your choice," Kate stated evenly.

"Maybe I will," Connie said sullenly.

Emil paced around the room; all eyes were on him. "Possibly— *very* possibly—we are being influenced negatively...by others, and this is why we quarrel."

Vicki glanced around. "Influenced? By who? Someone here?" she asked, obviously apprehensive.

Emil shook his head. "No, you will not see them. They are invisible to us, but they are here nonetheless."

"I sense *something*," Anna said. "Feels like lots of confusion."

"And mistrust," Evelyn added. Her lined and wrinkled face broke into one of her famous, mischievous smiles, a smile that transformed her into a young girl. "Okay, Mr. Emil, would you be so kind as to explain further?" she asked warmly.

"My pleasure," he answered, returning her smile.

The exchange between Evelyn and Emil, so obviously loving, shifted the energy to a higher level. Everyone relaxed.

With the air of a professor about to give a lecture to his students, Emil took a seat at the front of the room and asked, "Do you remember what Saint Germain said to us at a channeling last year? About our being the way-showers for many on the planet, and about how we would be showing others...uh, how did he say this exactly?"

"Oh, I remember!" Vicki exclaimed. "He said we'd be showing the world how to come together in a community based on true brotherhood and true sisterhood."

"Yes, that is what he said," Emil replied. "He said also, or at least he *intimated*, that there were those who would not appreciate our efforts and who might not want us to succeed."

Jeff scratched his head. "I don't remember him saying *that* exactly."

"Ah, yes, you are correct, I am not in the exact remembering," Emil admitted. "Nevertheless, Saint Germain did give us this message."

Jeff nodded, not quite understanding, but content to trust Emil on this point.

"I believe you're right," Evelyn said. "Saint German *was* saying something like that. He didn't exactly *say* it, but it was in between his words, if you follow."

Nancy chimed in, "I remember, it was when he talked about the secret government. What do you call them Sus...oh sorry, I forget sometimes. I mean Alana; what do you call these individuals?"

"The Gray Men."

"Yeah, the Gray Men. It was when he was talking about them," Nancy said.

Kate shivered. "Sounds crazy, but I can almost hear others laughing, like they enjoy it that we're having problems."

"You mean others we can't see?" Glenn asked, looking into the corners of the room.

"Yes," Emil answered.

Karen's eyes were wide with fright. "So, what do we do?"

Emil thought for a moment. "Mm, many things are possible. We may call in the Beings of Light and ask for their blessing and their protection. I have done much research on spiritual groups, and I have concluded that group invocation is very powerful."

Alana agreed with Emil; there *were* forces at work attempting to stir up disharmony in the group. Not *create* it; they didn't have to, for the seeds of disharmony were deep within each of them. The disharmony born of doubt. They wanted community, but they doubted the dream could come true. For thousands—even hundreds of thousands— of years human beings had been negatively conditioned about such things, *had been fed pictures of reality that said that dreams like this do not come true.* These unseen beings only needed to trigger those pictures. Alana knew that the group would have to transform and transmute this negative

Homecoming 37

conditioning if the community was to survive. "We could also smudge the room, even the whole house," Alana suggested. "In fact, it might be a good idea to do this before and after each meeting."

Veda agreed. "I know you are correct, for I, too, feel the negative energy. I also know that Saint Germain would not want us to be afraid or paranoid...just careful...and intending that we do everything we can to achieve our highest possibility."

Alana got her smudge sticks, lit the aromatic sage, and blessed the room. Veda then led them in a group meditation to call in the Forces of Light.

With the wonderful aroma of sage filling the room, and the meditation expanding their heart centers, everyone relaxed. Everyone except Connie.

Nancy dug her camera out of her backpack. "Look, this might sound silly and like I'm interrupting everything, but I'd like to take everyone's picture. Okay?" she asked. Nancy was a professional photographer and her camera was always close by, a part of her, like an arm or a leg. She had traveled to Southern California after the quake and had brought back many shocking pictures of the devastation, the concentration camps, and the mass graves. Her revelations had caused quite a stir at the Mount Shasta town meeting, upsetting some of the town's citizens: "No!" they'd yelled. "You're lying! My government wouldn't do such things!"

Except for Connie, who frowned and stared up at the ceiling in disgust, no one objected to Nancy's request—they knew she was "following Spirit" and they accepted this.

Nancy walked to the far end of the room and quickly snapped a few pictures. "If no one minds, I'd like to be the community photographer. I'd like to get it all on film, like now when we're talking and planning, and then later when we're actually doing the building. And in case I didn't tell you, I'm also a carpenter. I've helped build lots of houses. Just one of the guys," she said and laughed uncomfortably.

Alana saw the powerful male energy within

Nancy...*and* the inner struggle raging within her to align this male energy with her feminine aspect.
Connie fidgeted in her chair. "Now, can we talk about nuts and bolts for awhile? That okay with everyone?" she asked sarcastically.
"You mean the nuts and bolts of our community?" Jeff asked Connie.
"Yes! Like when are we going to *do* something besides sit around beating our gums!"
Alana was guided to sit quietly and allow the energy to swirl around her. And to do *nothing*.
No one responded to Connie's question. Tears of frustration filled her eyes, and with a huge sigh she jumped up and ran from the room, slamming the front door. A moment later they heard her car start with a roar, then heard her tires spinning on the gravel driveway.
No one moved or even looked at each other.
Finally, Kate said, "Nancy, can I ask you a question?"
"Uh-huh."
"Are you still living with Connie?"
"Yeah," Nancy replied.
A year ago, at the first group meeting, Connie had invited Nancy to share her house. Nancy was a "wanderer" who'd been traveling through Mount Shasta after the earthquake. Drawn to the group by Spirit and feeling an affinity with them, she'd decided to give up her wandering ways and make Mount Shasta her home. That's when Connie had made her offer.
"Something's going on with her. I can *feel* it," Kate said.
"So can I," Veda added.
"Any idea what it is?" Kate asked Nancy.
Nancy nervously twisted the ring on her finger. Taking a deep breath, she said, "I *do* know something, but it's real private. Connie doesn't know I know. I...well...I'm not sure if I should talk about it."
Alana appreciated Nancy's conflict. "We won't blame you if you don't say anything," she said softly. "But something's bugging her. I know she can be kind of gruff,

but I love her, and if there is something I can do to help, then I want to."

"Okay, I'm just going to tell you," Nancy said. "I have a room in her house next to her office. There's a little desk where she has the phone and where she puts the mail. A couple of days ago, I was wanting to make a call, so I went out to the phone, and there's this letter. Open. I'm not sure why I even *looked* at it—I *knew* it was Connie's business—but I *did*. It was from a clinic up in Medford. A cancer clinic. Connie has cancer. Bad. The letter said her other tests confirmed the original diagnosis. She's only got a few weeks to live."

"So *that's* what's going on," Kate said softly. "That's why she's gotten so depressed and angry all of a sudden. I mean she's always a *little*...oh well, you understand what I mean." Her face reddened in embarrassment as if she had done something wrong. "I'm not saying anything *bad* about her. Oh hell, you understand."

"Nancy, why didn't she *say* anything?" Vicki asked, puzzled.

"I'm not sure," Nancy replied. "She's pretty private. Maybe she's not the kind of person who easily shares this sort of stuff."

"That's why she left the letter for you to see," Alana said matter-of-factly.

Nancy's mouth dropped open. "You mean I was *supposed* to see it?"

"Feels that way," Alana replied.

Nancy considered this for a moment. "Hmm, I think you're right. So she *is* asking for help, only she can't quite come out and *say* it."

"And the next move is ours...*if* we want to take it," Alana added.

Everyone talked at once, but Anna's voice boomed out the loudest, "Sure we do. Let's figure something out."

"Anyone close to Connie?" Alana asked.

Evelyn shook her head and replied, "Like Nancy says, she's hard to know. Been in town a few years. Comes in the store every now and then, but never says much."

The energy in the room spiraled down as people struggled with their feelings of helplessness.

Alana's intuition whispered that someone in the room had information that would open a doorway.

"I know her a little bit," came a small voice from the back of the room. It was Karen. "A few weeks ago, she called me up out of the blue and asked me if I wanted to go and have tea at the Sunshine Cafe. She was so *sweet*. Asked me how I was feeling about...about my brother and all." Karen had to stop for a moment to wipe away her own tears. She blew her nose and then continued, "She told me a couple of things about herself. She lost a sister a few years ago, and I guess it was real hard. That's all I can tell you."

Alana smiled. "That's fine. Would you be willing to call her up and ask her if she wants our support?"

In a voice squeaky with fear, Karen said, "You mean you want me to call her up and tell her we know about her problem?"

Alana shook her head. "You don't have to put it that way. She already knows we know—at least on some level she does—so just ask her if she wants to come to our next meeting and get some support. That's all you'll have to say."

Karen looked relieved. "Oh sure, I can do that."

"Good. Tell us what happens, okay?"

"Sure."

"I have another suggestion," Alana said. "Something we can do *now*. Let's get into a circle, imagine Connie in the center, and do a healing on her."

"Great idea!" Anna exclaimed.

For the next ten minutes, holding hands, they sent healing energy to the center of the circle.

Karen opened her eyes and sighed. "I feel like she was actually here."

"She was—her *spirit* was—and that's all we needed," Veda said.

Jerry stretched and grinned. "Wow, that was wonderful. I feel like we've come closer together. It's great."

"Yes, we seem more focused. I guess that's the word," Glenn added.

"I feel it, too, folks," Evelyn said. "So maybe Spirit is telling us it's time to talk about our community."

Jeff agreed. "Great. Now what?"

The silence in the room was broken only by the occasional creaking of a chair as people shifted uncomfortably around.

Nancy offered a suggestion: "I think we need to *start* someplace. Like, where are we going to have our community?"

"And how are we going to pay for it?"

"And who do we let in?"

"And when are we going to *do* it?"

The questions tumbled out of their mouths, and they laughed and relaxed.

Brian said to Nancy, "I like your question. Where do *you* feel it needs to be?"

Nancy shrugged her shoulders. "Boy, I don't know, but Mount Shasta's beautiful, and I feel like I belong here, so why not Mount Shasta?"

"Land is dear here," Evelyn cautioned.

In her soft voice Veda added, "I believe that money and things like that aren't quite as important as, say, our right place. I believe there *is* a right place for us, and I agree with Nancy—it's *here*."

"Okay, Mount Shasta," Jeff said. "*Where* in Mount Shasta?"

"Evelyn's right, land is *very* expensive here," Anna said. "Anyone got an extra million or two lying around?"

More feelings of discouragement and helplessness filled the room, followed by another downward spiral of energy.

"Maybe Mount Shasta *isn't* the place," Brian said. "I've been here most of my life and I doubt there's anything available at a price we could afford and that feels like...how did you put it, Veda?"

"Our right place. I *know* we have a right place."

"I do, too; but I don't think it's here," Brian said sadly.

Another long moment of silence.

Andrew raised his hand. "I know of such a place," he said.

As was his custom, Andrew was sitting off in a corner; everyone turned to look at him. "Want me to tell you?" he asked seriously. They laughed and Andrew's usually somber face broke into a grin. "Well, me and my dog, we travel around the country, and lots of times we get a feeling to go this way or that. No particular reason mind you. So one day we found this here valley...west of town. I believe the Lord guided me there so I could tell you folks about it."

Evelyn scrunched up her face in disbelief. "Mm, I hate to burst anyone's balloon, but I do believe I've hiked everywhere around here, and no offense, Andrew, but there's no such valley."

"Yes, there *is* such a place," Andrew insisted. "About a mile west of town. Me and my dog, we stumbled on this dirt road...leads up over the hill and into a valley. The dirt road's right off the paved road that goes to the lake."

A chill ran up and down Alana's spine as Andrew talked.

Evelyn thought for a moment. "Oh, sure, I know the dirt road you mean. But Andrew, there's nothing at the *end* of that road. Doesn't go anywhere. Besides, I know that land like the back of my hand, and there's no room for a valley there."

Without the slightest trace of irritation or judgment on his face, just a look of pure knowing, Andrew inquired, "Ever been to the end of that road, Evelyn?"

Andrew's question caught Evelyn off guard. "Well, no, now that you ask me, no, I can't say I have. Guess I always just assumed it couldn't lead anywhere. And if you look at a map there's nothing there."

"But there *is*. The Lord told me to walk the road, so I did. Goes over a hill and into a real pretty valley. Got a creek and lots of trees and even a place for a big garden."

They stared at Andrew, then at each other, eyes wide. Jerry exclaimed, "Boy, this is weird. Like, I believe you, Andrew, but *I* hike there all the time, too, and it seems like it can't *be*. But I believe you. What's going on? A valley that's here and not here?"

Emil voiced his opinion, "Perhaps *we* are the only ones who will see this valley. It is the same with many sacred spots on the planet. Mother Earth sometimes hides her treasures and reveals them only to certain people."

"You mean the valley's not really there?" Kate asked.

"It is and it isn't," Alana replied. "Feels like maybe there's some kind of doorway or portal there."

Kate's face brightened. "Oh, *I* see. It doesn't make sense, but it makes *perfect* sense," she said and laughed.

"Let's go there," Jeff suggested. "You'll guide us, Andrew?"

"Sure."

They made plans to meet the following day.

"I have a suggestion," Veda said. "Actually, it's Saint Germain's suggestion. He really wants to talk with all of us and he absolutely will not wait," she said, laughing shyly. "Could we take a break, maybe get something to eat, and then come back here, say at seven, so I can channel for you?"

"Yes!" they all yelled.

They decided to go to the Sunshine Cafe for dinner.

Jeff took Alana's hand. "You coming?"

"I don't think so. I need to rest...or something."

"You feeling okay?"

"Yes. I need to rest, that's all. I'll have a bite to eat and maybe lie down for awhile. Go and enjoy yourself. I'm fine."

Alana went out on the deck to watch them leave, then stretched out on the chaise lounge. Sam padded along behind her and flopped down by her side.

She felt a heaviness within her; the heaviness turned into sadness and the sadness into tears. She cried for awhile, then got up to blow her nose. "So, what's going on? Am I taking all of this too seriously? All this community stuff?"

Possibly, but something else was going on, too.

Alana knew that her emotions were related to her inner

child: when her child felt bad, *she* felt bad. She'd also discovered that her child felt bad when she wasn't getting something she needed. Sometimes she needed to be comforted, sometimes to play, sometimes to talk and say how she was feeling.

Alana didn't understand what her child needed now, but she knew she needed *something*.

Veda had suggested an exercise Alana could do when her child was feeling needy or insecure.

"Sometimes your child wants to go to the one place she feels safe and protected and nurtured, and she knows *exactly* where that is," Veda had said. "For me, it's when I close my eyes and imagine we are outside in nature. My little girl loves going there with me."

"Mine too," Alana had responded. "I guess I never thought of intentionally taking her there. How did *you* think of it?"

"Saint Germain suggested it to me," Veda answered simply. Then she took Alana and her inner child on a guided fantasy, leading them to *their* safe place.

Alana lay back in the chaise lounge, closed her eyes, and opened her heart to her child. *"How are you doing?"* she asked.

Her child shook her head and did not answer.

"What would you like?"

Her child grinned and replied, *"Can we go to our special place?"*

Alana knew she would ask to go there.

She was about ten years old, naked, and very, very brown. In front of her, as far as she could see, stretched a white sandy beach. Behind her, a row of palm trees and behind *them* the cool green jungle.

Her heart leapt with joy! Home! Oh, she felt so good! So warm and safe!

From somewhere down the beach, a gentle flower-scented breeze brought the delighted laughter of children and adults playing and splashing in the water. She would join them later, but for now it felt delicious being alone. Well, not *really* alone, for she could feel her animal friends all around her, and she knew in a moment she would join them. She stretched out, wiggled her toes in the warm sand, and gazed up through the lacy fronds of a palm tree at the brilliant blue sky. She had not a care in the world and hardly even a thought. She sent her energy field—her aura—floating out, out, out, to touch the rolling surf; and, as her field touched the clear blue water, the dolphins called, "Come and play! Come and play! We love you! Come and play!" She laughed at the thought of the joy to come.

A moment later, as she imagined he would, a giant brown bird circled and landed, then waited. Climbing on his back, she sent him the thought-picture that she was ready to ride. Easily and effortlessly the bird rose into the air, lifting Alana far above the island. Looking down, she saw the others from her village playing on the beach. Shielding her face with her hand, she gazed out over the water, and there they were—the dolphins!—swimming and leaping, calling to her, racing ahead, barely touching the surface of the water. Far, far out over the ocean the bird carried her. The sun on her skin and the wind in her hair and the silky feel of the bird's feathers next to her nakedness felt good. The bird circled, turned, and swooped down until they were only a few feet above the sea. Saying goodbye, she slid off his back into the blue water and was instantly surrounded by cavorting dolphins. They talked to her, caressed her, and nudged her playfully this way and that, almost as if she was a toy someone had dropped into their midst. She broke away and swam by herself for awhile; and when she tired, a female dolphin came to keep her afloat. Alana climbed on her back, holding on to sea-slippery skin as the dolphin sped ahead faster and faster and faster, until Alana was sure they would crash onto the beach. But they didn't. They never did. Alana hugged her friend, slid into the cool water, and swam to the beach. Over and over she played the same game, riding out over the water on the back of the huge bird and coming back to shore with the dolphins. Finally, hours later, she lay down under the tree and fell asleep, exhausted.

Alana awoke from her inner journey joyful and renewed. Remembering the beautiful place she and her inner child had just visited, she said, "I want to live in this kind of world. I intend to. I intend to allow it for myself."

Chapter Four

By seven, Jeff and the others returned, rested and fed.

Jeff hugged Alana. "Hey, guess what we heard at dinner?"

"What?"

"The Feds are sending troops to Texas and Idaho and Montana. Lots of UN troops with them, too."

"Did they say why?"

Jerry answered, "Who *knows*. The TV people said the troops are to insure the public safety. I guess what happened in Montana totally freaked them out; you know, the thing with the Montana Freedom Fighters. Or maybe they know something they're not saying, cause...it doesn't hang together. Feels like overreaction to me, sending all those troops when nothing's really happening."

Glenn didn't agree. "Maybe not. There have been lots of federal people killed in the last few months. Remember the two Forest Service guys they found in Nevada? And what about all the federal buildings damaged or destroyed?"

"Yeah, okay," Jerry reluctantly conceded. "But still, we're talking about a *ton* of troops."

"Yes, there *were* a lot," Brian agreed. "Too many to deal with just a few troublemakers. Looked more like an invasion."

As Alana listened, she felt the forces at play in the

country: On the one hand, the anger of citizens who felt robbed of their dreams and their freedoms; and on the other hand, the government's growing panic that the social unrest in the West would erupt into revolution.

Looked at in this way, it *seemed* like a simple clash of opposing forces, both believing themselves in the right and both willing to fight. But her intuition told her that appearances were deceiving and to go deeper; and a deeper look convinced her that *someone*—the federal government or the military or perhaps the Gray Men's secret world government—had a hidden agenda. Of the three, she would bet on the Gray Men. They were clever and smart and so, so patient and, in her opinion, they were driven—obsessed—by the goal of total world domination. If her intuition was correct, *then much of the social unrest in the Western states was being deliberately stirred up to provoke a showdown between the dissidents and the federal government.* And the purpose of all these Machiavellian maneuvers? It was *this* she could not see.

The unfolding drama was like a play within a play within a play. Confusing. Spirit gave her some clues to help her fathom this intricate drama—her dreams and her visions were the most obvious of these clues—but she couldn't quite put it all together.

Like Alana, Nancy mistrusted the news media. She said, "We were watching this broadcast at dinner, and the funny thing is, for a minute I started to believe that these troops were actually going to *protect* us. They get you to start believing something by saying it's the truth, and you have to shake your head and say, hey wait a minute, is it *really* the truth? Creepy."

"Yes, they're powerful," Alana agreed. "That's how they got almost everyone in the country to take the debit card."

In a worried sounding voice Glenn said, "That brings up a good point. I still don't see how we're going to work our way around that stupid card. Even if we get our community started, and even if we grow our own food, we'll need to buy some things; but none of us has a card. And I

Homecoming 49

hear that more merchants are refusing to take gold and silver."

"I've heard the same thing," Emil added.

Alana shrugged her shoulders. "Don't know folks, but I'm not worried."

Meanwhile, Veda had slipped away to take her seat and to set up her recording equipment; she now waited patiently for them to sit down and center themselves so she could channel Saint Germain.

As was her custom, Veda led them in a short meditation; then Saint Germain's familiar voice boomed forth, "Greetings, beloved ones. And how are you this evening?"

His question was met with silence.

Saint Germain's dark and probing eyes scanned the room. He continued, "I do not usually ask to speak with you, for although this is allowed, I prefer the energy to be forthcoming from *you* for a meeting such as this; and yet on *this* evening I have requested just such an audience, for there is much, much to discuss. First, about your community. You are being guided and assisted in your venture. Are you in the understanding of this?"

No one volunteered to speak.

"Well, you *are*," Saint Germain replied. He remained silent for several long moments, causing some to wonder if he would speak again. Finally, he continued, "Much chaos and confusion and conflict swirls around you, for many in this your country are grandly upset with those who call themselves your leaders."

"Boy, you can say *that* again," Jerry exclaimed.

"Indeed. And at times this confusion and conflict finds its way into your little group, does it not? And you find yourselves at each other's throats."

A smattering of nervous laughter greeted Saint Germain's comment.

"Keep your hearts open and intend to move through this phase easily and effortlessly," Saint Germain suggested. "Do the inner work Spirit shows you is necessary and the confusion will pass. All is well. Your beautiful and longed for community is coming along grandly."

Still, no one spoke. They shifted around in their seats, stared at their hands, or at the floor.

"Much heaviness is in your hearts. Why is this so?" Saint Germain asked. When it was clear that no one in the room was ready to respond, he resumed, "Perhaps, like children who gather to create an imaginary kingdom, you fear some parental voice will call you to stop your foolishness and come in for dinner."

A few people chuckled uneasily, realizing that Saint Germain was accurately reading the doubts in their hearts.

"Or perhaps you fear that you are simply imagining all this in your minds and that none of your beautiful dreams will ever materialize."

Alana felt that Saint Germain was talking directly to *her*.

Kate was the first to speak. "We seem stuck. Maybe we *aren't* ready. Maybe we only *think* we are. I hate to say it, but...maybe we need to do some planning, see where we stand, work some of these things out and *then* go ahead."

"And the rest of you, how is it with you?" Saint Germain inquired. "Are you wanting to put your venture on hold?"

"No," Jeff answered. "Except, the whole idea feels so overwhelming. It's a year since we first talked about starting a community and what do we have? Nothing. It's...discouraging."

"Ah, but this is not the truth, you have a *grand* beginning," Saint Germain responded quickly. His remark elicited puzzled looks from everyone.

"We have a beginning?" Alana asked. "I don't see it. I have lots of faith in our community, but I don't see any real beginning. We have some gold and silver, if that's what you're referring to."

"Mmm, that is not what I mean," Saint Germain answered.

"Then what?"

Saint Germain remained silent.

"Brother Germain," Andrew began, "is this beginning you refer to the land I have told these folks about?"

Homecoming

"Precisely. You have found your land...the land that has been *waiting* for you."

"But no one's even *seen* it, except for Andrew," Nancy protested.

In his loving and lighthearted way, Saint Germain replied, "Most of you are thinking logically about this matter. It is not logical at all and cannot be apprehended in this manner."

"You've lost me," Anna said.

Saint Germain's gaze shifted to Anna. "How is it you know when something is right?"

Considering Saint Germain's question for a moment, she answered, "I just *know* it."

"Do you *think* it?"

"Unh-unh, I just *know* it."

"With what part of your self do you know these things? With your head?"

"No, usually with my solar plexus or my heart." She smiled. "Oh, *I* see. Are you saying we need to understand things from *these* centers?"

"Precisely."

"Feels like I'm still missing something," Glenn grumbled.

Glenn's lack of understanding did not bother Saint Germain at all, and he continued in his loving, patient way, "Very well, then, I will explain. When this one you call Andrew told you about your valley, what was your first reaction?"

"I had a rush in my gut," Jerry responded.

"I felt a tingling all up and down my spine," Evelyn added.

"Me too," Kate said. "Like an electrical current, except mine is more around my heart and my solar plexus. I've felt this before."

"Do you remember when?" Saint Germain asked.

"Yes, when I know that whatever is happening is *meant* to happen."

"Indeed, beloved one. And if each of you will remember when you first heard of this valley, you will discover that you experienced the same reaction...or one very similar, did you not?"

They agreed.

"So you see," Saint Germain began, "if you but trust this part of you—this part that *knows*—you will realize that although you have not physically seen this place, it is indeed your right place and your new home. Is this not true?"

They nodded in agreement.

"You *know* this to be the truth," Saint Germain repeated emphatically.

"Okay, so *now* what?" Vicki asked. "Do we simply go and buy it?"

"You may do this...if you wish."

"The land is for sale, then?" Emil asked, sounding surprised.

"Mm, not exactly."

"Then how will we get it?" Jeff asked.

"The land is already yours," Saint Germain replied. "It awaits you. You will see. Trust your knowingness that this is indeed your right place and that everything has been worked out."

"Yeah, lots easier that way," Jeff answered.

"Indeed. Beloved ones, move into your heart and your solar plexus. This is the most important work you can now do, more important than obtaining money or supplies. Trust your intuitions and trust what comes to you from Spirit. Are you all in the understanding?" Saint Germain inquired. When no one asked for more information or for clarification, he went on, "Very well. The second matter I wish to discuss also concerns you greatly. Consider all that has transpired in but a few months of your time: the unusual weather, the mighty quaking of Mother Earth, the death of your leader, the introduction of your new money, the loss of many of your freedoms, the coming together of this group you call the Corporation. Much, much has taken place, and more is to come. You are in the midst of a *quickening*. And this quickening births the coming together—the *clashing*—of what *appears* to be two opposing forces, *two apparently dissimilar and opposing forces*, those you call your Gray Men and those you call your ordinary citizens. We will speak of these citizens first. Many in your country do not like what has happened recently, and they are opposing the changes and the energies behind these changes. Is this not so?"

"Saint Germain, are you talking about the militias and the other people like them who want to resist the government and the Corporation?" Jeff asked.

"Precisely. Your initial impression might be that these two opposing forces represent vastly different points of view, that they are aspects of what you call the Forces of Light and the Forces of Darkness, *and that everyone on your planet, including you, beloved ones, will need to choose sides.*"

"Well, sure," Nancy agreed. "The people who oppose the Corporation and the Gray Men, these are people like *us*, people who want their freedom. I don't like the way they're doing their protesting, but I sure do sympathize. Yeah, I'm on *their* side. It's the only choice there is and it's the only way out of the mess we're in."

"Indeed, it would appear so," Saint Germain began, "and yet the opposite is true, for by taking *this* course of action you only deepen your involvement in the very thing you wish to free yourself from."

"Explain that please," Nancy requested.

"You do not oppose a thing that has no importance to you, you merely let go, knowing that its time in your life is at an end. When you oppose something—when you *resist* —you give this thing validity... *and* power. *Your very act of resistance has done this.* Indeed, *your resistance pulls toward you the very thing you wish to be rid of.*"

Anna caught on. "Oh sure. I've heard this idea before. Like when you hate someone and you want to stop thinking about them. It's hard, because when you *hate* someone you're saying they're still important to you; so they stay stuck to you. It's like love. When you love something, you pull it towards you, and when you *hate* something, the same thing happens, only it doesn't feel as good. Is this what you're talking about?"

"Indeed."

Anna went on, "I guess I've never thought much about it."

"I am suggesting that you do so now, for the fate of your community may hang in the balance," Saint Germain cautioned.

Vicki raised her hand. "Saint Germain, I think I see what you're talking about, but would you explain this some more?"

"Of course. These energies we have spoken of, these opposing forces, let us call them those who want their freedom and those who would take it from them. Now, the clash of these forces is precipitating a showdown in your country, a showdown you do not want to be involved in, for it will draw you into the battle and will mire you in the energy you wish to escape from."

The expression on Glenn's face clearly showed his exasperation. "But I thought the whole point of this community was to live in freedom. Freedom and peace and harmony."

"Indeed, it is," Saint Germain agreed. "And yet you will not achieve these beautiful goals by resisting those you *believe* would prevent you from reaching them."

"You're saying fighting is wrong. Well sure, but..." Andrew began.

Saint Germain interrupted him. "It is not that it is wrong to fight, for right and wrong as they are used on your planet are but illusions. I am saying that by resisting those you believe would deny you your freedoms and the other things you desire, what you are really saying is that you must *win* them, must wrest them from those you call the Forces of Darkness. This is *not* the truth. These gifts are *yours*. You need not win them. They *belong* to you. *They are your right.* To believe otherwise is to believe in your unworthiness to have these beautiful gifts."

Evelyn nodded. "We don't have to fight and we don't have to struggle, we just have to allow what is ours."

Nancy grinned. "I probably shouldn't say this, but doing things your way...well, I can see the truth in it and I *realize* it's the best way, but...well, it doesn't seem like as much fun."

Jerry laughed sheepishly. "That's how I feel, too. But I don't understand. I don't like fighting or resisting."

"The truth is otherwise," Saint Germain stated firmly.

"What do you mean?" Jerry asked.

"The truth is you *enjoy* the resisting."

Jerry didn't agree. "*I* do? Unh-unh, I don't think so. I mean sure, I've marched in a few protest demonstrations, but that doesn't mean..."

Alana interrupted him. "Saint Germain's correct, you *like* the protesting. *And* the resisting. We all do. The resisting gives us a sense of being *alive*, a sense of purpose. We always seem to need something, or someone, to push against, to say no to. Gives us a sense of who we are."

"Precisely, blessed one."

"Wow! You're right!" Cassandra exclaimed. "I'm always saying no to things." She put her face in her hands as another realization hit her. "Oh my God, I *like* saying no! No, you can't make me do this! Or no, I'm not that kind of person! Saying no makes me feel *powerful*."

Glenn laughed derisively. "I think we're in trouble folks. It's true about me, too. I've done this resisting all my life. I bet we all have, probably ever since we were born. How do we change such a lifelong habit?"

"Intend that you become conscious of all your patterns of resistance," Saint Germain replied. "Do this in a loving way. We will assist you if you but ask. Keep talking about this in your meetings. Help each other."

"Saint Germain," Emil began, "I agree that it's a good idea to eliminate resistance as a way to feel powerful or to feel good, but..."

"It is *imperative* that you do so," Saint Germain stated firmly, "for until you give up your resistances, you will find yourselves enmeshed in endless conflicts and endless struggles. You may feel that your struggles—your causes— are righteous, and you may call these struggles "fighting the good fight," but do not deceive yourselves, these conflicts pull you down into a lower vibration."

Emil didn't mind being interrupted; he waited patiently for Saint Germain to finish and then he asked his question. "If we no longer use resistance as a way to feel good, what do we replace it with?"

"How about love for ourselves?" Anna suggested. "And love for our community?"

Picking up where Anna left off, Cassandra suggested, "And love of the Mother and the Goddess."

"And love of the path we are on, of finding out who we truly are," Vicki added.

"Indeed, you are in the understanding of this," Saint Germain said. "There are other things you may invoke as well—other states of consciousness—but they all have this theme: that you allow the unlimited being of you to unfold...*on this your planet...now. Now, beloved ones. Now.* You must accept that there is no need to wait and that there is no need to prove your readiness or your worth. Allow your dream to manifest...*now.*"

"So, we can just go ahead with our community?" Jeff asked.

"Indeed. Why would you wait?" Saint Germain replied.

Jeff laughed. "I can think of lots of reasons."

"Yet each reason is based upon fear, is it not?"

"Probably."

"Or upon the feeling that you do not deserve that which you long for and which makes your heart sing?"

"Yes."

"There is no need to wait," Saint Germain stated. "Remember, you need not be perfect to have your community. Some of these issues of self-love, some of the doubts you all have concerning your worthiness, may be worked out *within* your community. Indeed, this is one of the grand reasons you would form such a community in the first place. Trust that you will know when to take a break and put things on hold for awhile. These times will be rare. Trust yourselves to know."

Alana asked, "Saint Germain, these opposing forces you mentioned, could you speak about the *other* side? What we call the Dark Side. Do you know what I mean?"

Homecoming

"Of course," Saint Germain replied. "Many on your planet dream a dream of total control, *a dream of the owning of all who dwell upon the Earth.* Many of you have wondered about the individuals who dream this dream. You know they exist, for you can feel their energy, and yet you understand little about them. Is this not so?"

"Yes," they answered.

"Indeed. And so, for a time, I wish to speak with you of these beings and of their history."

They knew Saint Germain's story would be a lengthy one, and so they took a moment to get comfortable and to fill their water glasses. Saint Germain waited patiently. When the stirrings and the rustlings around the room ceased, he continued, "These individuals have many names. You know them as the Gray Men. Others know them by the name Illuminati. They have other names as well. I will call them the Gray Men, for this is indeed an appropriate description.

"These beings have agreed, for a time, to represent the Darkness on your planet. This drama of the Light and the Dark has been played out many, many times on your beloved Earth. The Gray Men are merely the latest to play the part of the Dark Forces.

"These individuals—mostly men—began to come together during the time of the French Revolution. They were bankers. There were many wars during this period of your history, and the monarchs waging these wars were always looking for ways to pay for their armies. The Gray Men began to loan gold to these rulers to finance their warmaking. The interest charged was high, but the monarchs were more than willing to pay, for victory meant great riches and much land added to their kingdoms. The Gray Men became enormously wealthy in a very short period of time.

"The original Gray Men quickly saw the benefit of keeping their numbers small, for in this way they could keep their wealth—and their power—concentrated. Thus, over the centuries, the number of families involved has never grown to more than twelve or thirteen. You would know the names of some of these families; others you might not recognize.

"Their wealth soon grew to such proportions that it could not easily be hidden. The amount of gold and silver they could keep in banks, even their own, was minimal; and burying this gold and silver in the ground, or storing it in secret vaults, became burdensome and unmanageable. Faced with this dilemma, they came up with an ingenious idea: they bought a country in which to hide their riches. That country is the one you call Switzerland.

"In order to have the greatest possible freedom of action, the Gray Men also decided to keep themselves separate and apart from those around them. Thus, *they gave not their loyalty to any country or nationality or religion or cause*. They continue this maneuver to the present day, *vowing allegiance to themselves and to their families and to no one else*. In order to do business in their host countries, these entities often wrap themselves in the cloak of patriotism, and yet a close examination shows this is a sham, *for they care nothing about any country or any group of people*.

"The other lesson they quickly learned was the value of secrecy. From the beginning, they kept in the background, shunning publicity, carefully cultivating an innocuous public persona. Often, they present themselves as bankers or financiers or industrialists, wealthy to be sure, but no more than others. This also is not the truth. Their wealth and their invisible web of power are almost incalculable in your terms. The true amount of their wealth would astound you; you would think such riches could not possibly be amassed by such a small group of individuals. And they hide their wealth so expertly that a team of investigators, even one with unlimited resources at their disposal, would have little chance of understanding the Gray Men's true value. They remain secretive, and this is why your name Gray Men is appropriate.

"By staying in the background and by using their enormous wealth to manipulate governments, these beings quickly wielded enormous power and influence. Almost more than you can imagine. I will give you but one example: *Every war since the time of the French Revolution has been carefully planned by these individuals. Planned from beginning to end.* Your own Civil War, and the wars you call World War One and World War Two, are but three examples. These wars have been waged for the Gray Men's profit only and not for any other reason. All talk of democracy and freedom, or of individual rights, has been a cynical ploy to motivate young men to volunteer for slaughter.

"The Gray Men are powerful but not invincible. Occasionally, some individual, by their character, their popularity, or their innate sense of the truth, rises to prominence and appears to challenge their authority. If the Gray Men believe such an individual is a danger to their plans for total world domination they often simply have them killed. Sometimes, it is made to appear as if these individuals have been killed by a fanatic or by some mentally deranged person. Your own President Lincoln was ordered killed by the Gray Men. Also your President Kennedy and your leader Martin Luther King. Your Dag Hammarskjöld met the same fate. And many others, beloved ones. Those they decide not to kill, they discredit. Ruining a reputation is easy you know; you have only to plant a few well chosen lies or half-truths. The Gray Men are masters of this kind of dissimulation, and because they own the media and totally control what is read and heard by the masses, these lies often go completely unchallenged.

"These beings quickly gained control of most of the world's central banks, with the result that the currency in every nation—save perhaps two—is completely owned by them and has been for many decades. The currency in *your* beloved country is thus owned and has been for more than half a century. Because they own the central banks, the Gray Men can easily manipulate the economy in any nation of their choosing. Every depression, every financial crisis, every major economic downturn for the past two hundred years has been carefully orchestrated by them for their profit.

"They own not only all the major banks and other important financial institutions, *they also completely own all the major world governments.* When I say own, I mean not that they influence these organizations—*they own them.* They set the agendas and they make all the major decisions. Your governments and your leaders are but puppets. This is true of your presidents as well. Some presidents are in the understanding of the Gray Men and of their plans and are in agreement with them. Others are not. If a president is not in the understanding of this and begins to figure things out, he is warned; if he listens not to these warnings and begins to speak of what he knows, he is either killed or disgraced.

"Because they own all the major governments, they can create the appearance of divisions within the family of nations. That which you called your Cold War was but a show put on to distract the masses and to divert attention from what the Gray Men were doing. The country you call Russia and the country you call the United States have been one country for many, many years.

"All of your so-called minor wars and all of what are called your public scandals are also diversions, meant to distract the public's attention.

"For many decades, these Gray Men have been in contact with certain extraterrestrial beings, beings who wish to exert influence and control upon your planet. The Gray Men and these extraterrestrials have joined forces you might say. These extraterrestrials have given your Gray Men much advanced science: the ability to make what you call flying saucers, to travel in time, to create vast underground cities and bases, and to create robots so cleverly constructed you cannot tell them from humans. *They have also given them the secret of how to duplicate themselves.* And so now the Gray Men never need grow old, and not growing old they never need trust their heirs to properly carry out their plans for total world domination...*for now there are no heirs.*

"Understand...*these entities control your world; and in controlling your world, they control you.* Your media is the means for much of this control, *for what you receive is carefully orchestrated news. You are told what these individuals want you to know and nothing else.*

"But their control now begins to slip away, due, partly, to those who, like yourselves, are awakening to the truth; and also because some of their extraterrestrial allies have departed the planet. They realize that the time for manifesting their dream of total world control is getting short, for time is collapsing upon your planet. Are you in the understanding of this?" Saint Germain asked.

Most of those in the room shook their heads no.

Saint Germain continued, "It is written in all the records, and it has been prophesied for eons, that the end of the world *as you know it* is near, for your beloved Mother Earth is about to transform Herself, to lift Herself to a higher vibration, much as you lift yourselves to a higher vibration by the inner work you do. When Earth's transformation occurs—and the time is fast approaching—much that is presently allowed upon your planet will no longer be possible. The dramas of manipulation and control, the buying and selling of souls, the despoiling of the land, and the abuse of the beloved animals who inhabit this beautiful Earth will cease, for these activities cannot exist in a vibration of love and light. The beings you call the Gray Men are aware of this and they feel a sense of urgency, for on some level they realize their time is short."

"What are they going to do?" Jerry asked.

"They have done much already."

"You mean like the debit card and the Corporation?"

"And other things as well," Saint Germain answered. "Much of what they have set into place you do not see, especially that which you call frequency control and mind control. Your television plays a great role here, for much invisible molding and shaping of emotions and thoughts comes through this medium. Television is not just hypnotic—*it literally controls your frequency, and with this, your innermost state of being.* Television is but one way this frequency control is accomplished, however."

Dissatisfied with Saint Germain's answer, Jerry pressed on, "Sure, but *now* what are they going to do?"

"What do you think, beloved one?"

"Well, like you say, the time is getting short. These guys have lots of control, but not nearly what they want. They don't own the planet yet, so I guess they'll have to do something really big...and pretty fast."

"Precisely," Saint Germain responded. "But they will proceed with caution, for although they want complete control, they have no wish to fight a sizable armed uprising in your country, or in other countries around the globe. But the United States concerns them the most, for you are their greatest challenge, and if they can subdue you the rest is easy."

Glenn raised his hand. "Saint Germain, there's lots of unrest now. The militia movement is gaining strength, and lots of other people—ordinary people who aren't part of any group—want the government out of their lives. How does all this figure into what you are saying?"

"The individuals who would control you watch these events very carefully, for your country is like unto their laboratory. As I have said, they have no wish for a prolonged armed uprising; on the other hand, they cannot let these movements gain too much strength. Their wish is to use the least force they can to bring you into line."

"Are you saying there *won't* be a military takeover?" Alana asked.

"Mmm, not necessarily," Saint Germain replied. "Accomplishing their objectives by force of arms is always an option. One of many. These individuals have no moral or ethical reservations about such a takeover. Or any other course of action. *Their only concern is how much resistance they will meet.*"

Brian considered Saint Germain's words. "Okay, let's say they decide a military takeover isn't in their best interests. They still have to do something, don't they? Unless they can figure out how to give us all some kind of tranquilizer."

"This option is also being considered," Saint Germain stated. "These individuals have carried out many such experiments on your population and the populations in other parts of the world. Viruses have been sprayed over whole cities, chemicals have been secretly introduced into your drinking water, and the effects have been carefully and meticulously studied."

Karen made a face. "Boy, now *that's* scary."

"There is no need to be afraid," Saint Germain reassured her. "You have all intended that you would not be part of such experiments."

"Saint Germain," Evelyn began, "I know you don't like to make predictions, but could you tell us what *you* see happening? Is it something we've already talked about?"

Saint Germain paused a full minute before answering. "At the present time, another course of action—long considered and well thought-out—is more attractive to them. Their ace in the hole you might say." With a trace of a smile, he added, "Turn your attention to your media, for there has been a shift in focus and a shift in attitude concerning something that was once scoffed at and ridiculed. Understand this and you will understand what is planned for you."

Evelyn smiled. "Saint Germain, why do I have the feeling you aren't going to tell us any more?"

"Because to do so would be to interfere with the unfoldment of your destiny paths. You gain much by figuring things out for yourselves and by dealing with events as they occur in the moment. You have much information already, and if you but ask within yourselves, you will discover that you are in the understanding of much, much more."

Glenn's irritation was obvious. "So, that's all you're going to say?"

"Do you feel we are merely playing with you? Teasing you as it were?" Saint Germain asked gently.

"Something along those lines."

"To explain everything to you now would be to take away your power. You will see the truth of my words. We will meet again soon. It has been my pleasure to have been with you. I love you dearly. Good evening."

Chapter Five

Veda opened her eyes. "Wow, I was *gone*. I could feel Saint Germain's energy, but I don't remember a thing he said. Guess I'll have to listen to my own tape," she said and laughed shyly.

"Felt to me like he was saying, hold on gang something *big* is coming!" Nancy exclaimed.

"Yes," Evelyn added, "I got that, too. Wonder what he's talking about?"

"Hey guys! Come here! Quick!" Jeff yelled from the kitchen.

They trooped into the spacious kitchen and crowded around the small television, ingeniously, and Alana thought, obnoxiously built into the wall.

"For some reason I was prompted to turn the TV on," Jeff began, "and guess what, our President's about to make a big announcement. Something's cooking at the White House, folks."

On the screen, an attractive, smiling female newscaster was making an announcement. "In a moment, we will be joining the President for what the White House says will be a short but important news conference on the recent events in several Western states. But first, we want to show you the latest footage from...where is this from?" she asked, turning to her co-anchor. "Idaho," he replied. "Okay, Idaho. Early this morning, the newly formed Antiterrorist

Homecoming 65

Strike Force conducted a lightning-fast raid on a heavily armed militia stronghold."

While she talked, the camera panned the militia "compound," stopping to focus on the stacks of rifles, boxes of ammunition, grenade launchers, and a piece of equipment Jeff identified as a surface to air missile launcher. The scene shifted, showing several of the militia, dressed in battle fatigue, sitting on the ground, hands over their heads. They were guarded by ATSF agents and UN troops.

The newscaster continued, "According to the Justice Department, this group, calling themselves the Idaho Freedom Party, is the same one that has been sending threatening letters and at least one letter bomb to state and federal officials in Idaho. The man you are now seeing is Aaron Stockman, self-proclaimed leader of the Idaho Freedom Party and guru of the antigovernment movement." A tall, thin, blond man with piercing blue eyes stared directly into the camera, a trace of a smile on his tanned and weathered face.

Alana's solar plexus told her that someone was attempting to manipulate her and that at least some of what she was being shown was a lie. What part was lie and what part was truth was difficult to discern.

"Hey, those dudes are tough," Jerry said.

Vicki leaned closer, peering at the images on the screen. "Which ones?"

"The ones on the ground—the militia," Jerry replied.

"If that's what they are," Alana cautioned.

"Oh yeah," Jerry began, "I forgot, we're watching the manipulation machine, also known as the TV. Easy to make assumptions, isn't it? I mean, they show you a picture and tell you it's the truth and your first impulse is to say, oh sure, okay, I guess that's the truth."

Alana grinned at Jerry.

The newscaster's smiling face filled the screen. "Alright," she began, "President Storr is ready to give his address. We'll return and give you more militia footage after the Presidential news conference."

The scene shifted to the White House where President Storr waited to speak. As usual, he appeared tense and ill at ease. Alana peered closely at the President's image. Had he lost a few pounds since she'd last seen him? And the huge bags under his eyes, were they new?

"My fellow Americans," the President began, "early this morning, in a series of eight separate raids in four Western states, the Antiterrorist Strike Force, aided by troops from the United Nations, arrested several hundred people and seized tons of arms, ammunition, and drugs. These men and women, numbering approximately eight hundred in all, are hardened, organized, armed cadres of the antigovernment movement. They have vowed to eradicate all traces of the federal government in the Western states. They are armed and ready to fight!" the President shouted, pounding the podium to drive home his words.

He went on, "Shortly after the raids were completed, we found certain very incriminating documents, documents outlining plans for further antigovernment activities. Based on the information in these documents, and after conferring with the Justice Department and Brigadier General Williams of the ATSF, we have decided to declare martial law in the following states: Montana, Texas, Idaho and Wyoming. As I speak, Federal troops, assisted by United Nations peace keeping forces, are moving into these areas. These troops will enforce a dawn-to-dusk curfew." The President slowly drank from a glass of water, then announced, "I will now take a few of your questions."

Before the questioning began, the anchorwoman turned to her co-anchor and said, "Well, that's a bombshell, Cliff. We knew something big was about to happen—there have been all kinds of rumors flying around Washington—but martial law, that's something *nobody* expected. Pretty dramatic."

"The President must have his reasons, Jodi," replied the youngish and handsome co-anchor. "The government and the ATSF certainly seem to be on top of the militia situation. I'm sure they felt that the country's safety was in question."

Homecoming

"Right," she said, nodding her head. "Okay, they're ready for the questions. We'll go back to Washington."

A reporter in the middle of the room stood up. "Mr. President, was anyone hurt or killed in these raids?"

"One ATSF agent was shot in the leg. Nothing serious. I hear he's receiving treatment at a local hospital and doing fine. And two terrorists were shot. Both killed I believe."

"Why declare martial law?" a reporter in the back yelled out.

"We felt it was in the best interests of the country."

Harry Stapleton from United News Service stood up and asked, "But why whole states, Mr. President? Surely you don't suspect all the citizens of these four states to be terrorists. Couldn't you have restricted the martial law to the most troubled areas?"

The question obviously irritated President Storr. "Have you ever been plagued by hornets, Mr. Stapleton?"

"Well, sure, but I don't see..."

"How do you get rid of them? By capturing one or two?" the President asked sarcastically.

Harry Stapleton did not reply.

"No, you go after the nest and you *destroy* it! *The whole nest!* It's the only way!" the President said, gripping the sides of the podium.

A woman reporter from the back of the room picked up on Stapleton's question. "But, Sir, are you saying that *everyone* in these states is a danger to the country?"

"Of course not. Many in these areas are loyal, law-abiding American citizens."

"Then why statewide martial law?"

The President took a deep breath and replied, "We have reason to believe that the militia groups have infected other areas in these states. I am afraid I am not at liberty to say more at the present time."

A well-known black journalist from New York asked the question that was on the minds of many others in the room...*and* many others in the country. "Mr. President, are you considering declaring nationwide martial law in the near future?"

"No! Absolutely not!"

"But haven't there been reports of similar militia activity reported in all fifty states?"

"The areas I have named are the only ones to be under martial law," the President stated firmly.

"For now," Jeff added under his breath.

The black journalist continued, "Ah, Mr. President, what actual evidence—I mean *hard* evidence—do you have to indicate that these militia groups are a bona fide threat to the national security of this country?"

President Storr shook his head. "I can't comment on that, it would prejudice the coming legal proceedings. But I assure you that Justice has given me the results of their investigations and the evidence is *overwhelming*."

"But Mr. President, what have these groups actually *done*, except to criticize the government and to arm themselves," a well-known TV commentator protested.

The President held out his hands, palms up. "Sorry, no comment."

"Ah, baloney! That's such a cop-out," Glenn said disgustedly. "Bureaucrats always hide behind that one."

Another reporter, sitting directly in front of the President, inquired, "Mr. President, is today's action possibly a payback for the things Aaron Stockman has revealed lately? The things he's leaked to the press about you I mean."

The President's eyes blazed with anger. "What are you referring to, sir?"

The reporter smiled thinly. "Mr. Stockman has made some rather, shall we say, embarrassing accusations about you and those close to you. Is the raid on his headquarters in retaliation for some of these revelations?"

Jerry laughed and moved closer to the television to get a better view. "Oh boy, look at Storr. Is he pissed or *what*. This oughta be good."

Aaron Stockman had been a thorn in the President's side for several months, almost from the first day he had taken over for the fallen President Tipton. Among other things, Stockman had accused the President of illegal financial dealings as Vice President, had intimated that the President was medically impotent, and had claimed that he had often used call girls during his days as a Senator. Other, similar accusations were leveled at most of the President's staff *and* his Cabinet. Although the White House denied these stories, Aaron Stockman claimed to have documented evidence, evidence he had purportedly shown to several New York Times reporters. The rumor around the Washington press corps was that Aaron Stockman could back up *everything* he claimed.

"Mr. Spellman, isn't it?" the President inquired icily.

Spellman nodded.

Emil laughed. "You want to bet that this is the last press conference Mr. Spellman is ever allowed to attend?"

The President's voice was cold and controlled. "Mr. Spellman, *none* of these stories has ever been proven. *And*, I would ask you to consider the source."

Spellman was not finished with the President, however. "Sir, Mr. Stockman is a Ph.D. in economics from Harvard. Taught at several Ivy League schools. And wasn't he considered once for a cabinet post under the late President Tipton?"

"I have no knowledge of that," President Storr spat back.

"These accusations he's made against you and the others, isn't there to be a Special Prosecutor assigned to look into them?"

"That is simply a formality. There is nothing to these stories and there is certainly no truth to your *innuendoes* that we are on a witch hunt. That is precisely the kind of thinking that is dragging our country down into the gutter."

Spellman did not seem intimidated or contrite. Shrugging his shoulders, he said, "I have raised some legitimate issues, Mr. President."

Ignoring Spellman's last remark, the President took two more short questions and then ended the press conference.

Kate glanced at the group huddled around the television and said, "I have a creepy feeling about this."

"Like, what are you getting?" Jerry asked.

"That we could all be under martial law before long," Kate answered.

Alana disagreed. "Saint Germain said the secret government wants to avoid an all-out armed uprising. Remember? The Gray Men realize that's what would happen if they put the whole country under martial law now. So my guess is they'll watch and see what happens in these states—it's like one of their experiments—and *then* they'll decide."

Anna shrugged her shoulders. "Anyway, does it really matter to our plans for community?"

"It might," Brian said cautiously. "Martial law's pretty restrictive. We wouldn't be able to move around, like to get building supplies and the other stuff we need."

"But *everything* is restrictive now," Kate argued. "Look at the Corporation and the debit card. But we're doing fine. I think we just have to keep our hearts open and focus on our path. Let's not get pulled off-center by what the government or the ATSF or *anyone* else does."

Andrew put on his coat. "I hate to break up this here party, but I got to be heading on up the Mountain. Got to get some firewood and feed my dog. So I'll be saying goodnight to you kind folks."

"Okay, Andrew," Alana said. "Maybe we all need to take a break. But let's get together tomorrow and go see the beautiful valley you have discovered for us. What do you guys think?"

Everyone agreed.

"Karen, will you call Connie and invite her?" Alana asked. "Tell her the invitation is from everyone in the group."

"Sure, but what if..."

Alana shook her head. "Let's hold the thought in our hearts that she accepts. See you all tomorrow. We can meet here if you like, say around eleven in the morning."

Later that evening after everyone left, Jeff suggested they take a walk. Before leaving the house, he shouldered a small blue backpack.

Homecoming

The weather had warmed up considerably from the cold spell the week before, warm enough for Alana to wear the new green summer dress she'd recently bought in Ashland. Jeff admired her as she came down the front steps. "Hey, that's really cute."

Alana twirled around and smiled. "Think so?"

"Uh-huh. Look at those pretty legs."

"They're not bad...a bit chubby, but not bad. Come on, let's go. You're getting me kind of heated up. If you tell me how pretty I look again, I don't think we'll get out of here."

"We don't *have* to get out of here."

"Yes we do," Alana replied sternly.

"Then as a second choice—a *distant* second—want to visit our magic little creek?"

"Sure."

Turning down Old Stage Road, they walked arm in arm, enjoying the smells and the sounds of the warm fall evening.

Jeff sighed.

Alana hugged him and asked, "Where did that big sigh come from?"

Jeff chuckled. "You remember back in Marin County when we first noticed the weather changing? You told me you felt like everything was speeding up. Remember?"

"Uh-huh."

"Well, I didn't have a clue what you meant. I thought you were getting a lot of crazy ideas from your channeling group. But now I understand *exactly* what you mean. Things *are* speeding up. Faster and faster. Does it still seem that way to you?"

"Yes, even more now."

"Faster and faster and faster. Like..." He searched for the correct words. "Like we're on a collision course with something. Something *big*."

"Yup."

"Well, that's what the sigh is about. I'm getting some feelings about the thing we're headed for—or that's headed for *us*—and I'm...I guess I'm anxious. You ever react that way, sweetie?" he asked.

"Sure. What are you anxious about?"

"That's the part that's got me baffled. I can't pin it down."

"Want some help?"

His response was instantaneous. "Yeah, I'd like to know what you see."

At that moment, Sam picked up his ears, growled softly, and went crashing through the thick brush.

Watching him go, Alana said, "He probably smelled a rabbit. Lots of them around now and he loves to chase them."

"Ever see him catch one?"

"Nope. He just likes to chase them."

"Think we should wait?"

"Unh-unh. I've already sent him a picture that we're headed for the creek. He knows where it is. He'll find us."

Jeff took her arm and they resumed their stroll. "Okay now, tell me what you see," he said.

"What I'm picking up is, you have this picture of reality. Something like this: lots of big changes coming, you know, Earth changes...and maybe things the Gray Men are cooking up. The shit's going to hit the fan as they say and when it does it'll make your life harder...and well, kind of depressing. That's how you see things."

He didn't agree with her, and he was irritated by what she'd said. "I don't think so," he answered sullenly.

She realized immediately that he'd been triggered into a picture of reality, that he was now reacting from this picture, *and that it was a picture he did not want to see.* Familiar territory. Often, in the past few weeks, as they'd worked their way through their old conditioning, one of them would point out a picture to the other only to be met with a stone wall of denial and resistance. "Nope, that's not *mine*," the other one would say. This was the time to be as loving and patient, *and* as accurate and clear, as possible. Checking inside herself to make sure she was getting a correct reading on Jeff, she continued, a bit carefully, conscious that he'd just been emotionally triggered and conscious that almost anything she would say now might push

Homecoming

his buttons again. "It feels like something I said bothered you."

He shrugged his shoulders and stared off into the distance. "I don't think you're right. You aren't *always*, you know," he countered defensively.

She felt his stiffness...as if his emotional body had literally gone rigid. She cautioned herself not to judge him. She had been in this exact emotional place many times and would almost certainly be there again. Not a good feeling, being there. She reminded herself to open her heart and go softly with love. "Sweetie, what part of what I said makes you uncomfortable?" she asked gently.

"I don't *know*. *All* of it. It just doesn't fit."

She could hear and feel the frightened child in him. "But you can see that *something* is making you nervous and kind of edgy."

"Sure."

"And it has something to do with a picture you have. Right?"

"Who knows," he muttered.

"Well okay, it has something to do with the changes you're sensing."

"Yes, that fits," he agreed, his guard up.

"So..." she began.

He cut her off. "Let's drop it, okay? We're not getting anywhere."

"Okay," she replied. She wanted to push a bit to see if she could assist him in getting past his resistance—his "stuckness"—but she kept quiet, honoring his wish to stop. Remembering that *she* didn't like being pushed past this point helped, but not a lot.

They walked along in silence, occasionally hearing Sam in hot pursuit of his rabbit. She felt Jeff's frustration, felt him pulling away from her and into himself. His frustration hung like a dark cloud over both of them. *Breathe,* she told herself. Breathe...and let his feelings pass *through* me.

She listened to the night noises: the last of the summer crickets, the wind sighing through the tops of the tall pines, and the scurryings of little animals in the brush. What would happen? Would they have a nice walk? Or would they have to return? If the resistance was powerful enough, it could take the person a day or two to *admit* to being in a picture of reality and to begin the work of processing. A day or two—rarely more—but a day or two could feel like a *year*. Nothing to do about *that*, however, except be patient, take care of yourself, and let the other person do what they needed to do.

Sam appeared suddenly, panting, full of stickers, minus any signs of having caught the rabbit, but looking pleased with himself nevertheless. Alana reached down and petted him.

Jeff strode along stiffly, staring straight ahead, not ready to talk.

She wanted to take his arm, but thought better of it. Instead, she walked and waited.

She remembered stories of his childhood. His father, a career army man who never quite made it, moved his family every two years, so Jeff's was the typical life of an army brat. One day, in the middle of telling her some childhood memory, he'd looked at her with those big blue eyes, eyes that could melt her heart in two seconds flat, and said, "I lived in so many places, everywhere in the world, but I swear I can't remember ever having a *home*."

They'd met during her second year of art school, the memories of her hippie days with Frank almost forgotten. She'd sit for hours letting Jeff pour out his story, realizing after awhile *that this man had never had anyone to talk to*. Not his father, who loved him the best he could through the walls he'd erected around his heart; nor his mother, a sweet, shy woman who was drunk every afternoon by the time Jeff returned from school. So, when Jeff realized that Alana wanted to hear his story, he had talked and talked, until, physically exhausted, he would fall asleep in her arms. She would watch him for awhile, then put him to bed and tidy up his tiny apartment, careful not to do too much, mindful of the mothering instinct rising powerfully within her and wanting desperately to control it. She'd go back to her own apartment—really only one room with a bathroom down the hall—and return the next day for a simple dinner—both were poor—and for more talk. His childhood had been so bleak, so empty of human contact, so lonely, *hers* looked like heaven. She had cautioned herself not to feel sorry for him, but had anyway.

Why was she thinking of Jeff's childhood?

Jeff slowed his pace, sighed, and said, haltingly, "I hate this place...this emotional place I'm in. I don't have a clue how to dig myself out."

She kept quiet.

"I can feel myself getting kind of grumpy, sweetie," he said finally. "But it's my stuff. Doesn't have anything to do with you."

She relaxed, knowing that he was on his way to understanding.

They'd worked hard in the past few months, examining their pictures of reality, changing the ones that limited their capacity for self-love. Difficult, but also a wonderful learning experience. They'd learned, among other things, that when one of them was in the middle of a picture it helped to communicate this to the other person. If they could.

Being with Jeff now, watching him struggle with his picture, and paying attention to how *she* felt—Jeff's grumpiness was bothering her a bit, despite her intention not to let his mood get to her—Alana understood again the value of this communication. Human beings are so fragile sometimes, she thought. Even when we *know* it's the other person's picture we can still let it push our *own* buttons. So it really helped when the other person could say, as Jeff had just done, "Sweetie, this has nothing to do with *you*." This statement—the energy and the intent of this statement—sent love to both people.

Jeff was better at this than she was. He usually owned his irritability pretty quickly. She sometimes had a much harder time admitting her feelings.

She took a chance and said, "You *are* kind of grumpy. Feels like your kid."

Jeff was relieved to be pointed in a familiar direction. "My kid? You really think so?"

"Uh-huh. When one of us is feeling scared or angry or sad, isn't it usually our kid who's feeling that way?"

"Usually. But I don't see what's going on *now* with *my* kid."

She felt him begin to tense up again—to *constrict*—and she said, "Tell you what, we're almost at the creek; why not find yourself a nice comfortable rock to sit on and go inside and ask your child what's going on. You know how to do that. You do it *very* well."

"Okay," he answered, not sounding entirely convinced this was the best course of action.

They reached the creek, Jeff found his rock, and Alana walked down the road, giving him some space. She returned a few minutes later, a panting but happy Sam following her.

The stiffness was gone from Jeff's body; he'd let go of something.

He grinned. "You're right, my kid *isn't* feeling too good. Very insecure. He can sense the big changes about to happen, and he's afraid everyone on the planet is going to turn ornery and cranky. And that there won't be any room for love or cooperation. He feels kind of desperate and, and..." he stopped, the tears running down his face. "And..."

"And maybe like he wouldn't want to live in a such a world?" she asked softly.

He nodded, unable to speak. She held him and let him cry. Finally he said, "He feels like he wouldn't want to *be* here. What do I do?" he wailed.

She did the best she could. "Well, it's just how your little boy pictures the future," she said, smoothing his hair. "I have those feelings myself sometimes, like the whole world will get mean and nasty and like everyone will have to fight simply to stay alive. Like those Mel Gibson pictures."

Jeff blew his nose. "Oh you mean *Mad Max*. And there was another one....Yeah they *were* pretty grim. You know,

that's *exactly* how my kid sees it. Oh boy, no way, he says. No *way*."
"Sure, who wants to live in a world like *that*?"
"You think it'll happen?" the little boy in him asked.
"In some places, maybe. For us? Not unless that's our picture."
Jeff wasn't completely reassured. "Yeah, but if the shit really hits the fan we won't be able to escape *all* of it."
Alana spoke from the place of her inner vision, "Sure, there will be things to deal with. Some hard times. Lots of changes. But no matter how bad things get, there will be some people who will rise to the top. The challenge will bring out the best in them. Know what I mean?"
"Yeah, they won't let themselves be pulled into a downward spiral, no matter what's going on. They'll let go and follow Spirit," Jeff added.
"Uh-huh, and they'll realize that everything is an opportunity to grow, even the *big* changes that feel scary or impossible to deal with. Everything is an opening and an opportunity."
Jeff sat up and stretched. "So, I need to work on my picture. My *kid's* picture. I will. I want him to know what you just said. I want him to know he's *safe*."
"Feel better?"
"Lots."
Alana playfully ruffled his hair. "Got through another one of these, didn't we?"
"We did indeed," he replied. He shook his head. "It's weird, but sometimes I don't want to *admit* I'm in the middle of a picture, even when the little voice inside says I am. I don't understand."
Alana did, though. "That's how powerful these pictures are. We don't question them. We don't question them because we assume this is the way things are. We assume this is *reality*. *Our* reality. The *only* reality. We think we have everything figured out and it's too confusing to admit maybe we don't, so when Spirit comes along and taps us on the shoulder and says we need to check out a picture, lots of times we say go away, I don't *want* to."

"Thanks sweetie. Thanks for helping," he said. He put his arm around her and kissed her.

She gazed up into his eyes. "Mm, such a nice kiss. Definitely *not* a kiss from your kid."

"You noticed, did you," he said. "Did I tell you that you look very beautiful in that dress? And very, *very* sexy."

"I believe you did, but you can tell me again."

"You look beautiful."

"By the way, what do you have in your trusty pack?" she asked.

"A nice soft blanket."

"Oh," she said playfully, "did you bring it in case I got cold?"

"Well, not exactly. Why don't we spread it out here on the ground and I'll show you why I brought it."

She lay down next to him. "Now Sam, don't watch."

"Sam's sound asleep."

Jeff was right. Worn out from his rabbit chase, Sam *was* asleep. And snoring.

Chapter Six

The old Land Cruiser, with Jeff at the wheel and Alana sitting next to him, bumped and swayed over the dusty dirt road leading to "Andrew's" valley.

Evelyn and Vicki were in the back seat. Vicki shivered and clutched her coat to her body. "Brrr, sure got cold again," she said. "I've never seen the temperature change so fast. Think we're in for some more weird weather?"

"What?" Alana yelled over the roar of the Land Cruiser's ancient engine.

"You think the government's playing more games with the weather?" Vicki shouted.

"Yes!" Alana yelled back.

The Land Cruiser jumped a foot into the air, all four wheels leaving the ground, as Jeff went over a bump in the road. Alana held on for the inevitable crash as they returned to earth.

"Sorry," Jeff apologized, "I'll slow down. Still getting used to how it drives. The suspension isn't exactly in the luxury car class."

"Is there *any* suspension in this thing, sweetie?" Alana teased.

Jeff simply smiled. He'd found the old Land Cruiser a few days ago, had immediately fallen in love, and had bought it for almost nothing. "We'll need a four-wheel drive if we're going to live on a dirt road," he'd said. Alana knew he was right. Maybe some new shock absorbers would help.

A quick glance out the back window told Alana that the other cars were still following...but at a safe distance to avoid being engulfed by the huge plumes of thick dust spit up by the Land Cruiser's tires.

Jeff pointed to something up ahead. "There's the big rock. See, over there, up the hill a bit."

Alana spotted the boulder, the size of a small car, perched on the hill.

Jeff gripped the steering wheel with both hands as they hit a rough spot. "Andrew says it marks the half way point."

They'd been bouncing along on the dirt road for about five minutes. Alana did some quick figuring: Jeff was doing about twenty-five miles an hour, so they had come about two miles. And still climbing. Must be up about four thousand feet by now. Climbing at this rate, another couple of miles would put the valley around five thousand feet. Five thousand feet meant cold and snow. *Lots* of cold and snow. Too bad. But if the place was as pretty as Andrew said, she could deal with the cold weather.

"We've come a couple of miles. Another two or three to go," Alana replied.

Jeff frowned. "Boy, I dunno, that's a lot of dirt road in the winter."

"That's why we have your new little baby," Alana said, patting the seat of the Land Cruiser.

Jeff grinned at her. "Yeah, but we may need some kind of snow plow, too. Oh well, first things first. Guess we need to see if this place is really our new home."

They drove in silence for another mile. Jeff slowed down to negotiate a washed-out section of road, then put the Land Cruiser in low gear and inched up the steep hill, stopping as he reached the top.

"Oh my God, it's beautiful," Alana gasped.

They drove down the road, parked, and got out.

"I can't believe this," Evelyn exclaimed. "This is like, it's like..." But she couldn't finish her sentence.

Homecoming

With mouths open, the four of them stood staring at the jewel that was the valley.

About two miles long and perhaps half that distance wide, the little valley sparkled in the October sun. Bordered by thick stands of willow and alder, a tiny creek meandered along the valley floor. A gentle breeze brought the smell of water and of lush creekside vegetation, the familiar creek smell Alana loved so much, the smell she associated with being... *home*. On one side of the creek, a beautiful green meadow dotted with patches of purple and red wildflowers stretched halfway up the hill.

Alana stood transfixed. A bird called sweetly to her. A meadow lark? She couldn't remember, but she hadn't heard its music since she was about ten years old, and hearing it now she cried with joy.

The rest of the party parked their vehicles, joined them, and stood in silence.

The bird called again.

"Oh, look!" Kate yelled. "There, down by the creek! See? Three deer! No, four!" Hearing human voices, the deer glanced up, tails twitching; then, sensing no harm, bent delicate necks to resume feeding on the lush green grass.

"There's something about this place, something..." Brian began. Like Evelyn, he couldn't find the words to finish his thought.

Alana glanced at Andrew. "You were right, Andrew, it's beautiful."

"I kinda thought you'd see it that way. But I don't take no credit for this. It's the Lord's doing. He guided me here."

"Yes, he did," she agreed.

They spread out and walked slowly down the road to the valley floor.

"We could drive all the way. Looks like there's a nice flat place to park down there," Jeff said.

"We could, but for some reason bringing the cars in now doesn't seem appropriate. Maybe later," Alana replied.

Jerry pointed excitedly at something across the valley.

"Hey gang, do I see what I *think* I see? Over there, past the deer, are those fruit trees?"

"I do believe you're right," Evelyn answered.

Puzzled, Cassandra asked, "Does someone live here? I don't see any houses, but I get a weird feeling someone *lives* here."

Evelyn shook her head. "Funny about that. I called my friend Maria at Tall Pines Realty and talked to her about this place. First of all, her map doesn't even *show* a valley. But even stranger, she can't figure out who the property belongs to. She called the County Recorders Office, but they can't figure it out *either*. Pretty mysterious if you ask me."

Her eyes big with wonder, Veda said, "There's something *about* this place."

They laughed, knowing exactly what she meant.

They reached the valley floor.

"Which way guys?" Glenn asked.

"Let's cross the creek and explore the meadow," Alana suggested.

Glancing back over her shoulder, Vicki exclaimed, "Oh look! The Mountain!"

They all turned to see Mount Shasta, at least the top half of Mount Shasta, peeking at them over the rim of the valley.

Vicki laughed. "Why do I get the feeling the Mountain is watching over us? Almost like it couldn't let us out of its sight?"

As the group neared the creek, the resident deer, deciding that the humans were getting a bit too close, ambled further up the valley, to stand and watch and graze.

Crossing the creek, the group walked up the gentle incline to the meadow. Jerry stretched out on the soft grass and closed his eyes.

Something tugged at Alana's consciousness. "Aside from all the other unusual things about this place, notice anything odd about the temperature?"

"The temperature?" Vicki asked.

"Uh-huh. The temperature. What happened to your coat?" Alana asked her.

"Well, I left it in the car. I didn't need it. It's nice and warm here," Vicki replied.

Alana nodded. "It *is* warm, isn't it? Well, what do you guys think, is it warm here or are Vicki and I losing our minds?"

Brian agreed. "It *is* warm. But it was freezing cold when we left Mount Shasta."

"And we're up another couple of thousand feet, wouldn't you say?" Alana asked Jeff.

"Probably. Maybe even more."

"Its got to be about 70 here," Nancy said, not quite believing her senses. "And the temperature was what, maybe 45 in town? Should be colder here. *Lots* colder."

Andrew had walked on ahead to examine the fruit trees. Jumping up and down with excitement, he waved for the others to join him. "These here trees are young, five, maybe six years old! Someone just came here and planted them! Apples and peaches and pears!" he exclaimed happily.

Nancy inspected one of the trees. "Andrew, how do you know they're so young?"

"Cause I worked in the orchards down near Sacramento. I know about trees. Someone just up and came here and planted them," he repeated.

"But who?" Vicki asked.

Emil picked a ripe pear. "Fruit trees up here? I've always understood that fruit trees don't do well at higher elevations. Except for some kinds of apples. Right, Andrew?"

"Crab apples, they like the higher places," Andrew answered matter-of-factly.

"But these trees appear to be doing fine," Emil commented. He bit into his pear. "Wonderful! The best I've eaten in a long time."

Cassandra wiped away the pear juice dribbling down Emil's chin.

Kate walked over to a peach tree and got down on her hands and knees. "Look at all the fruit on the ground. The deer have eaten most of it, but you can tell these trees are pretty prolific."

Alana took in the magical scene spread out around her and asked, "Doesn't this valley seem kind of out of place?"

"Out of place? You've lost me," Jeff said.

"Remember when we went to Hawaii?"

"Sure."

"Remember the feel of the place? Doesn't this valley have the same energy?"

"Well, I guess..." Jeff started to say.

Brian interrupted him. "Yes, of course! It's not like a mountain valley at all!"

"Uh-huh, which explains the fruit trees and the grass and the warm temperature," Alana said. "I know this sounds weird, but it's almost like someone took the valley from some other place, maybe some tropical place, and moved it up here."

Glenn's mouth dropped open. "Uh, *moved* the *valley*?"

"I don't believe anyone really *moved* it, but still..."

"Why not," Nancy commented.

In her soft, almost inaudible voice Veda said, "I believe this beautiful valley has been waiting many, many years for us."

Connie looked at Veda questioningly. "Are you getting anything in particular? Is Saint Germain telling you something?"

"No. It's an intuitive understanding."

"Let's add one more unusual fact to the pot," Jeff suggested. "Did you see any tire tracks on the road as we drove in?" A couple of people shook their heads no. "Isn't it kind of odd, here is this beautiful place, five miles up a dirt road from one of the most popular lakes in the county and no tire tracks on the road?"

Glenn scratched his head. "Hmm. You're right, that road showed absolutely no sign of any traffic: no ruts, no tracks... *nothing*."

Jeff went on, "And something else. We're in the United States folks, but do you see any beer cans or plastic bottles or candy bar wrappers...or any other garbage?" He walked a few paces, searching the ground. "Nothing. Not even a scrap of paper."

Homecoming

As Jeff said, the valley was free of the debris usually found in almost any area visited by human beings.

Anna added her own observation. "Isn't it kind of hard to remember what the outside world is like?"

Evelyn puckered up her mouth. "Would you mind explaining yourself my dear?"

"There's another world out there a few miles away," Anna replied. "But can you remember that world clearly?" Glancing around at the circle of faces, she added, "Almost feels like *that* world doesn't exist."

Veda understood. "Yes. Absolutely. It is difficult to focus on anything except the beautiful energy of this place. The world—the *other* world—is there and yet...it isn't."

Connie shook her head skeptically. "Veda, how can that be?"

Veda's eyes changed as she peered into another reality. "This valley, all that we see in front of us, is *here*. For *us* it is here. For others, perhaps not. The Great Pyramids, Machu Pichu...other such places...are the same. There is a doorway, a portal, an opening. Some may enter and some may not. We have entered."

"*Precisely!*" Emil exclaimed excitedly. "I am writing a book about the sacred places of the Earth. I have been to most of them and it is *exactly* as Veda has described! All have the same feel to them. I call such places "reality benders." People see and experience many, many different things at these sacred spots. For some, the great Pyramid is simply a crumbling pile of old stones. For others, a sacred place that shines with a celestial beauty."

Evelyn chuckled. "I agree with you, folks. Feels right. But you know me, I'm practical about things. So let's get practical. Let's assume this is an energy portal. Is this important for our community?"

No one answered.

Veda laughed and her face turned a crimson red. "Oh dear, Saint Germain just told me something. That rascal, he *does* have a sense of humor sometimes." She cleared her throat, acting as if she was stalling for time. "He wants me to tell you that he has a few things to say to you. And, uh, he wants you to know this will be a very short channeling. His exact words were...uh...his exact words were: this will be a "quickie."

They laughed.

Veda hid her face in her hands.

Alana came to Veda's rescue. "What do you need us to do, Veda?"

Composing herself the best she could, Veda answered, "Oh, just find a place to sit and we'll do a short meditation."

They found comfortable places on the soft meadow grass, closed their eyes, went within, and welcomed Saint Germain.

"Greetings, beloved ones," Saint Germain said, his dark eyes dancing with good humor. "And how do you find your new home?"

Karen grinned. "So this *is* our home...for sure?"

"If you want this to be so."

Glenn looked sharply at Saint Germain. "Who does it belong to?"

"To all of you and to any others who share your dream."

Saint Germain's answer didn't satisfy Glenn, however. "Sure, but that's a figure of speech, isn't it? What I want to know is, who does the valley *really* belong to? Who owns the deed? Who would we talk to about buying it?"

"He is out of the office at the moment," Saint Germain answered and smiled.

"Who is?" Glenn asked.

"The being who owns the property."

Alana caught on. She laughed. "Saint Germain, are you talking about Prime Creator?"

"In...deed," Saint Germain replied. "And I hope you appreciate my play on words."

"Indeed," she replied and chuckled. "So there *is* no owner?"

"An owner can be found, a deed produced...if you require this," Saint Germain responded.

"Well, no, I guess not, but..." Alana began.

"*You* are the owners," Saint Germain reiterated. "Can you begin to allow that you have dreamed this valley into existence? That you have, shall we say, pulled it out of *another* reality, where it has always been, and inserted it into *this* physical reality?"

Evelyn sat up straight—all five feet of her—and asked, "Saint Germain, can I play devil's advocate for a minute?"

"Of course. I know him well. He will not mind if you impersonate him for awhile."

"You're in rare form today," she bantered back.

"I rather thought so myself."

Evelyn continued, "Let's say we go along with the idea that we've dreamed this place into existence...or pulled it from some other dimension. I kind of agree with you, although when I *think* about it, I'm afraid I'm losing my marbles."

"You will understand the truth of this dream *and* the truth of *you* when you move out of what you call your left brain mode of thought," Saint Germain replied.

"Okay," Evelyn began, "but let's get practical. Let's say we start building here. And let's say we decide to be legal, so we ask the building inspector to come out and approve our plans and our buildings. Then what?"

"You need not invite anyone here unless you truly desire to," Saint Germain responded. "You select those you invite into your home, do you not? You do not simply open your house to all who wish to come and go as they please."

"But Evelyn has a good point," Brian persisted. "What if we *did* invite someone here? Like the building inspector?"

"He would not see what you see," Saint Germain answered simply.

"What *would* he see?" Brian asked.

"He would see what he *expects* to see. He would see a valley as he thinks a valley should exist in this locale and at this altitude. There would be a few tall pines, but no green grass and no trees bearing fruit."

Anna grinned and said, "I bet you're going to tell us he wouldn't see our buildings, either."

"Indeed, he would not. And he would wonder why you had called him on a wild goose chase. And he would return to his office and complain about that bunch of airy-fairy New Age hippies playing practical jokes on him."

"Will anyone else be able to see what we see here?" Anna asked. "Or are we the only ones?"

"Some of your brothers and sisters, a few of those who share your dream, will find their way here and will see what you see. They will be able to walk through the portal as you have," Saint Germain answered. He waited a full minute before continuing. "Many here are experiencing difficulty believing the truth of my words. Why is this?"

Glenn spoke for the disbelievers. "Because much as I might *want* to believe you, things like this simply don't happen."

"You mean you have not personally experienced this kind of event," Saint Germain corrected him.

"But that's all I have to go on."

"Do you believe others when they say they can see fairies and elves and nature spirits? And can carry on conversations with them?" Saint Germain asked.

Glenn thought for a moment, then replied, "Yes, actually I do. I mean I believe *some* of these people."

"Yet you yourself cannot see these beings."

"No."

"Are they truly there or are they not?"

"They are for the people who can see them."

"And why is that?"

"Well, because...I guess because they really believe in the possibility..."

"Indeed."

Glenn sighed. "I see what you're driving at. Let me think about it."

Saint Germain continued, "Beloved ones, it is not my intention to make our visit a lengthy one, but before I go let me say this: You are special entities. You have come to this planet with a dream, and the dream is, as I have said to you before, to create a community of true brotherhood and of true sisterhood. In accomplishing your goal, you will be the way-showers for many, many others." He peered deep into their hearts and spoke to them there. "But to bring your beautiful community—your dream—into manifestation you must see events from a larger perspective. *Do not judge what is possible by what you have experienced in this you call your past.* This way of thinking will limit you greatly.

"Believe in dreams and in magic. In dreams, you know, all the rules of common everyday reality are, as you are fond of saying, thrown out the window. In your dreams, if you desire a banana you have only to imagine a banana tree and one manifests instantly before your eyes. Returning to what you call your "real" world, you do not believe that such things can take place. Only in dreams, you insist. Yet this is not the case. You will soon understand the truth of what I am saying, for the time is fast approaching when the *official* rules you *believe* govern your world will no longer apply and many things will be possible." Good humor and love poured forth from Saint Germain's dark and mysterious eyes. "And now I will bid you good-day. Enjoy your dream, beloved ones. It is beautiful and it is real. You have only to touch the soft grass upon which you sit or cast your eyes around at the other treasures of this place to know that. Trust yourselves...and trust that you *are* the dreamers, the *awake dreamers*."

Veda breathed deeply a couple of times and opened her eyes. "Well, that *was* short," she said, sounding surprised.

"*And* confusing," Nancy added.

With a twinkle in her eyes, Evelyn countered, "That's only because we don't understand what we've done...yet."

"It is like this," Emil began, "we dream of inventing some fantastic thing, something—some *gift*—we wish to bring to the world. Yes? We work hard. Many times we almost give up. Then, one day, as if by magic, the gift is before our eyes, finished. We stare at our creation and we scratch our heads, not quite comprehending that *we have done it*!"

"We have, haven't we," Cassandra said, putting her arm around Emil.

Jerry stretched out and lay his head back on the grass.

"Weird, really weird. Like, I've wanted to be part of a loving community for a long time. I searched for it in the sixties when I was doing my hippie thing, but I never found it. Back then I always thought I'd find a community that was already started and go live there. I never imagined *I* would have to start one. *Me*? Oh boy... *help*!"

They laughed.

Kate understood. "I have the same feeling. I always thought someone else would do it, someone who...who *understood* these things better. Better than me anyway," she said.

"Like who?" Glenn wanted to know.

"Well, like some intelligent and loving extraterrestrial who landed in his space ship—or *her* space ship—and showed us poor humans how to birth a community," Kate replied.

"When I think about starting a community, I feel kind of overwhelmed," Cassandra added.

Alana took exception to Cassandra's way of looking at this. "Overwhelmed makes it sound like you're helpless to do anything."

"Okay, what word would *you* use?" Cassandra asked, feeling like she'd just been corrected by her mother.

"The word that comes to me is...awe," Alana answered. "I am in *awe* of this event that is unfolding. This community. *Our* community. I am in awe of what I have created. What we all have created."

"In awe?" Jeff asked.

"Uh-huh. Because you know what, we can *do* this!"

Glenn raised his eyebrows as if he did not *quite* believe her.

Alana saw Glenn's disbelief and quickly countered, "Yes, we can! Here's the way I see it. It's like a story: When this beautiful Earth decided to transform herself, a bunch of us got together on the other side—in the other realms where we also live—and we talked about how we could be part of this wonderful event. And we decided that *some* of us would come here and establish communities, the kind of communities Saint Germain is talking about."

She closed her eyes, then went on, "I can see the leader of our group. She's looking around at us, asking for volunteers. And guess what? When she asked who would come here to assist in Earth's transformation, we all raised our hands and volunteered!"

"I don't remember doing that," Brian said, half serious, half in jest.

"Neither do I," Alana admitted. "And remembering *is* one of the keys. But don't you feel like in these past months something is pushing its way into your memory? Some dream? Some agreement we made? Some purpose for being here? Something like that?"

"Yes. It's vague but it's there," Brian agreed.

Lying or sitting on the luxurious meadow grass, with the comforting sound of the creek a few feet away, and with Alana's story fresh in their hearts, they went inside and remembered their dream.

A few minutes later, Alana said, "I have a couple of suggestions. First, that we hold our next meeting here, all of you who want to anyway."

"When?" Vicki asked, excited.

"Tomorrow!" they shouted.

Alana smiled. "Yes, tomorrow." Then, turning to Connie, she continued, "And the second suggestion involves Connie. I am *very* glad to see you," she said, putting her arms around Connie.

Connie shook her head as if she didn't deserve Alana's hug or her kind words. She cried. "It was hard to come back. I feel like I was such a shit to you guys, especially you, Jerry. I'm sorry. I..."

"Hey Connie, it's okay. No offense taken," Jerry said, obviously speaking from his heart. "How do you feel?"

Connie picked a blade of grass, twirled it in her fingers. "Not real good. I guess you all know I have cancer." She broke down sobbing. "It hurts...and it makes me mad. I know it doesn't make any sense, but I can't help it, that's how I feel. But I don't want to take it out on you guys. I won't. I...I..."

"I intend not to," Alana helped her.

"Yes, thanks. I intend to own my anger and..." She stopped, eyes wide with emotion. "But I am so *scared*."

Many came and hugged her. Evelyn sat down, put Connie's head in her lap, then told her own story. "I had cancer many years ago. Breast cancer. I had both of my breasts removed. I guess you folks don't know that, no one except Anna. She was there for me." Evelyn reached over, took Anna's hand. "I couldn't have gotten through that dreadful time without you. Did I ever tell you that?"

"Many times, sweetie."

"You were like a rock for me."

"Hey, I know I'm tough, but a rock?"

Evelyn grinned. "Yes, a rock you silly goose. You know what I mean." Then to Connie she said, "So why not lean on us and let us help you? Would you accept our help?"

Connie's eyes filled with tears. "But why would you want to help *me*?"

"Oh dear," Evelyn said. "Anna, what did I say to you when you offered to help me?"

"You started crying and you said, 'Why do you want to help *me*?'"

Connie glanced from Evelyn to Anna and back to Evelyn. "You really said that?" she asked Evelyn.

"Yes...more than once if my memory serves me."

"You really want to help me?"

Evelyn smoothed Connie's hair. "Of course. For starters, I have a friend Kathleen who's a wonderful herbalist. Herbs can help you. You can talk to some of the people she's worked with; they'll tell you. So why not make an appointment with her?"

"Okay, I will. Thanks. My doctor wants me to start chemo and radiation. I'm sure she means well, but I don't want to. When my sister had cancer they put her on that stuff, but...it only made her sicker."

"Yes, yes," Evelyn said knowingly. "You can always do those things later if you want to...or if Spirit prompts you to. But let's try some of these alternatives first. They're *very* effective."

"Okay."

Guided by her intuition, Alana suggested, "Let's do a toning, a healing toning for Connie. Everyone know about toning?" Seeing the puzzled expressions on some faces, she explained, "We're going to make sounds. Make whatever sound comes to you. Let yourself be guided by Spirit." To Connie she said, "And if you're willing, we'll put you in the middle of the circle and we'll intend that the toning brings in the healing energies of this beautiful Universe."

Connie agreed, so they formed a circle around her and they toned.

The sounds began softly: wind sighing gently through the trees. Then louder: water rushing and tumbling over rocks. Then sweet sounds: birds singing to each other, mother animals calling to their babies. Low sounds: the surf crashing upon the beach.

Drawn by the love pouring forth from this group of humans, Others—Unseen Others—came to watch and to add *Their* voices: The Ancient Ones, guardians of the Earth and of this sacred spot; Angelic Beings from the heavens; and the Devas and Nature Spirits who called the valley home. They added their voices to the human voices and they all sang for this woman. The sounds rose and fell, blended and melded. Afterwards, many in the group wondered which of their friends could have made such beautiful, celestial tones.

A soft light surrounded them, a light they could have seen if they had opened their eyes at that moment.

As if by prearranged signal, the sounds stopped. No one spoke. They held hands for awhile, then they left the valley, the valley that was to be their home. They left with joy in their hearts, knowing that they would return soon to continue the adventure.

Chapter Seven

Black, unmarked helicopters, heavy caliber guns poking ominously from every conceivable opening, sped fast and low over the wooded countryside, while heavily camouflaged troops roamed the forest below, silently stalking some unseen enemy. As these pictures flashed across the television screen, the newscaster brought them up-to-date on the day's events:

"Heavy fighting is reported in Northern Idaho, near the Canadian border. Also around Billings and Missoula and other scattered locations in Montana. And we have unconfirmed reports of armed resistance in Texas. Although the reports are vague at this time, the fighting appears to be confined to militia and ATSF forces. We understand that several militia groups have managed to surround and pin down a federal strike force in Idaho. Heavy losses are reported on both sides. The head of the newly formed ATSF, General Williams, has dispatched several thousand reinforcements to the three affected states."

Karen and Nancy, along with Jeff and Alana, watched these events unfold on the television.

"The country's really coming apart," Jeff remarked darkly.

Karen bit her lip to keep from crying. "God, hasn't there been enough death in this country? How can they *do* this when millions of people just died in the quake?"

Homecoming

"The government's pushing people too far," Nancy said.

"But how many people have to die?" Karen sobbed. "When my brother Tom and all those other people in Los Angeles died, I could kind of understand, but this...this is just *stupid*! You people are really stupid!" she yelled at the television.

Alana put her arm around Karen, feeling her pain and her outrage.

Although months had passed since the quake had rumbled through California, tearing the land apart as if it was made of paper, suddenly it all came back to Alana: she and Jeff sitting in the Sunshine Cafe as the quake hit. Then the pain and the numbness...and the *waiting*. And the crazy days following the quake—the lies and the cover-ups. How many had died? No one would ever really know. Despite the army blockade still sealing the state in half, some people, like Nancy, had managed to sneak in and out and to report what they'd seen. But they brought back little information, and Southern California remained shrouded in secrecy and in darkness.

What was next for their battered, wounded country? Alana wondered.

The scene on the television switched to the Governor's office in Boise where a distraught Governor Milton Anderson was about to hold a press conference. He angrily pushed away the microphones thrust in his face.

"Governor, do you have any more news about the confrontation up near Bonners Flat?" a reporter asked.

"I don't know any more than you do," the Governor barked.

"So you can't tell us whether the ATSF troops are still under heavy fire?"

"No."

A woman reporter yelled to get his attention. "Governor! Governor Anderson! What do you make of this, sir? What's *happening* in this state?"

The Governor gazed directly into her eyes and replied angrily, "We have a civil war on our hands."

"That's pretty strong language. The fighting seems fairly isolated. Don't you think..."

"What I *think* is we have a civil war on our hands! You think the fighting will remain isolated? No! There will be more!"

"Could this have been avoided?"

"Of course!" the Governor snapped back. "We warned Washington. The folks here have about had it with Washington! They are *fed up*! And the raid on militia headquarters was the last straw!"

"But Sir, these groups pose a threat to the country, don't they?"

With a disgusted expression on his face, the Governor sarcastically replied, "Why don't you people take a good hard look and then *you* decide who's the real threat to our country! No more questions!" He walked away to join a group of aides motioning for his attention.

Jeff headed for the door. "Come on gang, let's go. It's almost nine and we promised the others we'd meet them at ten."

But the television wasn't through with them yet, and before Jeff could turn it off, the familiar logo signaling a special news bulletin flashed across the screen. The picture shifted to a studio where a stunned newscaster reported, "We have just been handed this bulletin: In a daring and well-organized early morning raid on the Federal building in Boise, Aaron Stockman, self proclaimed leader of the militia movement, has been freed and has again fled into the hills. The lightening fast raid by twenty or so of Stockman's followers was so well organized and so swift it took Federal officials completely by surprise. There are no reported casualties. We will keep you posted."

Alana felt the movement of energy in the country. Wild and restless and angry energy. Soon this energy would shape itself into events, events that would forever change the destiny of all who lived in the land.

With the television images fresh in their minds, they left the house, squeezed themselves into the Land Cruiser,

Homecoming

and headed for the valley, quiet and subdued, pondering what they'd just seen. Leaving Mount Shasta, they crossed over I-5 and turned towards the lake. Nancy leaned forward, rested her arms on the back of the seat, and said, "You know, I've been thinking about all the violence. The government and the Gray Men can't much like it that citizens have all these weapons and are fighting back."

"That's probably the understatement of the year," Jeff quipped.

Nancy continued, "So why didn't these guys figure out some way to disarm the country? I'm not sure exactly how I feel about guns—I guess I don't like them much—but if *I* was in power I sure as hell would've taken them away."

"I *hate* guns," Karen declared vehemently.

Alana thought back to the late eighties and early nineties. "I think there *were* lots of attempts to have gun control. Especially after President Reagan and James Brady were shot. Remember?"

"Sure," Nancy answered. "Oh, you're *right*. That's when the control stuff really started."

Jeff added, "I bet the Gray Men had gun control on their agenda for years. Those shootings gave them a good excuse to push for it. It was good timing: a popular President shot and Brady injured for life. Lots of people climbed on the bandwagon."

They swung around the end of the lake, passing a few scattered tents—the weather was too cold for many people to be camping—and the half deserted RV park. At the far end of the long lake, the sparkling white sails of a small sailboat glittered on the deep blue alpine waters.

Jeff turned onto "their" dirt road and slowed down.

Alana continued their conversation. "Why *didn't* they follow through? These guys are *very* smart. I bet they did some market research and decided that pushing for controls would've precipitated more violence than it was worth. They never did figure it out, though, they just kind of dropped it."

A few minutes later, Jeff pulled up alongside Glenn's Volvo. They walked down to the creek to join the others.

Alana sensed the change in Evelyn as soon as she saw her. Usually upbeat and full of energy, today she looked sad and dispirited.

"Connie's pretty sick. She's not coming," Evelyn announced. "Anna's with her."

"It's hard for you," Alana said simply.

Unable to speak, Evelyn just nodded.

"Because of your own cancer?"

Evelyn's blue eyes filled with tears. "Yes, I guess I still mourn for my own breasts. You might not think of it to look at me—not much meat on these bones and never has been—but I had a pretty figure when I was young. And then I got the cancer and they cut my breasts off and threw them away...like rotten meat. I wish..." She clenched her fists in frustration.

Nancy finished her thought for her. "You wish you'd known about the herbs and other ways to heal?"

Evelyn nodded, tears streaming down her face.

Kate took Evelyn's hand and said, "Come on, let's all go over and sit under one of the trees by the creek and we'll talk. You need some support," she said to Evelyn.

With a sigh, Evelyn hunched down, her back against a rock, and stared at the water. "I don't know why this upsets me so much. Shouldn't," she said gruffly, untying, then retying a shoe lace that didn't need fixing.

Alana and Kate exchanged glances, sent a telepathic message that asked, "Who will speak what we both know?" It was Kate who said, "Evelyn, do you feel it was *your* fault you lost your breasts?"

"Course not silly. *I* didn't cut them off. It was that knife-happy doctor. Talked to me like I didn't have a choice, like I might...might die if I didn't let him go ahead with his stupid operation."

Kate pressed her point. "Sure, but maybe you feel you...well...you should have learned more about other healing methods. Maybe you judge yourself for not having at least *tried*."

Evelyn was silent and then a huge sigh escaped her, followed by fresh tears. "Funny you should say that. I've often wondered if I could've found another way. But..." She sighed again. "I didn't do anything, just let him cut on me."

Vicki was closely following Evelyn's story. "When was this, Evelyn?"

With a faraway look in her eyes, Evelyn answered, "Oh, years ago. I was fifty. I'm eighty-four now, so..."

"You're eighty-four?" Brian exclaimed, not believing what he had just heard.

"Yep. Had my birthday last week."

"Why you old coot, why didn't you tell us?" Vicki scolded her.

"Oh, I don't make much commotion about my birthdays any more. They come and go."

Kate wasn't finished yet. "So, what do you think about what I said? Think you might be blaming yourself?"

"Could be. Guess I have to chew on it a bit," Evelyn replied. She untied, then retied the *other* shoelace. "Yep, feels like that's what I've been doing. Guess it's time to let it go."

Alana asked, "Is there some other reason why Connie's illness upsets you?"

"She's pretty sick."

"You feel *you* have to cure her?"

"Oh, no, she has to do that. We can help, though. In fact, I called my herbalist friend and we have an appointment set up for Connie for day after tomorrow."

"You feel she's going to die, Evelyn?" Alana asked softly.

Evelyn smoothed the grass with her hand. "Might."

Alana nodded. "We'll just have to do what we can."

The talk about Connie's illness, about Evelyn's own bout with cancer, and about death quieted everyone and they retreated into their private thoughts. Then the energy of the valley revitalized them. They stirred and stretched, ready to go on to something else.

Nancy said, "Hey, I have something weird to tell you guys. Remember I said I wanted to be the official community photographer? Well, I took a few pictures of us here yesterday. Only none of them came out. They were all fuzzy. I thought maybe my camera wasn't working, so I took a couple of pictures last night. But they were *fine*. There's something about this *place...*"

They laughed along with Nancy.

"Maybe this here valley isn't ready to have her picture taken yet," Andrew said somberly.

"You're right, Andrew," Nancy said. "Guess I'll wait and try later."

Jerry was eager to talk about his favorite subject. "You hear the news today? About the fighting?"

They waited for his report.

Jerry rolled over, cupped his chin in his hands. "You know something, I think it's gonna spread. I have friends in Oregon. They have a group up there. Not a militia exactly, but they have lots of militia contacts. There's a *ton* of people ready to fight. They've got all kinds of weapons and underground bunkers and..." Suddenly, his mood changed and he mumbled, "I guess the whole thing's got me kinda bummed out."

Glancing shyly at Jerry, Veda said, "There is no reason to upset yourself. We need not be part of that energy."

Alana noticed that whenever Veda spoke, Jerry listened to her intently. *Very* intently. *And* with a certain look in his eyes. And she had caught Veda sneaking looks at Jerry, too.

"You're probably right. I go off on these tangents sometimes," Jerry replied apologetically.

Veda reached over and put her hand on his shoulder, reassuring him. "No, it's *good* you say these things. Many of us share your feelings. Correct?" she asked the group.

They agreed.

Looking relieved, Jerry asked, "So, how do *you* handle this, Veda?"

Alana named the look she saw in Jerry's eyes: *adoration*.

With her hand still resting on Jerry's shoulder, Veda answered, "I focus on the 'God I Am.' Saint Germain has taught me how. He's also taught me to expect that others will have their karmic dramas to play out, for this is what is happening on Earth at this time. I watch their dramas, I send love to all of them, but I do *not* participate."

Karen looked skeptical. "Sure, but don't you believe what's happening is wrong? All the killing and the violence?"

Veda took her time responding. "No, not wrong. Not right, either. There are simply some people who need to fight, and they must have others to fight *with*. It is for their learning."

Kate nodded. "And you don't need to be involved in their dramas. Right?"

"I don't, and I'm grateful for that," Veda answered. Looking suddenly self conscious, she took her hand from Jerry's shoulder, then added, "None of you do, either. Otherwise, you would not have gathered together in this group. You would be in some other group. One of the militias perhaps. But certainly not in *this* group."

Nancy jumped to her feet and paced around. "But I get so *angry* when I see what's happening in this country!" she yelled, banging her fist into her open palm. "Sometimes I just want to go and knock some heads together! Doesn't that make me just as bad as those idiots out there who are shooting at each other?"

Veda smiled. "And have you actually gone out there and knocked heads together? Or done violence to someone?"

Nancy kicked some dirt, sending up a little swirl of dust. "No," she muttered.

Alana added her own thoughts. "I have the same feelings sometimes, and I don't like it; but I don't want to beat myself up for it, either. I don't know..." Her voice trailed off. "Maybe it's okay to get angry sometimes, maybe we all have one or two things that will *always* make us mad, no matter *how* evolved we become. Jeff can't stand to see animals mistreated."

"Yeah, it drives me crazy," he admitted.

"But he doesn't go out and beat anyone up. He...what *do* you do, sweetie?"

"I rant and rave for awhile and then I let it go. Until the

next time I see someone being mean to an animal, and I rant and rave some more."

Kate grinned at everyone. "We spend a lot of time sitting around talking, don't we?"

"Maybe it's what we do best," Cassandra replied.

"Maybe," Vicki began, "but there's more to community than *this*." She got up and stretched. "Come on gang, let's have some fun. Let's *play*. My goodness, we haven't even explored the valley yet."

"*Our* valley," Kate corrected her.

"Yes, *our* valley," Vicki laughed.

"Great idea!" Alana exclaimed. "By the way, Jeff and I brought a picnic. Nothing fancy, but..."

"So did I," Kate said.

"Me too," Jerry added.

"Well, hey, maybe we'll just stay here for a couple of days," Jeff said. "We have plenty of food. And it's warm enough. Gotta be at least 10 to 15 degrees warmer than in Mount Shasta, wouldn't you say?" he asked Alana.

"Uh-huh."

Vicki playfully pulled Alana to her feet. "Come on guys, let's go."

They headed off towards the other end of the valley, walking together for awhile, then breaking up into smaller groups. At the first opportunity, Jerry and Veda quietly slipped off by themselves.

Alana nudged Jeff.

"What?"

"Do you think..." she began, looking in the direction of the retreating couple.

Jerry and Veda were half way up the hill. They watched as Jerry offered Veda his hand, helping her over some boulders.

"You mean Jerry and Veda?" Jeff asked.

"Yes," Alana replied. "There's something about those two." She searched for the right words. "It's like their energies line up. I bet their charts are compatible and..."

Jeff interrupted her. "I don't know, sweetie, Veda's pretty shy."

"Not *that* shy."

Jeff laughed.

They hurried to join Karen and Kate and Andrew and the five of them walked along the creek.

Alana breathed deeply. "Oh God, I love this water," she said. She took off her shoes and splashed along in the creek. "Can't you guys just see us living here?" she asked happily.

"I can," Karen replied, joining Alana in the water. "Are we going to build houses?"

"Sure," Jeff answered. "In the spring. Or maybe..." He paused to consider something. "...maybe with the warmer weather we could start this winter."

"What kind of houses?" Karen wanted to know.

"Up to you guys," Jeff replied. He surveyed the land, and Alana could tell that he was seeing the community coming to life. "This place is perfect for several small houses or cottages. See, it's the way the trees are situated and it's all the little hills and valleys. Lots of nooks and crannies. I bet you could build ten small houses here and you'd hardly even see each other. Very private."

As Alana gazed out over the valley, she could almost see the houses, could almost smell the smoke rising from chimneys, could almost hear the sounds of people happily going about their daily tasks.

Jeff was curious about Kate. "What about you, Kate? You see yourself living here?"

Kate's face expressed worry and sadness. "*I* can. I'm *going* to...but my husband Ted, he's still set against the idea, so..."

"He's still mad at you for being in the group?" Alana asked.

"Ted's stubborn. He won't change his mind."

"Can we help you?"

"Unh-unh."

There was nothing else to say. They walked along quietly, occasionally glancing up to watch the others: Veda and Jerry sitting under a huge oak tree, facing each other, deep in conversation; the rest of the group, with Anna leading the way, struggling up the last few steep yards to the rim of the valley.

Alana's child was busy with more possibilities. "You think we could have a pond?" she asked Jeff.

Jeff pointed the way they had come. "Back there a ways…see…where the creek takes a turn and there's a flat spot? That would be a perfect place."

"And we could have ducks and geese?" Alana's child wanted to know.

"Sure."

Karen caught Alana's mood. "And we could swim in the pond? I bet we could." She clasped her hands together. "I can't wait!"

"How long will it take to build everything? And get settled here?" Kate asked Jeff.

"Hard to say. Ordinarily, I'd guess a year or two. But in this magic place? Who knows?"

Andrew was hanging back by himself. "And you, Andrew, can you see yourself living here?" Alana asked.

Andrew stared down at the ground. "I'd sure like to. Guess I could always find a spot and pitch my tent. Be out of the way."

Karen didn't understand. "Why would you do that, Andrew?"

"Oh, I got this here all-weather tent. Real cozy. I'm kind of used to it. My dog Mollie, she likes it, too."

Andrew's answer didn't satisfy Karen. "But wouldn't you like to have a house? Or a cabin?"

"Naw, I don't need something fancy. A tent will do me fine."

Alana didn't quite believe him.

They reached the end of the valley where the creek came cascading down from a higher elevation, splashing noisily over huge granite boulders. A water ouzel, walking along on the bottom of the creek searching for food, popped her sleek head out of the rushing stream and regarded them warily.

The noise made talking difficult, so they sat for awhile, watching the ouzel, listening to the tumbling water, feeling the fine mist on their faces. Then they retraced their steps and joined the others.

Alana peeked inside the basket of food she and Jeff had prepared. "Well, guys," she began, "we could talk some more—do some more planning—*or* we could eat. Personally, I vote for eating. It's around one o'clock, isn't it?"

"More like eleven," Kate said.

"Yeah, eleven sounds right," Glenn agreed. He peered at his watch, shook his wrist. "I must have banged it on something. Can't be three o'clock."

"Mine says the same thing," Vicki said, sounding surprised. "But three? We just *got* here."

Jeff studied the sun. "Ah, folks, I do believe we've just discovered something else odd about this valley: it does funny things to time."

"What do you mean?" Glenn asked.

"Well, look at the sun. I'm no astronomer, but that sun is farther towards the West than it would be if it was twelve. I bet your watches are correct, I bet it *is* three."

Cassandra looked puzzled. "Are we in some kind of time warp?"

In her soft and gentle voice, Veda offered her own explanation, "I believe we are in a place where the ordinary rules for time do not exist. I believe time can expand and contract much easier here than in the outside world."

Alana agreed and she added, "Perhaps this is the way time really *is*."

"Expanding and contracting?" Nancy asked.

Alana thought for a moment. "I'd say it's *subjective*. You know how it is when you're enjoying yourself or when you're totally engrossed in something and you lose track of time? Maybe time changes or molds itself to fit *us*. Or maybe time is simply an illusion and doesn't exist anywhere except in the third dimension. And if this valley is in *another* dimension, then we'd be free of time and that might feel strange at first. Kind of disorienting...disorienting and maybe expansive, too. I'm not exactly clear how this works, but I bet we can learn lots about time in this valley. Let's pay attention and share our experiences," she said, unwrapping a sandwich and taking a bite. "But right now I'm *starved*."

They moved to the meadow, to a spot where they could see Mount Shasta, and ate their picnic lunch. Half way through, Anna showed up.

"How's Connie?" Karen asked.

Anna sat down wearily, put her hands over her face, and rubbed her temples. "She's resting. Feeling better. She wanted to come, but the pain is getting pretty intense."

"Essiac will help a lot," Evelyn said. "My friend Kathleen gave me a pamphlet to read. Wonderful stuff."

They told Anna about their exploration of the valley and about their unusual experience of time.

"Well, here's something *else* kind of interesting," Anna said, piling her plate with food. "You all know I have this, uh, man friend, Steve. Well, I kind of ran into him on the way here, and I invited him to come and see the valley."

Jeff raised his eyebrows. "Don't you think we'd better wait until..."

Anna held up a huge hand. "Hold on, I know what you're going to say...I think. Let me finish the story." She took a bite, chewed thoughtfully and continued, "He was going to follow me in his car. So, he gets onto the road and wham, his car stalls. Couldn't start it no matter *what* he did."

Alana and Evelyn exchanged knowing glances.

Anna went on, "We push his car to the side of the road and he gets in *my* car. Great, everything's peachy, so we go maybe a hundred yards and he doubles up in pain. Stomach cramps. Okay, we stop for a couple of minutes until he feels better, then we go another hundred yards...only *now* he has a headache. Bingo! The light goes on: Steve isn't supposed to visit the valley, at least not yet. So I took him home and put him to bed."

"Put him to bed, huh? Now we know what took you so long," Brian teased.

Anna tried to hide her embarrassment, but to no avail. "Unh-unh, it's not what you think. I put him *right* to bed and came *right* over here." Seeing the good-natured smiles, she gave up defending herself and joined the fun. "But I did tell him I'd drop over later…just to check and see how he's feeling, mind you."

"Sure, sure," Jerry quipped.

Anna stuck her tongue out at Jerry, then turned to the group and asked, "So, what do you think about what happened with Steve and me?"

With a smirk on his face, Jerry teased, "I think you should have stayed and played "nursey." Maybe a sponge bath."

Anna slowly and deliberately put her plate of food down on the grass and stared at Jerry, her face giving no hint of what was to come. Then, with catlike quickness, she pounced on top of him, pinned him to the ground, and tickled him. Squirm and twist as he might, he couldn't throw her off. Giggling uncontrollably, he squealed, "Okay, okay, I give up! Oh God, stop!" Anna took her time. She sat on top of him for a few more seconds, patted his cheek affectionately, and calmly returned to pick up her plate.

Jerry sprawled out on the grass, exhausted. He grinned at Anna. "Boy you're strong."

With a deadpan expression, Anna replied, "You better believe it, buddy."

Veda smiled at Jerry with much affection and much love, making no attempt to hide her feelings.

Staring at Jerry with an expression that said: I *dare* you to even open your mouth, Anna repeated her question, "What do you guys make of what happened on the road?"

Looking very innocent, like he was the last person in the world even to *think* of making a smart-ass remark, Jerry kept quiet.

Kate answered, "Like you said, Steve isn't supposed to visit here yet."

"Maybe it would be a good idea not to invite anyone here, at least until we can figure out who the valley will accept," Evelyn cautioned. "What do you think?"

"Why not let Spirit decide," Alana suggested.

"Remember, Saint Germain said some people will be drawn here and will be able to come through the doorway. Let's see who shows up and let's trust that they're the right people."

Everyone agreed.

They finished their lunch, put the rest of the food away, and relaxed.

Alana lay down on her back, hands under her head, and gazed up at the cloudless blue sky. "Yesterday I became aware of something that's, well, kind of odd about..."

"Yes, we know, kind of odd about this valley," Vicki chirped.

Alana laughed. "No. Well, yes of course, but that's not what I meant. No, this is something different. This is about *us*, about the composition of our group. We have no children."

"Except for Jerry," Anna said seriously.

"Hey, not fair," Jerry protested.

Alana joined the fun. "Yes, except for our one resident middle-aged child, we have no children." She waited for the giggling to die down, then went on, "We have all kinds of people here...all ages...some married, some not. We have different religious persuasions. But no children. I got to thinking about what a community would be like without kids, and I'm not sure I like the feel of it."

"Ours are all grown and married," Vicki said.

"Thank the Lord," Glenn added.

Vicki poked him hard in the ribs.

Jeff reached for Alana's hand. "We thought about having children when we were first married. I'm not exactly sure why we didn't, but I believe..." He squeezed Alana's hand. "I don't want to speak for you, sweetie."

"No, go ahead."

"I believe we didn't need the experience. I believe we both had lots of kids in other lifetimes, and..."

"Hey, listen to *you* talking about other lifetimes," Glenn kidded him. "Couple of months ago you sure pooh-poohed *that* idea. Next thing you know *I'll* be talking about *my* other lifetimes."

"I certainly hope so," Vicki said. "You'd understand yourself better."

"Well, maybe, but..."

Jeff held up his hand. "Anyway, the bottom line is we just didn't want to have kids."

Kate took a chance and asked, "You think children would get in your way somehow?"

Alana's intuition immediately alerted her to pay attention.

Jeff took his time before answering. "I'm not sure. I like being around children. *Some* children."

Obviously choosing her words carefully, Kate asked Jeff, "What about having them here in the community?"

Jeff answered without thinking. "The idea kind of scares me."

With a knowing look on her face, Kate continued, "Like you wouldn't be able to get away from them? Like they'd follow you around and bug you and pester you until you'd feel like drowning them?"

Jeff laughed nervously. "Yeah, something along those lines."

It was Alana's turn to ask a question. "Katie, what are you getting at?"

After a long silence, Kate replied, "I have two children of my own. A boy and a girl."

Kate's revelation surprised Brian. Since the earthquake, Kate and her husband had been living in a cottage at the back of his property, and he'd never seen any children. "You have *kids*?" he asked.

Kate hid her face in her hands for a moment, then went on with her story, "They are by my first husband. They live with him, but...I want them back. I gave them to him when we got divorced. My life was a mess, and the thought of raising kids was too much. I'm not proud of what I did, giving them away, but I did it and I guess I needed to." A tear slid silently down her cheek, fell onto the soft meadow grass. She looked around the group and said, "I want them back. How would you feel about having them here?"

Before anyone could respond, another voice—a small,

wavering voice—announced, "There's another child, too." It was Karen who spoke. She tried to smile, but mostly she looked as if she might jump out of her skin as everyone's attention suddenly focused on her. "I'm pregnant," she said. "About three months."

"Oh, I didn't know you were..." Vicki began, then stopped, her face red with embarrassment.

Karen finished Vicki's question. "Married?" She shook her head. "I'm not. Right after the quake, when I was so upset about my brother being killed, this friend of mine...well, he came over a couple of times and let me cry on his shoulder. He was really sweet. And then one night I guess...things just...happened. He's helping me with my expenses and all, but I don't want to get married and neither does he...so I guess if you take me into the group you take my baby, too," she said, the defensiveness obvious in her voice.

Vicki beamed. "I feel like I'm going to be a grandmother. I kind of like the idea."

"Personally, I'd be honored to have you and your baby in our community," Cassandra said.

"Me too," another murmured.

Karen burst out crying. "Oh, *thank* you! I was so afraid you wouldn't want me. *Us* I mean."

Alana looked pleased. "Great, there's *one* child on the way. Now, how about yours, Kate?"

"Well, they're a bit older," Kate responded, worried. "Not babies exactly. Maybe they wouldn't fit in."

"Why not bring them to one of our groups," Alana suggested. "We can meet *them* and they can meet *us*, and we can mutually decide if we all want to live together. How does that sound?"

"Great. They're coming for a visit next week. I'll bring them then."

With that settled, Evelyn got up and stretched. "I don't know about you youngsters, but my bones are getting tired. This old body needs a nice soft mattress to lie down on for an hour."

"Yes, I'm getting tired, too," Karen said.

"Time to go I guess," Vicki said sadly.

They collected their gear, and each said good-bye to the beautiful valley that was quickly becoming their home.

Chapter Eight

The next day dawned clear and cold with the threat of snow. Alana put on a heavy winter sweater, made herself a cup of blackberry tea, and sat by their big picture window watching the heavy dark snow clouds gather around Mount Shasta. Her thoughts drifted to the valley. Closing her eyes, she saw the creek, the green meadow, and the bright patches of red and purple flowers. She'd meant to bring a few flowers back so that she could look them up in her flower book. Maybe next time. Warming her hands on her tea cup, she sighed and felt a familiar feeling in her heart and in the pit of her stomach: a *longing*. She *longed* to be in the valley, surrounded by the beautiful, magical energy of the place and away from...from all the darkness and the violence in the outside world. A disturbing thought assailed her: was the valley becoming an escape? A way to avoid life? She hoped not.

She and the others had originally planned to visit the valley today to search for building sites, and she had eagerly anticipated this. But one by one they'd called and cancelled, agreeing to go tomorrow instead.

Well, she told herself, if she couldn't go to the valley, at least she would see some of her friends today—Anna and Evelyn and Brian, and maybe Jerry, were coming for a potluck around six. Didn't help much, though, she still longed for the valley. She finished her tea, and with a last glance at the Mountain, went into the kitchen, washed her cup, then poked around in the refrigerator. Satisfied that she had plenty of food for the potluck, she went outside and sat on the front steps, feeling more and more like an abandoned child.

She had the sudden urge to jump in the car and go to the valley by herself. Only...only it didn't feel like she was supposed to.

She could have gone to town with Jeff. He'd found a couple of local carpenters who might help with their building and he was going to talk to them.

"Why not come?" he'd said. "I'd like your reading on these guys. And I'll take you out to lunch."

She had declined. "I have a few things to do," she'd answered, although she couldn't think of *what* things exactly.

They'd been sitting on the front steps. Jeff seemed in the mood to linger. "By the way, we haven't decided what kind of house we want. Any thoughts?"

Alana's child had the answer to *that* question. "We always talked about a round house, remember? We said we were round house people."

"That means a yurt or a dome. Any preferences?"

"Let's get some books and brochures and do some dreaming. We have time, don't we?"

"Depends on how quick we want to begin building. We don't have to build from scratch you know."

Alana made a face. "You mean like a mobile home?"

"Unh-unh. I mean like a kit. Or a prefab. There was a company over on the coast a few years ago that made beautiful prefab yurts. Remember, I showed you pictures of them?"

"Not me, sweetie. Maybe one of those other women in your life."

"Oh, you mean before *we* got married."

"Yup."

"Hmm. Maybe. There were so many I can't remember."

Alana swatted him playfully with the rolled up *San Francisco Ledger*.

Jeff laughed and hugged her and said, "I've got to get going. See you later."

Alana still had the paper. She opened it and spread it out on the porch. For years an avid reader of newspapers — sometimes devouring two or three a day—lately she had tired of the sameness of the stories. And of the lies. Although not better than the rest, the *Ledger* was the paper she usually bought. Perhaps because it lied so *creatively*. She browsed through it occasionally, reading between the lines, paying more attention to what was *not* reported than anything else.

The *Ledger's* front page blared forth the news of the intensified fighting in the Western states. Outbreaks of violence were now reported in *five* states, although, curiously enough, California was not one of them. More ATSF troops—*and* more United Nations troops—were being hastily mobilized. Heavy casualties on both sides. End of story.

Another front page story told of the incessant rains pounding the Southwest. Fifteen days without any letup in sight. Lots of flash floods. Two hundred dead.

The other item that caught her interest concerned the increased number of UFO sightings in California—lots of unexplained green lights streaking across the midnight sky and lots of saucers, especially over the desert regions. Old stuff...*except* the *tone* of the story was different. In fact, now the tone of *all* such stories was different. A few months ago, the media's attitude toward UFO sightings and the like was extremely negative: they either didn't mention them or they downplayed them or they labeled those who reported them as publicity-seeking crackpots. Now the media treated these people *as individuals with important information to give.* Why? She knew that the secret world government controlled the media and that they always had a hidden agenda in reporting the news; they used their control of the media to shape public opinion and to mold thoughts. Why this sudden change in attitude toward things extraterrestrial? Very curious.

She finished the paper. Now what? A walk perhaps? No. Then what?

"Spirit, what do *you* want me to do?" she asked. She sat for a moment listening inside, then felt the gentle prompting that was Spirit's way of communicating with her: She was to go into Mount Shasta. No reason why, but then Spirit never gave a reason why. She got her coat and hat. Sam gazed up at her expectantly and wagged his tail. "No, you stay here now," she said sternly. But he followed her to the door and she relented. "Oh, okay, come on, but you have to stay in the car." Sam took this news in stride.

She drove down Old Stage Road, Sam in the back seat, his nose stuck out the window. He alternated between sniffing the air and warmly—and wetly—licking her ear. She reached back and gave him a one-arm hug, very glad he'd come.

She hadn't been to town for several days, maybe even a week. Right after moving to Mount Shasta last spring, they had spent lots of time in town, sitting in the Sunshine Cafe, drinking coffee, and watching the people. But lately...well, they preferred being with their group of friends, the group that was fast becoming their family.

Reaching the outskirts of the city, she began to feel gloomy and depressed. Dammit, where was the sun? Glancing up, she saw only heavy dark clouds—snow clouds—blanketing the sky. And she hated the snow! Suddenly, she regretted coming. She wanted to be back home. Or better yet, in the valley. She stifled the urge to turn around and go back. Spirit wanted her here for some reason.

She parked the car, leaving Sam to guard it, and decided to walk for awhile. Everyone she passed on the street looked depressed and tense and empty inside, as if they had been turned upside down and all the life force drained out of them. No, that can't be, she told herself. Must be the mood *I'm* in. I must be projecting my own feelings onto *them*.

She decided to stop thinking and concentrate on walking. She meandered along Mount Shasta Boulevard, stopping occasionally to peer in store windows. She turned up a side street past rows of well-kept houses with their beds of brightly colored flowers and manicured lawns. Mount Shasta was not a large town, and she soon came to the outskirts. She felt the ground beneath her feet and she felt the connection—the grounding—to Mother Earth. On impulse, she walked into the city park and sat on a swing. Gazing up at Mount Shasta, she swung herself gently, lost in her daydreams, and when she'd had her fill of that, she walked back downtown for another reading of hearts and minds.

It was the same: peering inside the people rushing past her, she read emptiness and despair. And then she realized what she was *really* reading: *They had no dream to warm them and to keep them going.* And with no dream, they had no purpose, only emptiness and waiting...waiting...waiting for something to happen to give their life meaning.

Now she felt worse, much worse than when she'd first come into town. She reminded herself—again—that reading hearts and minds was risky business...*unless* she remembered to let these thoughts and emotions pass *through* her. They were not hers. They belonged to these others. Read them and *let them go!* Her serenity demanded it! She breathed deeply, then mentally cleared her aura and her energy field, much as she might do in a smudging, and felt instantly better.

So engrossed was she in her own thoughts that for a moment she didn't recognize where she was. Oh, yes, Mount Shasta. But *where* in Mount Shasta? A man and a woman hurried by, giving her a funny sideways glance. No! I'm fine! she wanted to yell at them. I don't know where I am, that's all! Forcing herself to focus on her surroundings, she recognized some familiar landmarks: There was the old train station...and the Forest Service building. Then she laughed, for she was standing squarely in front of the Sunshine Cafe. Inside, two friends were playing chess at a corner table. She would find warmth and companionship there, people who knew her and loved her.

But that was not her path today. Impulsively, she spun around, retraced her steps, and headed for an old, established Mount Shasta cafe at the other end of town, a place she'd been only once and hadn't much liked. Pulling her coat tighter around herself to protect against the sharp, biting wind, she hurried down the nearly deserted street, not even noticing when she passed Evelyn's bookstore, and not feeling the first few snowflakes drifting around her face, stinging her eyes.

Harry's cafe was empty except for a lone customer staring into his cup of coffee and three bored looking waitresses, one, young, in her twenties, and the other two in their fifties or sixties. The television was on, tuned to a national news station, the sound barely audible over the whir of the huge corner heater and the chatter of the waitresses.

Still not sure why Spirit had prompted her to *this* spot, Alana sat down at the counter. "Coffee please," she said to one of the older waitresses, a woman with sad, tired eyes. She braced herself for what was sure to be a weak, unsatisfying cup of coffee. "On second thought, make that tea, would you? How about some lemon tea...if you have it." The waitress smiled and returned a moment later with her tea.

"Anything else I can get you, hon?" the waitress asked.

"No, I'm fine," Alana replied. Wanting to make conversation and to draw the woman out, she asked, "Anything interesting on the TV?"

"More about the fighting," the waitress replied and laughed derisively. "Men!" she spat. "What in the hell are we going to *do* with them? Know what I mean, honey?"

"Well, I'm not sure," Alana replied, hurriedly pouring her tea to avoid the woman's intense stare.

Alana shifted her gaze to the television where ATSF forces and UN troops marched along on some unidentified rural road. With a disgusted expression on her weather-beaten face, the waitress said, "Look at them. Little boys playing soldier." She poured a huge amount of sugar into her coffee, stirred it absentmindedly and continued, "Oh hell, things never change I guess. My husband went to fight in World War Two. But back in *those* days we thought going off to war was a great adventure. We were going to make the world a safe place. Know what I mean?"

"Uh-huh," Alana mumbled into her cup.

The younger waitress wandered over and sat on a stool at the end of the counter. Chewing her gum busily, she looked inquiringly at the two women and asked, "You talking about the fighting?"

"What else," the older woman replied. She smiled at Alana. "By the way, name's Edna. And this here is Haley. Haley just moved into town. And what's your name, hon?"

"Alana."

"My, what a pretty name. Sounds foreign. Are you a foreigner?" She didn't wait for Alana's answer. "We get lots of foreigners here, don't we Haley? Anyway, I was telling Alana here about the Big War. My husband came back more or less all in one piece. Lots of the boys didn't, though."

The customer, a middle-aged man, called out, "Hey Edna, mind if I turn the TV up? Sounds like something important is happening!"

"Doubt it...but suit yourself, Mel."

He turned up the volume, catching the newscaster in mid sentence: "...believed the fighting was more or less localized. But we are now getting reports of civil disturbances in several other states," he said. He read from a paper someone handed him: "In New Hampshire and Maine, in Ohio and Pennsylvania and in Georgia, there have been reports of violence and looting. The violence appears aimed at the government, with many federal buildings damaged or destroyed. Just who is in back of all this, whether the work of militias or possibly others dissatisfied with Washington, we aren't sure. But you can *bet* that the ATSF will respond as they have in other hot spots around the nation." The newscaster stopped reading, lifted his eyes, and looked directly into the camera. "And what is Washington's response? No one knows, for there has been an almost total blackout of news from the White House. Many around the Capitol are readying themselves for the President to declare a national state of emergency, or even martial law, but it's anybody's guess what will happen, or when."

"Okay Mel, heard enough?" Edna barked. "Scoot your little butt closer to that damn thing if you want, but turn it *down*, will you? We're trying to have an intelligent, civilized conversation over here. Jeeze, the TV gets on my nerves sometimes."

Deciding perhaps that he *had* heard enough, Mel left the television and joined them.

They want to talk, Alana realized. They want to talk...and *I* want to listen.

Alana now knew why Spirit had impulsed her to come into town and into this cafe—Spirit wanted her to read the hearts and minds of the people here. These *particular* people. Why? She didn't understand, but maybe she didn't have to understand...yet.

"Lots of violence these days," Alana said, hoping to get the conversation going again.

"That's why I moved here," Haley volunteered. "I lived in San Francisco; but it's crazy there. You walk down the street and people look at you like they'd cut your throat if you looked at them wrong. Creepy, know what I mean?"

Alana nodded.

Edna agreed. "People are mean today. Mean spirited. Even up here in Mount Shasta we're beginning to see the meanness."

"Drugs, that's the problem," Mel volunteered.

Edna wasn't sure she completely agreed with *that*. "Maybe...but it's gotta be something else, too," she said. "Wasn't always like this," she added, as if apologizing for the present miserable state of affairs.

Alana felt the sadness well up in Edna's heart.

"Wasn't always like this, was it Mel?" Edna repeated. "Remember back in the forties...even the fifties...we had some fun and life had some meaning. You worked hard and raised your family. People got together and helped each other out. And you could walk down the street without being mugged." She shook her head sadly, looking much older than her years. "But not now. Now you walk into a store or the Post Office and you don't know if some damn nut case is going to pull out an AK-47 and start blasting away. Jeeze, it's creepy."

"It's not like that up here," Mel protested.

"You watch. It won't take long. It's like a cancer and it's spreading fast. We'll get it," Edna warned.

Alana felt Edna's confusion and her pain. Life was not turning out the way it was *supposed* to, and she didn't understand why or what to do.

This — the pain and confusion of broken dreams — was what she was sensing in the hearts and minds of those she passed on the Mount Shasta streets. Overwhelmed by broken promises, by the disintegration of the old familiar ways, by the lies, people were withdrawing inside themselves, unhappy, angry, waiting.

"How do you deal with the way things are now?" Alana asked, really wanting to know.

Edna looked into Alana's eyes, sensed her sincerity. She was silent for a moment, and then a tear slid down her weathered cheek, a tear she was quick to brush away. "I'm just tired you understand. Usually don't get all blubbery like this," she apologized.

"Of course."

"I don't know about your question. Guess I don't do *anything*. Just mind my own business and hope things will get better. But you know what really gets me? I got two of the prettiest grandchildren you ever did see. Here, I'll show you a picture." She proudly showed Alana and the others a picture of a boy and a girl, both about three. "You know what really gets me? What do I tell them about this world? How do I get them ready for it?"

"I don't want to have kids. Too weird now," Haley said. "I just want someone to *do* something."

"You mean do something about what's going on in the country?" Alana asked.

"Uh-huh. Someone's got to *do* something," Haley repeated vehemently.

"What about the Corporation? You think they're doing anything?" Alana asked.

Haley spit her gum into a napkin, carefully wrapped it up, and replied, "They started out okay, and they've got some good ideas...but I don't know, they seem like all the rest now."

Mel added, "You know what's wrong with the world? They want your money. Everyone wants your money."

The two waitresses nodded in agreement. "Men!" Edna snapped.

"Nope, nope. It's money. It's what money does to you," Mel insisted.

"Somebody's got to do *something*," Haley said. "Otherwise we'll all kill each other."

Mel offered his solution: "We need a leader. Now you talk about the old days. Remember FDR?"

Edna scrunched up her face. "He was okay."

Mel continued, "He was a real leader. Took a gander at the country and saw the mess we were in and *took over*. Gave us *direction*. Told us what we needed to do and by gum we *did* it! And he wasn't after our money, either. Had lots of his own. There's nobody like him now. All the good ones are gone now."

"Mel honey, for once I agree with you," Edna said.

By now, three more people had joined their little group.

"Eisenhower was the one I liked," a woman customer offered. "A kind man. But a military man. Knew how to give commands."

Alana was surprised. *And* alarmed. "You believe the military should take over?"

"Well, maybe not the whole military. Someone like Eisenhower would be okay, though, someone to take *charge*. But someone *kind*, like he was."

"You know anybody like that?" Alana asked the group.

No one did. The energy spiraled down then, and after a couple of minutes of desultory small talk, one by one they drifted away.

Alana sent them all love and light, finished her tea, and left.

Driving home, with the images of the townspeople fresh in her heart, she knew that the country was filled with such people—afraid and sad and waiting for some direction, for someone they could believe in and for someone to tell them what to do.

Jeff listened to her story, then added his own observations. "Hmm, that's interesting. I've picked up the same thing, especially since the ATSF and the militias have been tangling. People are scared."
"Panicked is more like it."
"Yeah," he agreed.
She told him her dream of the blood-red sky and of the birds flying upside down. *And* of the radio announcement she could not quite hear. "The radio announcement...it was so *real*. You know how dreams are sometimes."
"Uh-huh."
"I'm going to hear that announcement someday. I know it. Gives me goose bumps."
"But in the dream you couldn't understand any of it?"
"I only caught a few words. It was an announcement from Washington. Really important. But I couldn't take my eyes off the birds and the sky, so I didn't get to the radio in time and I missed most of it. I *wanted* to hear it, but I couldn't," she replied, clenching her fists in frustration.
Jeff trusted her dreams. "You think you're getting a premonition of something that's going to happen?"
"Yes."
"Like another quake? Or..."
"As big as that, or bigger, but...not a quake. Nothing do to with Mother Nature."
"Hmm. A real mystery." He thought for a moment. "As you were talking, I was getting kind of excited. Has that kind of energy. Know what I mean?"
"Exactly."
He continued, "But scary, too."
"Yes, both."
"Nothing we can do except wait I guess," he said. "Not to change the subject, but I think I found a couple of people to help us with the building. A man and a woman. Both carpenters. Nice people. They're excited about our project

and not in the least worried that we're going to ignore the building codes. And guess what else? They know the folks I was telling you about, the ones who build the prefab yurts. They gave me the address. Want to go over to the coast one of these days and take a look and see if you could live in a yurt?"

Jeff was practically jumping up and down at the thought of checking out the yurts. Alana loved the part of him that got excited like that. "Sure," she replied. "And maybe some of the others want to go, too."

The "potluckers" arrived at six-thirty.

"Veda wanted to come but she has friends visiting," Jerry announced.

He's happy, Alana thought. She could sense Veda's energy around him, surrounding him like a warm blanket. Good.

They ate and talked, bringing each other up to date as good friends do after even a short absence.

Anna spoke what they all felt. "I miss the others. I wish we were all here together."

"Me too," Alana said. "But I guess this is how it'll be sometimes. We won't always meet as one large group."

"Boy, I sure don't like the sound of *that*," Jerry said. "But you're probably right."

They ate quietly... *and* a bit somberly.

Brian was the first to speak. "The fighting has spread. Pretty bad now."

"I heard," Alana said. "Three or four more states."

Brian shook his head. "Unh-unh. More. Twenty at least. And it's not just the militias anymore. There's lots of fighting in the cities. Ordinary people. Remember after the quake and the Market crash how everyone in the cities came unglued and how they sent in the troops? Well, same thing's happening now. The situation is totally out of control."

Jeff was busy building himself a gigantic sandwich. *And* listening intently to Brian's news. "I wonder why we haven't seen any fighting here?" he asked. He took off the top slice of bread, added more sprouts. "There's fighting everywhere, but not here. And there's lots of people in the county who hate the government, especially now that the Corporation's decided to keep their troops in town."

"Fighting's getting closer," Evelyn said ominously. But before she explained, she reached over and playfully stuck an olive on top of Jeff's sandwich. "Just what it needs, don't you think?" she asked, her blue eyes twinkling.

Alana was interested in Evelyn's news. "What do you mean it's getting close?"

Evelyn suddenly looked serious and a little frightened. "There's fighting up in Eugene. Heard about it on the car radio coming over."

Jeff was about to add another olive next to Evelyn's. He stopped. "Eugene? Boy, that's only a couple of hundred miles."

"How bad, Evelyn?" Alana asked.

"Don't know exactly."

Jeff lost interest in his sandwich. "Eugene's awfully close. Kind of brings it home, huh."

"You think it'll work it's way down here?" Jerry asked.

Brian thought about it. "I'm not sure if we'll have that kind of violence here. But we don't have to. Let's say things get out of hand on the West Coast—*anywhere* on the West Coast—it could still get in the way of our community."

Anna looked worried. "Like how?"

"I don't *know* exactly. Maybe some kind of martial law or..."

"Or a military takeover?" Anna asked.

"Possibly," Brian responded. "We've been close to a takeover several times in the past."

Alana didn't agree. "I don't see that happening, guys. I know the country's ripe for it, but I still believe the Gray Men want to avoid a confrontation. Martial law or a military takeover, that would *really* get people riled up. They want control, but they want it as easily as possible. Which means without lots of violence."

Jerry was skeptical. "I don't see how they're going to

pull *that* one off. Sort of too late, what with all the ATSF guys and the militias killing each other."

Alana related her dream. "My dream is telling us something is about to happen. And crazy as it sounds, I think whatever's coming will benefit us. I think it'll be so big we'll be left alone."

Evelyn told them of *her* dream. "No birds flying upside down," she began, "but I had the same feeling...you know, something *big* about to happen. Only it felt like the country was being invaded."

"It is," Brian commented wryly. "Look at all the UN troops."

Evelyn shook her head. "Unh-unh, felt like another kind of invasion."

"I had a similar dream," Anna said. She frowned. "Fuzzy though. I can't remember any details."

As Alana listened, she knew—*absolutely*—that these dreams were *preparing* them for something. What? Asking Saint Germain probably wouldn't help; he would tell them they needed to figure this one out by themselves. So, nothing to do but wait.

Suddenly, and without any warning, Anna sat up straight and yelled, "It's a test!"

Evelyn almost jumped out of her chair. Holding her hand over her heart, she gasped, "My dear, let us know when you are going to do that, will you?"

Anna smiled sheepishly. "Sorry, it just came out. But it *is* a test."

Half expecting another blast from Anna, Jeff moved his chair back a safe distance. "Okay. *What's* a test?" he asked cautiously.

Waving her arms around excitedly, Anna exclaimed, "This! *All* of this! The fighting! The rioting in the cities! The crazy weather and the quakes! All the negative news on the television! It's a test to see how focused we can stay!"

Brian scrunched up his face in doubt. "You mean it's been created just for *us*?"

"No," Anna answered. "Everyone has created these

events for their own learning. For *us* it's a test of our focus and our commitment."

"Oh, sure, I understand," Brian said. "I think," he added doubtfully.

Jerry helped him out. "It's like this; we *could* let all this stuff bum us out. We could all go around moaning and complaining how we can't have our community because of the violence and because of all the possible things the government might do...like a military takeover and that kind of stuff."

Jeff agreed. "Only we don't have to let that happen. We don't have to let ourselves be pulled off course. We can go on very calmly with our plans, because we don't have to get involved in this drama unless we *need* that experience."

"And we *don't* need that experience," Evelyn added emphatically.

They looked at each other, *knew* they understood, and knew that no more words were necessary.

They enjoyed each other's company for awhile, brainstormed about their community, got high on their own energy. Alana served them peach pie; then they left, agreeing to meet again in two day's time to talk some more about their community.

Alana suggested a walk. "Our nightly stroll. Pretty soon we'll be taking our walks in the valley," she said happily.

Jeff felt her joy. "Our own valley to walk in whenever we want. Sounds wonderful."

She took his arm. "I noticed you didn't bring your pack this evening," she kidded him.

"Hey, I knew I forgot something. I can always go back and get it. Or maybe we can get Sam to go back."

"No, just give me a nice big hug."

Jeff put his arms around her.

Sam sighed and plopped down to wait, disgusted at this turn of events.

Jeff felt some tenseness in her. "You feeling okay?"

"Yes...except whatever I was picking up in town today is still in me someplace. In my aura or my energy field. I can't do this anymore, I mean store things like this. I need to find a way to let other people's emotions and energy pass through me. *Really* pass through me."

He saw how she took everyone's problems into herself, tucking them into a corner of her heart, and it worried him. He hugged her. "It would be wonderful for you to learn how to let go of that stuff."

Alana nodded.

"You *sure* you don't want me to go back and get the pack?" Jeff asked.

She laughed. "No, let's walk." A couple of minutes later she said, "I have the oddest feeling that we're going to be alone very soon."

"You and I?"

"No, the *group*. The *family*." This was the first time she had said the word family out loud and she liked the way it sounded. She went on, "Here's how I vision it: We're on a boat; we're leaving the harbor, and the rest of the people — I mean almost everyone else in the country—is standing on the shore watching us go. And the distance gets farther and farther...until we almost can't see them. It's like that."

"How does this vision feel to you?"

"Good question." She thought for a moment and answered, "Mostly okay. I'm kind of scared—or excited— that we're going off by ourselves. And I'm sad the others aren't going with us, because I don't think they are. And I feel bad about something else. The people on the shore, they want someone to give them direction, to tell them what to do. They want it *and it will happen*...soon. I wish they could do things for themselves, but they don't want to, or they don't believe they can, and I'm sad about that." She squeezed his hand, then swung both their arms way high the way children do when they are happy. She continued, "Mostly, though, it's a good feeling. *Exciting*. Yes, exciting. This trip we're embarking on, it's like going home after being away for a long time. Yes, that's what it is...it's a *homecoming*."

"A homecoming. Sounds great."

They strolled some more, then Alana asked, "By the

way, where *is* your pack? Maybe you could find it when we get home. We could get the blanket out and spread it out on the porch. Just to look at the stars mind you."

"Sure. I'd love to look at the stars with you. And I know exactly where it is."

Alana smiled and snuggled close to him.

Chapter Nine

"It can't get much worse!" Nancy yelled, beating her fists on the carpet.

"Sure it can! And it's *going* to!" Glenn yelled back, his face red with anger.

"Shit! Who made *you* the authority?"

"I've been around! Believe me things can get worse! So don't fall apart for Christ sakes!"

"I'm *not* falling apart! But you…"

Jerry leaned forward and held up his hands, pleading, "Hey guys. Relax…okay?"

Nancy and Glenn stopped yelling, but they continued to glare menacingly at each other.

A dark, invisible cloud had crept into the room… *and* into their hearts.

Alana sighed. Her head throbbed. After only five minutes, the meeting—an important planning meeting—had turned into a shouting match. Not an auspicious start. Why were tempers so short tonight? The full moon? Perhaps. But something else was going on, something Alana couldn't quite figure out. The energy in the room just seemed… *contentious*. Right from the start.

Anna came over and put her arm around Nancy. Scowling, Nancy shrugged it away. "Okay, okay, I'm fine," she said angrily.

Without saying another word, Anna calmly plopped her

large frame down next to Nancy, not in the least upset by her refusal to be comforted. After waiting a moment, she asked, "Want to talk about what's bugging you?"

Looking like a child who wanted to be left alone to pout, Nancy yelled, "No! Have someone *else* talk! I'm tired of talking!" She crossed her arms, closed her heart, and ignored everyone. Then, a few seconds later, she relented and said, "Okay! You want to know what's bugging me? The country's in a civil war! We're going to have fighting here. *Real* soon! Then what? You think they'll let us build our houses? I sure as hell *doubt* it. I'm just...I'm just God damned frustrated! Why can't these idiots *stop* it! I've waited all my life for this kind of community, and now...now everything's going down the tubes!" She fought to hold back her tears.

Alana had to admit the news *was* bad. In only forty-eight hours, every grievance, every buried hurt, every hatred had malevolently and odiously bubbled to the surface. The morning news brought reports of out-of-control riots in every major city, even in the smaller towns and villages, the places usually immune from such violence. People shooting each other...over a look...or a word. Over *nothing*! The country had gone mad!

It was as if in the middle of the night someone had sprayed some evil virus over every city and town in the country. A virus that turned people mean and contentious...and *hateful!*

Now, the virus had crept through the walls of *this* house to infect *this* group of people, *this group of people who a few hours ago had opened their hearts to their dream of a new and loving way of life.* Yes, something was in the room, something dark and angry, casting a net of hopelessness and despair around everyone, then tightening it, threatening to squeeze the life out of their beautiful dream.

To make matters worse, she and Jeff had their *own* problems. They had argued sharply just before the group had arrived. One of those sudden, "crazy" arguments about... *nothing*. Worse, they hadn't had time to clear the contentious energy. She *hated* that.

Homecoming

The pressure in her head worsened.

The dark, argumentative energy swirled around everyone, crept into every brain and heart.

"I heard they're moving the tanks out of Redding. Some of them are coming up here," Andrew announced ominously.

"Damn it, Andrew, we don't need to hear that crap!" Brian snapped. "And anyway, how do you *know*! Have you actually *seen* them!"

Andrew visibly flinched. "Well, not...not exactly," he stammered. Glancing furtively at the faces turned in his direction, he went on, "But a friend of mine, he was hitching through Redding and he..."

"So it's a rumor, just a stupid rumor," Brian said disgustedly.

The unbearable tension threatened to blow the room apart, scattering bodies and dreams alike.

With a horrible, sick feeling deep in the pit of her stomach, Alana fantasized people bolting for the door. Any second now. Then what?

The tension in the room increased. People fidgeted, stared at the floor, examined their hands, twisted watches and rings, picked at their clothing. Half of them were out of their bodies. *All* of them were extremely uncomfortable.

All of them...except the two children.

Kate's twin children, a girl Camille and a boy Jonathan, had arrived sooner than expected and Kate had brought them to the meeting. Alana was struck by their eyes. Beautiful violet eyes. Thoughtful and intelligent eyes. *Adult* eyes. Not the eyes of typical seven year old children. And their skin was so beautifully tanned. Very unusual looking youngsters.

Alana's heart sank as the unpleasantness started; she wanted to protect the children from the ugliness swirling around the room.

She need not have worried. Whereas the adults were agitated and coming unglued, *the children calmly took in everything without getting upset.* At one point, when everyone seemed to be yelling at once, Camille glanced at

Alana with such calmness and understanding and compassion it sent shivers up Alana's spine.

Alana said a silent prayer: Please Spirit, I really want these children in the community. Please don't let them be turned against the group by what's happening tonight. *Please let them know we're not always like this.*

The cloud of dark energy spared no one.

Evelyn leaned her tiny frame forward, her angry eyes raking the group, her body posture saying she was ready to fight. "I don't see why everyone's so damned upset! You all got burrs up your butts or what?"

Nancy glared at her. "We're upset because the whole country's..."

Alana had *had* it. "Stop!" she yelled. Forcing herself to lower her voice and stay calm, even though she didn't *feel* calm, she continued, "Wait. Maybe we need to do something, some deep breathing or a meditation or something..."

"No!" Cassandra screamed. "You *always* do this!"

"You mean me?" Alana asked, pointing to herself.

"Yes!"

"Do *what*?"

"You always play... *leader*. Or *mother*." The word mother was uttered with anger and contempt.

"Mother?"

"Yes, *mother*! Don't you suppose... don't you suppose for once you could let us alone? And let us figure things out for ourselves? *Just for once*?"

Feeling hurt, the best Alana could do was to respond, "Okay, I will."

"Good!"

But Alana couldn't let go of it yet. "Are you saying I'm trying to mother you?"

"Something like that," Cassandra replied, her voice oozing sarcasm.

Now Alana felt the need to defend herself. "No I'm not. Not really. Except, sometimes you... you seem confused and like maybe..." She knew she was in trouble the minute the words came out of her mouth.

Her eyes blazing, Cassandra screeched, "Are you saying I can't take care of myself?"

"No," Alana answered meekly.

"Oh really?" the little voice inside Alana inquired. *"Do you really see Cassandra as a powerful, capable person?"*

"I think so. I know I like her."

Her inner voice was not fooled. *"Liking her has nothing to do with it. Do you see her as powerful?"*

"Not always."

"Most of the time, even? Honestly now."

"No, honestly I believe she has trouble focusing. She needs guidance."

Alana squirmed inside as she admitted her real feelings about Cassandra. She squirmed because, dimly, she knew she was seeing *herself*. She wished she was alone. But she wasn't alone, she was in a group of people, most of who were expecting her to say something. She stared at a spot on the far wall just to the right of Cassandra's head.

The two children watched quietly. Had Alana been observing them, she would have seen Camille reach over, take Jonathan's hand, squeeze it for a second, then let it go.

Veda offered a suggestion: "Do you suppose we could all be quiet for a moment? Not meditate, just be silent?" Her voice, so soft and loving and so clearly coming from her heart, calmed everyone.

The mood in the room lightened as they took her advice.

Vicki was the first to speak. "Veda, I feel like we're floundering. I'm afraid the group is coming apart. Do you suppose Saint Germain might give us some direction?"

"I've already asked him," Veda replied. "He won't. He wants us to work this out ourselves." With a little smile on her face, she added, "He says it's a test."

A chorus of groans met Veda's remark.

Veda giggled. "That was my reaction exactly."

"Didn't he say *anything* else?" Karen asked, sounding desperate.

"Yes. He said we were having a lover's quarrel."

Jerry was lounging on two green overstuffed pillows, apparently asleep. All of a sudden, he sat up, alert and obviously quite wide awake and said, "But hey, that makes sense. We've all asked for this community. But when you ask for something you really want, then whatever's in the way of it happening has to come to the surface. Right? Like when two people get together and they want the relationship to work..." With a quick, shy glance at Veda, he hesitated, unsure whether to go on. "Well, all I mean is...they're probably going to trigger each other's pictures. So why wouldn't it be the same in the group? Heck, it's one big relationship, isn't it? Makes sense that we'd trigger each other's pictures and that we'd quarrel sometimes."

With a confidence Alana hadn't seen before, and a willingness to talk that completely surprised her, Veda took over. "So, let's figure out what the pictures are and work on them. We have lots of insightful people here. We can assist those who are in conflict...if they want," she said. With a loving glance at Alana and Cassandra, she asked, "Do you want assistance?"

"Yes," Alana answered, not at all sure she did.

"And you, Cassandra?"

"I'll try."

Alana's irritation immediately surfaced. No! No! No! She wanted to yell. Don't *try*! *Do* it!

Alana's inner voice pestered her. *"Why does Cassandra's way of being in the world bother you?"*

"I don't know. Please go away!"

Anna made a suggestion. "Everyone here feels like they're miles apart." She motioned towards Alana and Cassandra. "Why don't you two sit closer together...and *we* can move in a bit closer, too."

Alana and Cassandra inched towards each other, carefully avoiding any eye contact.

Being physically closer appeared to make everyone self conscious.

"Now what?" Karen asked nervously.

Kate was sitting directly across from Alana and Cassandra. "Cassandra, what got you so upset?" she asked.

Homecoming

The question obviously irritated Cassandra. "I already *told* you, she's always trying to mother everyone. It bugs me."

Brian didn't agree. "Hmm. I don't get the same feeling. Sure, she takes charge lots of times, but I don't get the mothering part."

"I can't help what you see," Cassandra replied petulantly.

"But I don't get it, *either*. I mean about the mothering," Kate added.

Feeling very much on the spot, Cassandra said to Kate, "All I know is, Alana treats me..."

Kate interrupted her. "I have a suggestion. Instead of talking to *me*, talk to Alana."

Turning slightly to face Alana, but with her eyes downcast, Cassandra repeated, "Sometimes it makes me feel...no *you* make me feel like I'm about ten years old. I'm *not*. I'm twenty-six. I was even married once."

Before Alana had a chance to respond, Evelyn stepped in and asked Cassandra, "My dear, what was *your* mother like?"

Cassandra's face darkened. "I really don't want to talk about my mother."

Kate looked sympathetic. "Pretty bad, huh?"

Cassandra's mouth quivered. She nodded, fighting to keep back the tears.

Kate put a reassuring hand on Cassandra's shoulder, then handed her the box of tissues.

On some level Kate and Evelyn had agreed to temporarily take charge of the group. Evelyn now took over. "What about you, Alana? I was watching you, and every time Cassandra spoke you had a certain look on your face. Know what I mean?" she asked, grinning mischievously.

"Uh...sort of," Alana stammered, knowing, somehow, what was about to happen and feeling naked and *very* insecure.

Evelyn continued her gentle teasing. "Want me to show you?"

"Sure."

Evelyn screwed up her face, portraying impatience and exasperation.

"That bad?"

"Yup."

"I don't do it like *that*," Alana argued.

Kate took over. "Okay, no problem, let's go back to Cassandra. Cassandra, you think you might be putting your mother's face onto Alana? Possibly?"

"No!"

"You sure?"

"I'm sure!"

Lovingly and patiently, Kate persisted, "Does Alana remind you of your mother at *all*?"

Sensing Kate's genuine caring, Cassandra relaxed. "Well, sort of. They both come on like they know what's best for you."

"But I don't do that!" Alana protested, hearing the defensiveness in her voice.

"Yes you do! Admit it, you *like* to mother people!" Cassandra yelled.

Alana opened her mouth, but nothing came out. Wetting her lips, she *willed* herself to speak. Nothing! Not even a squeak.

Kate scooted closer. "Hmm, something's not working here. Is there anything we can do to help you two?"

The two women stared straight ahead, solemn-faced, silent.

Alana felt alone and afraid. She knew that part of her was unwilling to work things out with Cassandra. She wasn't alone of course—others in the group were *also* unwilling to resolve their differences. This couldn't continue. They had to realize that they were all mirrors for each other, and that, being mirrors, *when they looked into the other they were seeing themselves*. Literally seeing *themselves*. If they refused to acknowledge this truth, preferring instead to point the finger of blame and to find fault with the other, *they would be resisting the inner work the mirror told them they needed to do,* and the community would fail. Would wither and die. And their dreams with it.

With almost everyone mired in helplessness and frustration, the energy in the room rapidly spiraled downward.

Quietly, nonchalantly, the children moved closer to the two women, Camille next to Alana and Jonathan next to Cassandra. More than nonchalant, they seemed almost *disinterested*. But Alana immediately noticed a sensation in her body—a *tingling*—as if a slight electrical charge was coursing through flesh and bone. Although alarmed at first, when she relaxed she found the feeling pleasurable. She *felt* better. Not great, but better. More optimistic. And easier on herself. Yes, she was resisting seeing the mirror—the mirror that was Cassandra—but she had always worked through her resistances before and she would this time. And the others? They would do what they needed to do. No problem.

"Let me take this inside," Alana said. "I'm sure I have something to learn. I guess I have to do some processing," she added, surprised how easy it was to admit this.

Cassandra's resistance also dissipated, and, almost as if the words were being gently and lovingly pulled from her, she replied, "Me, too. I have some work to do, too." Then, to Alana, "Maybe we can talk some time. Not right away, but...sometime."

"Sure."

It was as if the sun had suddenly appeared *in the room*, beaming down love, warming hearts, melting the stubborn resistance of a few minutes ago, easily and effortlessly.

Everyone breathed a sigh of relief.

The walls did not remain down long, though. A few minutes later, Nancy and Glenn ended up in another shouting match. Several others also had problems. The contentious, conflictual, angry energy returned and wouldn't budge.

Alana's uplifted mood evaporated. She felt discouraged and pessimistic. They would never learn how to get along!

Again, the children assisted. Quietly and unobtrusively moving closer to the "stuck" ones, they somehow—mysteriously—helped the energy to shift and the resolution of conflict to begin.

Alana watched with amazement. Who were these children? Kate's of course, the physical resemblance was obvious. But that didn't answer her question: Who were they? And how were they performing their magic?

They worked on themselves for over an hour clearing old energy and helping each other see their pictures of reality.

Surveying the group, Evelyn asked, "What do you all think? Can we live together? Kind of like getting married you know."

They laughed, a nervous laugh for some.

"*I* want to," Vicki declared. "I realize I have things to learn, but I can do it. Besides, I'm already married, so that part doesn't scare me a bit."

More laughter.

Nancy was next. "We've really got to *want* this!" she said. "When Glenn and I tangled, I felt like hightailing it out of here! Seemed easier. Not sure why I stayed. Guess I really want to live with you guys," she added and grinned sheepishly. "I've always run away before. If something didn't feel good, I was *out* of there. I'm tired of that, so I'm staying…and *I will work on myself*."

Nancy's intention, so clearly coming from her heart, touched them all.

"We're going to bring up lots of our stuff…pictures and patterns and things like that," Brian warned.

"We already have," Karen said.

Andrew fiddled nervously with the straps on his pack. Finally getting up enough courage to speak, he said, "I want to say sorry if my talk about the tanks was bumming you out. Sure didn't mean to."

Jeff shook his head. "It's not just you, Andrew. The people who were bothered by what you said, that's *their* issue. I don't get it exactly, but…"

"It's the way Andrew talks sometimes. It's his *attitude*," Anna volunteered.

"Which is?" Brian asked, an edge to his voice.

"Nothing personal, Andrew," Anna began, choosing

her words carefully, "but you get, uh, very negative sometimes, and it pushes peoples' buttons. Shows us what *we* need to work on."

Andrew scratched his head, genuinely perplexed. "Someone else told me that once, about being negative. Can't say I rightly understand."

"You always see bad times and disaster everywhere," Evelyn said gently.

"Well sure, that's the way the world is, ain't it?"

Several people covered their mouths, hiding their laughter, which only increased Andrew's discomfort.

Evelyn glared at the smirkers. Then to Andrew she said, "The world isn't always such a tough place, my dear, although I think maybe it has been for you."

"I left home when I was eleven," Andrew said. "Never went back. Been on the road ever since, doing the Lord's work. I got no complaints mind you...except I get to missing folks every now and then."

"Course you do," Evelyn sympathized. "That's why you're here, isn't it?"

Unable to talk and obviously uncomfortable, Andrew stared at his hands and nodded.

For the first time since she'd known Andrew, Alana could sense some emotion breaking loose and bubbling up to the surface.

Jeff changed the flow of the energy, telling them of his experiences with the two Mount Shasta carpenters. And about the yurts. "Anyone want to come with us when we go to the coast to check them out?" he inquired.

Evelyn did. Also Anna and Brian.

"As long as we're talking about houses and those kinds of things, can we talk about money?" Nancy wanted to know. "I don't know about you guys, but I'm flat broke. I'd sure like a house, but, shoot, I couldn't even pay for a foundation."

"Ted and I are in pretty much the same situation," Kate admitted. "Or just me I guess, since he wouldn't be coming anyway."

"Me, too," Karen added.

"I'm in the same boat as the rest of these guys," Anna glumly announced. "No money."

Alana didn't like the way the conversation was going.

As they related their stories, it was clear that the only people with enough money were Glenn and Vicki, Connie—who had *some* money—and Jeff and Alana. Everyone else lived from month to month, with little if any savings.

Nancy looked dejected. "Oh well, I guess we had to face this sooner or later. It was a nice dream, but without any money we can't do it. Or maybe *you* guys can live there," she said, staring at the "money" people. "And us poor folk can visit," she added sarcastically.

"We've got the land," Jeff said, hoping to cheer Nancy up.

It didn't. "Great, but how are we going to live there?" she asked morosely.

"Me and my dog, we plan to live in my tent. Maybe you all could, too," Andrew suggested.

Nancy frowned. "Maybe in the summer, for a few months, but in the winter? In the snow?"

"Maybe it won't snow in the valley," Vicki said hopefully.

Nancy's frustration erupted. "Shit! Be real you guys!" she yelled. "It's always this way everywhere I go! There's the "haves" and the "have-nots." And I'm always one of the "have-nots"!"

As he listened to Nancy, Glenn's whole body stiffened. "Are you blaming *us* for having the funds to pay for a house?" he asked angrily. Alana wondered if the two of them would fight again.

"Christ I'm tired," Nancy said, her voice almost a whisper. She put her hands over her face, rubbed her temples. "I'm tired of being on the outside looking in. That's all I'm saying. I grew up on the wrong side of the tracks in a Texas border town. Can't get more wrong than that. I thought this would be different...but it's the same old shit."

"I can't live in a tent, not with the baby coming," Karen said dejectedly. "I'll probably have to say good-bye to all of you and go someplace else."

Hopelessness and despair and frustration permeated the room again, worse than before.

Anna sighed. "Seems like just a dream, doesn't it? Do we actually think we can just go and live on this land? *Someone's* got to own it."

Evelyn did her best to stem the negativity. "Nope, nobody owns the valley. It's *ours*."

Anna threw her hands up in the air. "But what good does *that* do if we haven't got any money? We couldn't *build* anything. That takes money. Lots of money."

"Maybe Saint Germain was wrong," Kate said sadly. "Maybe we aren't the way-showers after all. Maybe *another* group will show the world how to build a loving community." She glanced around hoping someone would say something to change her mind. No one did. "Damn I'm frustrated!"

"Hey, maybe we can borrow the money," Brian said hopefully.

Glenn didn't think so. "Not likely. The debit card makes that pretty tough. We'd have to find a private lender."

"But it's possible, isn't it?" Brian persisted.

"Sure, anything is possible," Glenn replied. He really wanted to give them some hope, but his experiences on Wall Street told him not to expect much in the way of miracles. He continued, "It would have to be someone pretty special. We wouldn't even have title to the land. Pretty risky for a lender."

"But *we're* special," Karen argued.

Glenn nodded, thought about saying something, then changed his mind.

Legs tucked up underneath them, the two children sat quietly watching the renewed outburst of hopelessness. Alana felt frustrated. Why didn't they help? They did before, why not now? Obviously, they possessed some special kind of power...or *something*. Why withhold it? Then Alana realized that the children were doing exactly what Saint Germain would do: *they helped for awhile, but they didn't rescue anyone*. They *guided* people; they showed them new ways of being, then stepped back and said: this is how it feels, now *you* do it.

Jeff offered a suggestion. "I realize lots of you are bummed out. I am, too. But maybe if we *do* something, something positive, like...well, let's draw up some plans, like where we want our buildings, or..."

"Great idea!" Kate exclaimed.

"Hey guys, can't do it! I gotta go!" Nancy yelled, getting up to leave. They watched as she got her coat and quietly slipped out the front door.

"I'll stay," Cassandra said. "I don't have any money, but I'll stay and help do some planning...although I don't feel like the energy's here now."

"Perhaps this is the time to say goodnight," Veda said, looking downcast...*and* very tired herself. "But before we go, could we all get into a circle and hold hands? I believe we need to be connected."

With everyone holding hands, Veda closed her eyes and invoked: "We ask for guidance on our journey and especially in the birthing of our community. Please, you who are of the Love and Light vibration, be with us and help us to see the path to our highest possibility." Then, to the circle of people she said, so softly that many had to lean forward to hear, "Open your hearts, and in the center of your hearts put this dream of community. And remember, you *are* the way-showers. You have come to Mother Earth to bring this dream into manifestation. Remember also that on some level the dream has already taken place. We have but to allow it. Remember this and nothing can stop us."

They were silent for a moment; then one by one they let go of each others' hands, gathered their things, and quietly said their good-byes.

Alana was talking to Evelyn about a book she wanted to buy when she felt a gentle tug on her sleeve.

"Can we say hello to Sam?" Camille asked.

"How did you know...?"

Jonathan replied, "Our mother told us you have a beautiful dog. Do you keep him outside?"

"No, he's in the kitchen."

HOROSCOPE
SYDNEY OMARR

ARIES (March 21-April 19): Without apparent effort, you'll be at the right place at a crucial moment. Your words, actions are taken seriously. Flirtation lends spice; you'll be exhilarated, as vigor makes a comeback.

TAURUS (April 20-May 20): Secret ally provides information previously prohibited. Emphasis on change, travel, variety of sensations. Ultimately, however, you'll sing the praises of "home, sweet home." Scorpio involved.

GEMINI (May 21-June 20): Accent aggressiveness! Highlight sales ability, personality; win friends and influence people. This means don't sit back watching the world go by — shape your own future! Pisces is in the picture.

CANCER (June 21-July 22): What appeared long ago and far away will practically be at your doorstep. Focus on spirituality, publishing, journey that leads to soul mate. Capricorn, Cancer natives involved.

LEO (July 23-Aug. 22): Vindication! People say, "It ain't bragging if you can do it — and you did it!" Commendation received from one in a foreign land. You're becoming international! Aries plays dramatic role.

VIRGO (Aug. 23-Sept. 22): Erase the word "impossible" from your vocabulary. You'll be doing the impossible. Take initiative, imprint style, exude personal magnetism, sex appeal. Money withheld will be paid. Leo involved.

LIBRA (Sept. 23-Oct. 22): Intuitive intellect featured. Stress elements of unorthodoxy, surprise. Join forces with Cancer native who has your best interests at heart. Aquarian, also in picture, promotes finances.

SCORPIO (Oct. 23-Nov. 21): Play role of silent partner. Exert influence in an unobtrusive manner. People quietly seek your counsel. Social affair elevates morale, promotes love relationship. Gemini involved.

SAGITTARIUS (Nov. 22-Dec. 21): A roadblock to a relationship is removed — don't brood about the past, instead take optimistic view of future. Scorpio person in scenario. Proofread new material.

CAPRICORN (Dec. 22-Jan. 19): Study Sagittarius message. Focus on communication, education, dissemination of information. Excitement at home base — Aries individual stirs controversy. Refuse to be intimidated!

AQUARIUS (Jan. 20-Feb. 18): You'll be called upon to be the peacemaker. Provide words to music, encourage people to settle differences without being obsequious. Relative, long absent, makes a dramatic return. Libra!

PISCES (Feb. 19-March 20): You could be dubbed practitioner of the mystic arts. Answers are found behind the scenes. Transform tendency to brood into positive meditation. What you need is closer than might be anticipated.

IF JULY 8 IS YOUR BIRTHDAY: When a crisis exists, you are called upon to fix it. You display an amazing talent for bringing order out of chaos. Capricorn, Cancer natives play prominent roles in your life. You are intense, dynamic, and maintain the highest standards where morality is concerned. You insist on nothing less from those you love.

LUANN

ONE BIG HAPPY

FRUMPY THE CLOWN

MARY WORTH

Camille was concerned. "Has he been bad? Are you punishing him?"

"No sweetie, he's in the kitchen because he *wants* to be. Sam doesn't like crowds. Come on, let's go in and say hi. He'd love to see you."

The two children immediately flopped down next to Sam and began petting him.

With her arm around Sam's neck, Camille looked up at Alana and asked, "Why are you sad?"

Taken completely by surprise, Alana mumbled, "Oh, you mean me? No, I'm not sad."

"Yes you *are*," Jonathan stated, and with such conviction and such force that Alana could not deny the truth of his words.

"Yes, I am."

"We knew you were," Camille said. "We were watching you. And sometimes you were watching *us*," she lisped.

Alana smiled; Camille seemed like a typical seven year old—*some* of the time. "How did you know I was sad?"

Jonathan rubbed Sam behind the ears and answered, "Cause you looked just like mom does when she thinks of our dad."

"You mean Ted?"

"No, he's our stepfather," Jonathan corrected her. "Mom and dad are divorced. Our *real* father's name is Andrew, like *your* friend Andrew."

"I see. So, I had the same look?"

Camille stood up. Putting her hands on her hips, she drew herself up, took a deep breath, and in a scolding voice said, "Yes, and when we told you, you did the *very same thing* our mother does."

"And what is that?" Alana asked. She was enjoying the children immensely.

"You said *no!* I'm *not* sad. Why do you and mom *say* you aren't sad when you *are*?"

"I guess we don't want to admit our feelings sometimes. Don't *you* ever do that?"

Camille and Jonathan emphatically shook their heads no.

Without thinking, Alana reached over and touched Camille's arm. "You have such beautiful skin. You must be out in the sun a lot."

Recoiling from the touch, Camille glanced at Alana, a momentary flicker of fear in her eyes. Then, as if nothing had happened, she hugged Sam and purred, "Pretty dog. You love living here, don't you?" Camille hesitated, as if thinking about something. Then, with another quick glance up at Alana, she whispered, "If we tell you a secret, promise you won't tell?"

Alana hoped they weren't going to tell her something awful. "Okay, promise."

"*We* don't care," Camille began, "but our mother does and we promised her we wouldn't tell. But we can tell *you*."

Alana sat down on the floor next to Sam and the two children. "Great. What's your secret?"

"This isn't our real color," Camille answered.

"Oh, you mean your skin? Oh, I'm sure it's not. You have a beautiful tan. I bet your skin must be very fair looking."

"Unh-unh, our skin is blue," Jonathan said in all seriousness.

"Blue?" Alana couldn't help herself—she laughed. "Oh, you're *kidding* me," she said. A glance at the children told her they were indeed serious. Blue skin? What medical problem could cause blue skin? "Oh, I'm sorry. Is there something wrong? No, that's not what I mean exactly," she stammered, feeling very flustered. She gathered herself together as best she could and asked, "I'm not prying, and you don't have to answer...but do you have something wrong with you? Not enough oxygen maybe?"

The two children regarded her calmly. Jonathan said, "No, there is nothing at all wrong with us. We just have blue skin. Not *real* blue. Just...*sort of* blue. Mom doesn't want anyone to find out. She made our father, I mean our *real* father Andrew, promise *over* and *over* and *over* again not to tell anyone."

Camille added, "She was afraid people would think we

were freaks. She wouldn't show us to anyone when we were babies."

"Are you sure?"

"Uh-huh, we remember," Jonathan replied solemnly.

Alana believed him.

"When people came over to see us she put face powder on us and kept us all wrapped up. She told people we had a skin rash," Jonathan added, sounding a bit offended.

"But you didn't?"

"Course not, silly," Camille giggled. Suddenly looking very thoughtful, she went on, "But she's *still* afraid. Now she's really afraid, cause we're in school and dad can't keep us home all the time. So she takes us to the tanning place, and we sit there until our skin is all nice and brown. And no one knows."

Something in Camille's voice prompted Alana to ask, "How do *you* feel about that, sweetie?"

Camille's expression clearly showed her sadness. "I like our skin. It's pretty."

"I see," Alana said, although she really didn't. These children completely mystified her. Blue skin? Reaching far back into her memory banks, she grasped at something, something about children with blue skin. But the understanding slipped away.

Mystified or not, she was taken by them. *Very* taken. Her heart opened wide and she would happily have visited with them for hours.

Kate appeared at the door, coats in hand. "Ready to go?" she asked the children.

"Yes," they answered in unison. "Can we come and visit Sam?" Camille asked her mother.

"If it's okay with Alana."

"Sure, anytime," Alana replied. She got up on her knees, gave each child a hug, and felt that same gentle tingling...*and* a rush of love and joy that nearly toppled her over. She didn't want to let them go. Feeling naked and defenseless and absolutely overwhelmed, she said, half jokingly as if to cover up her loss of control, "Wow, you two are good huggers."

Camille laughed and wrinkled up her nose. "We know what you mean. Come on Jonathan, time to go," she announced. She took her brother's hand and very adultly led him out of the room.

Alana's head was spinning and her heart was pounding. "What was *that* all about, Sam?" Sam thumped his tail on the floor, got up, and padded out into the front room to say hello to Jeff.

Alana heard the front door close, heard Jeff bolt it, heard someone's car—Kate's probably—roar to a start.

Briefly, she luxuriated in the children's loving energy, feeling uplifted and positive. Then, as before, these good feelings gradually faded and she was left with other thoughts. Like the meeting, the meeting that was supposed to launch their community but that ended up showing them how far away they were from the manifestation of their dream.

Jeff walked into the kitchen, took one look at her face and asked, "What's up?"

"Thinking about the meeting," she answered, hearing the irritation *and* the judgment in her voice. Where were her good feelings of a few minutes ago? The love and the joy of being with the children? What was happening anyway?

Jeff fed Sam and put the water on for tea. "So, want to tell me what's upsetting you?" he asked.

Feeling completely, overwhelmingly depressed, she answered, "*Everything.*"

"Hmm. Anything in *particular*?"

"Attitudes."

"You mean the negativity?"

"Uh-huh."

"There *are* some unhappy people, aren't there?"

Alana smiled ruefully. "That's the understatement of the year, sweetie. Depressed is more like it. They're giving up."

"You think?"

"Didn't you *hear* them. Half of them are ready to quit!" she shouted angrily.

"Only the ones who don't have the money."

His reasonableness bugged her. She wanted him to *agree* with her, to see the total disaster *she* was seeing. She stared straight ahead, her mouth set grimly.

"Did I say something to bother you?"

"I feel like it's all going down the drain," was all she could say.

"*Now* who's giving up?"

"I'm not, *they* are."

"But don't give up on *them*."

Alana threw her hands up in the air, obviously irritated.

Jeff didn't let her theatrics stop him. "Look at it from their point of view," he said. "They have no money, so they think they can't be part of the community. We *do* have the money."

"So?" she said defensively.

"So, maybe it's time to be patient and to help them. I'm sure we'll have our own issues. Like...well, like the thing between you and Cassandra."

Alana didn't want to be reminded of *that*. Just another unresolved issue in her life, one more to add to the growing pile.

"Maybe this isn't the time to talk," she said, trying to control the anger she felt.

"You pissed at me?"

"No."

"Then what?"

"I'm pissed at this stupid God damned world! It's coming apart! People killing each other! The Gray Men ready to eat us for lunch! And a group of people with a beautiful dream who can't get it together! Damn! Damn! Damn! Damn!" she yelled.

Jeff knew she needed to express her frustration and so the yelling didn't bother him. He waited, then asked, "Feel better?"

"Yeah, some. But not much."

"Can I say something?"

"Sure."

"It's about what you're doing. Sure you want to hear?"

"Yeah, go ahead," she answered glumly.

"Take care of *yourself*, sweetie. And let *them* take care of *themselves*. You can't pull them along."

"But what if…"

He finished her thought for her. "What if some of them don't get it? What if they give up?"

She nodded, the tears beginning to course down her cheeks.

"Then they do," he said simply.

"Will they?" she asked in her little girl's voice.

"Some…maybe. Not all. We'll have to wait and see. Want some tea? I'm going to make some."

"Thanks."

There was nothing else to say. They drank their tea in silence.

Alana went to bed depressed and confused.

Chapter Ten

November 1998:

Alana's dark and gloomy mood did not begin to lift until Tuesday, three days later. At ten that morning, she and Jeff, along with Brian and Evelyn and Anna, squeezed into the Land Rover and headed for Fort Bragg and the yurt factory.

Alana's inner child loved to travel. And, knowing they were headed for the coast also lifted her spirits, for the ocean had always been a special place for her. A place of renewal.

But best of all, they were going to inspect the yurts! She had gotten a book on "round" houses from Evelyn's bookstore, had poured over the pictures of yurts, and had read their history. They were beautiful dwellings, and when she closed her eyes she could see one or two of them nestled snugly in the valley. They just *fit* there. *And* she could see herself happily living in one.

She felt better as soon as they pulled out of the driveway. Better, but not great. The general grouchiness afflicting everyone at the last meeting continued to bother her. She brooded over their inability to work out their differences and move into harmony and balance. Once or twice, her brooding had plummeted her into a painful, gnawing fear that they weren't ready and that their dream of community was just a child's fantasy. That was the worst.

And, her heart ached for her country, for the unthinkable had happened—the hatred and the fighting had spread to all fifty states! The country had gone mad and, like some deranged, insatiable beast, was gnawing and ripping at its very flesh. Frightening! The government had stopped pretending that this was simply an isolated outbreak of domestic unrest. They knew it was a war—a civil war.

And, as in any war, the casualties mounted. Since the outbreak of the violence, more than nine thousand Americans had been slain—mostly civilians. Added to those killed were thousands of wounded and maimed.

The United Nations was considering a resolution to send thousands of additional troops to the United States and was demanding that these forces be under UN command. Foreign troops on US soil commanded by foreign generals! Incredible! If someone had told the average American that the United Nations would send "peacekeeping" troops to the United States in 1998, they would have reacted with disbelief. Bosnia perhaps. Or Uganda. Even South America if the situation worsened in Brazil or Bolivia. But the United States? Never. Not in a million years. Yet the day had come...and with mind-numbing swiftness.

Alana had brought her newspaper and was reading them some of these stories. Evelyn chuckled and said, "Feels like the United Nations is taking over, same as in all those other countries we used to read about. Those...*third world* countries. Remember them? Only now it's *us*. Does that mean..."

Alana picked up on her thought. "That we're a third world country now? I'd say so. What goes around comes around I guess."

The violence, the anarchy, and the UN troops were only part of the story, however. The earthquake in California, the stock market crash, the devastating depression that had felled the United States a few short months ago, all had contributed to the downfall of the once proud and strong country. The sending of the United Nations troops was simply the last event in a long series of events.

Alana believed that the Gray Men had been planning the demise—the *economic* demise—of the country for many, many years. These individuals had always regarded the United States as the most important piece in their plans for world domination. If they could break the United States, if they could economically enslave the population, the rest of the world would tumble. And they had succeeded.

Almost.

Almost, but not quite. With victory seemingly assured, something had gone wrong; and that thing was the civil war now raging across the country. The Gray Men had not planned on a civil war, and Alana imagined them gnashing their teeth as the insane, out-of-control firestorm of violence leapfrogged across the land, threatening to destroy everything in its path. The Gray Men did not want that—charred cities and a ruined infrastructure and a decimated population would be an empty victory. Could they stop the civil war? Probably, but they hadn't much time.

Alana watched and waited to see what these clever beings would do. Gifted with seemingly supernatural powers of perception, they always saw the road up ahead more clearly than most, so she was sure they had foreseen the possibility of a civil war, unthinkable as this was even a few short weeks ago. And she was also sure they had formulated a plan. But what would they do, that was the question.

"Anything else of interest in that gossipy rag you're hooked on?" Jeff asked humorously, referring to her self-proclaimed "addiction" to the *San Francisco Ledger*.

"Well, let's see if I can find you something," she replied. "More crop circles reported in Iowa." And she held up a picture of the perfect geometric shapes laid down in an Iowa cornfield.

"Beautiful," Anna said.

"Funny, we never used to hear about those," Evelyn commented. "Now the paper's full of them."

Evelyn's remark made Alana think about her dream, and especially of the announcement coming over the radio, the announcement she could not quite hear. *What was that dream telling her?*

"Hey sweetie," Jeff said. "Hello, Earth to Alana."

"Oh, sorry. I guess I was gone for a minute."

"Anything else in the paper?"

"Lots about the fighting. And here's a story about the Corporation. And she read, "After a weekend meeting at their Virginia headquarters, the Corporation has decided to tighten the penalties for those caught trying to circumvent the debit card laws. From now on, the Corporation spokeswoman stated, anyone found using gold or silver or any other unauthorized medium of exchange will be arrested."

Anna was worried. "Wonder what that will do to our plans?" she asked.

"Ah, those idiots are blowing smoke," Evelyn commented dryly.

Their laughter filled the car, lightening the tension they were all feeling.

Halfway to Redding, they passed a convoy of troop carriers—the ATSF logo stenciled on the side—racing North up I-5, the way they had come.

"Hmm. Mount Shasta?" Jeff wondered.

Alana shook her head. "Eugene or Medford is my guess. Heavy fighting in the mountains around Medford."

Forty-five minutes later, they turned West onto Highway 299, the two lane road that wound its way along the beautiful Eel river. The river, an iridescent blue-green, sparkled in the afternoon sun.

Jeff pointed to tree branches and bits of debris a few feet down the embankment. "Wow, look where the water came during the floods! Almost up to the road!" he exclaimed.

In some areas, the flooding that had preceded the monster quake had permanently changed the face of the state, sweeping away thousands of houses, crumbling roads, and inundating once fertile farmland.

"They're having some flooding in Arizona," Alana said, remembering the story in the *Ledger*.

"I heard that half of Phoenix is being evacuated," Brian said. "Ten thousand people dead, lots of them from disease." He saw the surprised looks on their faces. "Jerry told me. He got himself a shortwave radio and he's been listening to what's happening all over the country. He says they're only telling us a little of what's going on."

Although Alana was well aware that the news was managed, still this surprised her. "Ten thousand? I heard a couple of hundred."

"Yeah, well, they're lying. You hear about the wildfires in Maine? Should be snowing there, right? But they've got temperatures over a hundred and these fires that are burning up towns like crazy. And another big quake off of Chile. Caused a tidal wave that took out half the coast."

Evelyn felt the energy begin to spiral downwards and she didn't like it. "The Earth will survive folks," she said. "And so will we. We're not being burned up or washed away are we?"

"No," they answered in unison.

"Darned right. So let's enjoy our trip."

The yurts were beautiful and not as expensive as Alana thought. She fell in love with them as soon as she saw them. She and Jeff settled on a thirty foot diameter model, plenty big enough for their needs but not too big to dominate the valley. Jeff asked Steve, the owner, if he would consider taking gold or silver in payment and he readily agreed.

"We'll get the yurts to you in about two weeks," Steve said. "I'll tell you what...if you don't mind, I'll come along with my delivery guys and help you set them up. No extra charge. I've always wanted to see Mount Shasta. Sound okay?"

"Great," Jeff replied and drew Steve a map of how to get to the valley.

As they walked back to the car, Jeff said, "No problems about using our gold and silver coins. That's a relief."

Alana had a sudden inspiration. "Jeff, what about buying another yurt? We could easily afford it."

"Another one? What for?"

"For someone else in the group. Maybe a couple of people could live there...you know, until they can manifest their own money. Or maybe we'll donate it to the community. Yes, I like that idea; let's give it as a gift," Alana said happily.

Jeff agreed, and so they went back and bought another yurt.

Back in the car, they told the others what they had done.

"You bought two?" Anna asked, surprised.

"One for us and one for the community," Alana explained.

Evelyn had leaned forward and quietly kissed Alana on the cheek.

They didn't discuss who might live in the second yurt. No one seemed concerned.

The next few days were busy ones for the community. Vicki and Glenn ordered two domes, one for themselves and one as a "gift." Jeff could feel Alana's hand in this "gifting."

After some figuring, Brian decided he could afford a small house.

The community was growing.

Accompanied by the two Mount Shasta carpenters, they made several trips to the valley to prepare the building sites.

A week after their trip to the coast, they held another get-together. The negativity and interpersonal strife, although less intense, soon crept back into the meeting, showing them that they had not yet figured out how to clear these energies.

Alana counseled herself to be patient.

Nancy was still missing. Connie told them the following story: "Right after the meeting, she took off for home, threw a few things in her bag, and left "like a bat out of hell." Haven't heard from her since."

Homecoming

Alana hoped Nancy would return, but, wisely, let go of any expectations. Nancy would do what she needed to do.

Six days later, on a crisp November morning, two flatbed trucks carrying the yurts—in sections and ready for assembly—rumbled along the dirt road leading to the valley. The community cheered as the trucks cleared the crest of the hill and wound their way down to the valley floor.

The two drivers shed their heavy winter coats as soon as they parked the trucks. "Hey, it's warm here. That's weird. Colder'n hell over on the coast. Mount Shasta, too," one of them remarked.

Jeff checked his thermometer. "It's 70," he announced proudly. Even more amazing, the previous night's "low" was a rather balmy 50. Mount Shasta had shivered at 38.

With the help of the men from Fort Bragg, the yurts were up by five the next afternoon. Although these were just the shells and much interior work remained, still the yurts were up! Two dwellings were in place! They walked around, touched the outside walls, walked in and out of the front door, peeked through newly installed windows. They smiled and hugged each other and laughed at the magic of it all. The community seemed much, much more real now.

"You folks have a beautiful place here," Steve said, lovingly eyeing the valley. "But you're way off the grid. How are you going to get electricity?"

Jeff and Emil had researched this and they happily explained that the electricity for the valley would come from a variety of sources: solar panels would generate much of it; also, Jeff had recently found some simple and efficient wind generators, so they would be an important element in the system; and they were considering the possibility of using a stream-powered turbine.

Steve listened, nodding occasionally. "Sounds great. If you need any more people, give me a buzz. Been looking for a place like this. And let me know how the yurts work out. Hope you have a problem or two; I wouldn't mind an excuse to come back for a visit," he joked as he climbed into his truck.

After the men from Fort Bragg left, the group gathered in the yurt that was to be Jeff and Alana's new home.

"It's so *big* in here," Vicki exclaimed, "But it doesn't look big from the outside."

"That's the thing about round houses," Alana said, sounding like the proud mother of a new baby. "They're pretty deceptive. Beautiful, huh? You'll see when you get your dome. It'll have the same feeling."

"And the ceiling is high enough so we can add a loft," Jeff said, obviously proud of his new home.

"We can hold our meetings out here now...yes?" Emil asked. "Oh, I guess there is no way to light this house."

"No problem," Jeff said. "We can use kerosene lanterns for awhile. Some of them put out as much light as a large light bulb."

Cassandra walked around the yurt, peering out all the windows. "It's amazing how *private* this is. I'm looking out towards the next building site and I can't see it."

"All the sites are like that. Neat, huh?" Jeff commented.

"You really believe there's a way for all of us to live here?" Karen inquired meekly.

Alana could sense Karen's inner struggle to allow abundance for herself. She had little in her life—almost no personal possessions—and with the baby coming... She fought the urge to take Karen in her arms and reassure her that everything was okay.

"I have to tell you guys something," Kate said, tears in her eyes. "Ted says he's going to turn us all in. He's mad about me leaving him and moving out here and..."

"You've decided for sure!" Anna yelled.

"Yes. You are my family and the valley is my home. I will find a way," Kate said simply. "But we fought last night, and he said he's calling the county officials to come out here."

"I bet they don't even find the place," Jerry said, trying to sound more sure than he actually felt.

"Or they'll get stuck on the road like Anna's friend did," Brian laughed.

Alana fought down a moment of panic at the thought of

county officials nosing around their valley. "Let's go on with what we're doing. If we need to deal with the county, we will. But I doubt that'll happen."

"I'm sorry," Kate apologized.

"Unh-unh, don't take responsibility for Ted," Evelyn said. "Just keep focused on your dream."

"How do you feel about leaving him?" Cassandra wanted to know.

Kate shrugged her shoulders. She sighed, then said, "I'd rather not. I know I haven't painted a nice picture of Ted, but he's okay. Just scared. And afraid to change. Oh well, I'll have my children here in a few days, as soon as they get all their stuff from Andy's, so I guess everything's fine."

Alana eagerly awaited the arrival of Kate's children. She knew they would add to the community, probably in ways no one could imagine.

"Oh, by the way, Nancy's back," a weary-looking Connie announced. "She got in late last night and we talked for awhile. She isn't sure she wants to be part of the community, but..."

"Because she doesn't have the money?" Glenn asked.

"Uh-huh. She *wants* to be here, but she's...she's proud. Doesn't want a handout," Connie replied.

"I can understand that," Anna sympathized.

While the others talked, Veda had quietly slipped out to her car and had returned, holding something behind her back. She shyly approached Jeff and Alana. "I have a housewarming present for you," she said and handed Alana a large crystal. "I have had this for many years, but it told me that its place is in your home."

Alana held the crystal next to her heart. "Oh my, it's beautiful," she gasped. "Feels *wonderful*. Thank you," she said and embraced the young woman.

Jeff held the crystal for a moment. "We'll find a special place for this. Thanks, Veda," he said.

The sun was beginning to disappear behind the rim of the valley. Knowing it was time to go, they drifted outside, slowly, one by one.

Reluctant to leave yet, they gathered together and visited for a while longer.

"Who's going to occupy the other yurt?" Vicki wanted to know.

"Who wants to?" Alana asked.

"I got my tent," Andrew said. "So I'm fixed good for now."

Karen raised her hand. "Could I?"

"Sure," Alana said. She could sense how difficult it was for Karen to ask for this, and she wanted to hug her.

"Me too?" Anna asked.

"And me?"

"And me?"

They all laughed.

"You are welcome to it, all of you. You folks decide what works best for you," Jeff said.

"Don't forget now, there will be an extra dome before long," Vicki reminded them. "Oh, this really *is* working out," she said happily. "Could we do a toning before we leave?"

They held hands and toned, and even though it was November, the crickets sang along with them; and a lone bird called sweetly from one of the willow trees near the creek. The toning became a whisper, then stopped, replaced by the soft, soothing sounds of the water rushing and sloshing over stones. They sat quietly and then said their good-byes to the valley.

The community cheered the arrival and the erection of the two domes. Now they had four permanent structures! The composting toilets had also arrived. The solar panels and the other equipment they needed to generate electricity were due shortly. Everything was coming together ...easily and effortlessly.

They celebrated Thanksgiving in the valley, beginning with a late afternoon picnic on the meadow and then moving inside one of the yurts when it got dark. Alana lit some candles. They sat in a circle, and in the flickering glow of

Homecoming 159

the candlelight they talked and shared the joy in their hearts. It was past midnight when they left for home.

As the community grew and prospered, the rest of the country plunged headlong in the opposite direction, into total anarchy! Like some deadly airborne plague, the fighting and the violence spread to all corners of the land. No place, not even the most tranquil corner of the country, was immune.

Although most of the media coverage continued to focus on the "war" between the militias and the ATSF troops, this conflict now represented but a fraction of the violence. Mostly, now, it was "ordinary" citizens who accounted for the turmoil and the killing. All of a sudden, these ordinary men and women went berserk. It was as if someone had implanted a device in them that, once activated, screamed to their brains: Burn! Loot! Kill! They roamed the streets in gangs, robbing stores. They shot each other on the freeways simply because someone cut in front of them. They burned churches and synagogues and mosques. They beat their children and their spouses and their pets.

Someone poisoned the drinking water in several Midwest cities. In Topeka, Kansas, fifteen thousand people died before the warning went out not to drink the water.

In many Southern cities, huge mobs of screaming, rock-throwing people suddenly, and for no apparent reason, stormed the jails and the prisons, freeing prisoners and locking the guards up in their own jails. Sometimes, instead of locking them up, they simply murdered the prison personnel, often in quite gruesome ways.

Urban areas were the worst. The inner cities had teetered on the edge of anarchy for decades. Now, all traces of civilization vanished as inner-city dwellers destroyed the places they had come to hate. These citizens soon discovered that fire was the fastest way to express their rage, and so they set their cities ablaze. Detroit and Chicago were burned to the ground. Oakland and Newark suffered a similar fate.

The ATSF and UN troops did little to stop the destruction of America's cities. When questioned about the lack of effort to contain the urban holocaust, the President responded that the federal government did not have the personnel to police these areas. Local government was responsible for containing the violence, he had added. Alana and others suspected there was another reason for the government's inaction.

Being in a position of authority *anywhere* in the country was proving dangerous. Whatever was pushing people over the edge, they directed their pent-up anger and frustration towards authority figures, viciously attacking anyone in uniform. Law enforcement personnel were shot at for no apparent reason. In the inner cities, police and fire stations were mobbed and literally torn apart.

A growing number of officials, deciding that the present mood of the country made their job too dangerous, simply turned in their badges. Most stayed on the job, however. Some of these paid a price.

Mount Shasta was the scene of one such drama. Two California Highway Patrol cars racing up I-5 to help in the Medford fighting were blown up with antitank guns.

Alana and Jeff passed the scene of this violence just as the tow trucks were pulling the charred remains of the patrol cars from the ditch alongside I-5.

"It's reached Mount Shasta I guess," Jeff commented sadly.

Mount Shastans were obviously on edge and extremely stressed—several parking lot fist fights and numerous tavern brawls attested to this—but the six highway patrolmen were the first to be killed.

Alana silently watched the tow trucks pull the first of the patrol cars up onto the highway. Her intuition told her that it would take very little for the violence to spread, even to traditionally peaceful places such as Mount Shasta. "Maybe I was wrong," she said sadly. "I honestly thought the government, or someone, would have found a way to stop this. But maybe they can't. Maybe we've reached a…what do you call the thing that happens in an atomic explosion?"

"Oh, you mean a critical mass," Jeff asked.

Homecoming 161

"Yes, maybe we've reached critical mass and the whole thing's going to explode no matter what anyone does."

"You think it's time to pack up and go live in the valley?" Jeff asked, hoping she would agree. "We could fit everyone in. Might be a tad crowded, but we can do it."

"I still feel..." she began, then stopped and sighed. "Oh, I don't know, let's take a vote at the meeting tomorrow."

They arrived home to find a message from Jerry on their answering machine.

"Hey guys, what's up?" Jerry's cheerful voice asked. "Called to inform you that our leader is having a news conference. Yeah, *another* one. The guy's a ham. But anyhow, he's going to be on the tube at five. That's all. See ya later."

It was a little after five. Jeff flicked on the television, catching President Storr listening to a question from one of the front row reporters.

"Sir, are you saying that we can do nothing to quell this...this national tragedy?"

"No, I did *not* say that!" President Storr angrily replied. "We are doing everything we can. I *said* we are overwhelmed!"

"But Mr. President," an obviously agitated reporter sputtered, "you cannot let the anarchy continue! Are you aware that not ten miles from here an all-out riot is taking place! That our city and others across the country are being torn apart! And Sir, I mean *literally torn apart!*"

The President, obviously tired and on edge, snapped, "What do you propose we do? If you have any good ideas please present them!"

"Well, can't we..."

The President did not let him finish, "And I deeply resent your innuendo that we are not doing enough! We care deeply about this country and we are doing everything we can!" he thundered.

The President's outburst quieted the room for several seconds. Then a back row reporter called out, "What about the United Nations troops that were supposed to help? Where *are* they?"

President Storr regained some of his composure, then went on, "We requested their aid a few days ago. My military advisors tell me that the deployment of these troops will take a minimum of two weeks."

"You mean we are on our own for the next ten days or so?" the reporter asked, worry in his voice.

"Yes."

"Mr. President, why haven't you declared martial law?" the same reporter asked.

The President's shoulders sagged. "The violence has gone too far for martial law."

Another reporter jumped to his feet. "But we need help! Why hasn't the national guard been used? In my state of Minnesota the guard hasn't even been put on alert!"

"I am not familiar with the situation in your state. There are some states where the national guard *has* been deployed. But..."

"But what?"

"In most cases the guard has refused direct orders to quell the violence."

"They refuse to fight?"

"Yes."

"Mr. President, isn't it true that none of our regular armed forces has been put on alert, either? That we are holding the line with ATSF troops and a few United Nations forces and local law enforcement?"

"What is your point?" the President snapped.

"Well, Sir, the situation is clearly out of control, so why not use all the force we have?"

"Using regular armed forces would further increase the violence," The President responded, obviously choosing his words carefully.

"But how can the situation get any worse?"

The President ignored the question. Instead, he faced the cameras and implored, "We are hoping...no, we are calling on you, the American people, to *stop this senseless violence!* We have no wish to have an all-out war! Please,

please, I *beg* you, you who are listening to this broadcast, stop the violence! Lay down your weapons! Let us sit down and work out our problems!"

"But Mr. President, that makes no sense!" a frustrated television newscaster called out. "You *must* use the army. Otherwise we are lost. You *must*, Sir!" Many of his colleagues nodded, obviously agreeing with him.

The President hesitated, and another reporter shouted, "And if you don't, perhaps there are those in Washington who will see that this is the only way!"

The President's face drained of all its color. "What do you mean?"

"I mean, Sir, you need to take some decisive action! I mean, Sir, you need to give over command to those who understand how to deal with anarchy!"

The President furrowed his brow, sighed and responded, "Are you suggesting...?"

"I am suggesting that you let the military deal with this mess!"

"And abandon the Constitution of the United States of America?"

"The Constitution is pretty dead right now, wouldn't you say?"

The President and the reporter stared at each other. No one moved or made a sound as the enormity of what the reporter had proposed sunk in. The President took one more question, then left the news conference.

Jeff turned off the television. "I wonder how many others see things this way?"

"Quite a few I bet," Alana answered. "The Constitution doesn't mean much to most people now. They see the country being destroyed. They're scared and they'll probably agree to almost anything."

"Hey, sweetie, how about if I do some packing? We could spend one or two nights in our new home. What do you say?" Jeff urged.

Alana sensed his fear. She could understand it, for she was barely able to control her own. Over the past few days, she had cleared many fear pictures; but sometimes the fear crept back, wrapping its icy tendrils around her heart. She opened the blinds on the windows overlooking the Mountain. "Sure, why not," she replied.

"Good, I'll..."

Alana's heart skipped a beat! "Oh my God! Over there!...that bird...flying upside down! Like my dream! Look!"

Jeff looked where she was pointing. "Oh no, unh-unh. I mean it's not what you're thinking. They do that all the time. They're playing. Nothing to worry about."

Alana hoped he was right. But somewhere inside herself she knew it was otherwise.

Chapter Eleven

The event that changed the lives of everyone in the community, in the country, and in the world took place on a day when dark, ominous, snow-threatening clouds blanketed most of Mount Shasta. In Chicago, it *was* snowing. In Washington, cold but clear.

The President had just entered a meeting with the Joint Chiefs of Staff for an update on the nation's deteriorating condition.

Aaron Stockman was in *his* underground headquarters, deep in the Idaho mountains, conferring with *his* chiefs of staff.

After spending the past two nights in their yurt, Alana and Jeff had come to town for candles and lamp oil and other assorted supplies.

Coming out of the hardware store on Mount Shasta Boulevard, they spied a woman running up the street, her hair flying wildly in the wind, her coat open and flapping around her body. She was gesticulating wildly and yelling something, but the wind carried her words away and they could not hear. Suddenly, she ran into the street, oblivious of the danger. A car screeched to a stop, coming within a foot of hitting her.

"It's the stress," Jeff said. "People are getting crazy."

Alana wasn't so sure. Her intuition told her something else was taking place.

The woman was now a half block away and still yelling. "They're here! Oh, God, God help us! They're here! We're being invaded!" she screamed. She collapsed, exhausted, a few feet from where Jeff and Alana were standing. A man ran over, knelt down next to the woman, and called her name: "Elaine, what's the matter?"

The woman was breathing hard and mumbling. Alana was sure she was in some kind of shock.

"It's my neighbor, Elaine," the man said. "What's wrong with her? Is it epilepsy?"

Alana shook her head no. She put her hands on either side of Elaine's body, pulling white light into her to calm her. Elaine opened her eyes and looked up at the crowd gathered around her. "Oh God, please help us. Oh God, please help us," she mumbled.

"Elaine, what's the matter. Can you tell us?" Alana asked.

"They're here."

"Who's here?" Jeff wanted to know.

"*Them*!"

Following her intuition, Alana asked, "Them? You mean beings from outer space?"

Elaine nodded weakly. "They landed in Washington. They're going to kill us all. Kill us with their death rays."

"How do you know?" Alana asked.

"I heard it on the radio."

Alana smoothed Elaine's hair. "You are fine," she said soothingly. "You are fine. Do you know that?"

"Yes," Elaine answered. And then, "No, no..."

"You are fine," Alana repeated, pulling more healing white light into Elaine's body.

Elaine closed her eyes, relaxed. "Yes."

"Can you stay with her? Maybe get her out of the cold?" Alana asked Elaine's neighbor. "She's okay, but she needs to rest for a bit."

"Sure," he agreed.

Jeff and Alana headed for the Sunshine Cafe and the closest television.

"Sweetie," Jeff said, walking fast to catch up to her,

"she heard it on the radio. I think it's some kind of hoax. Remember back in the late thirties when Orson Wells did a radio broadcast called "The War of the Worlds" and everyone got scared because they thought it was the real thing? This feels like..."

Alana shook her head and hurried along. "Unh-unh, something's happening."

A car pulled up alongside them, and a man, obviously drunk, leaned out the window and yelled at Alana, "Hey baby, why doncha get in the car with us! Tell your boyfriend there to take a hike. Come on...whatcha say?"

When Alana ignored him, the man persisted, "Ah, come on, we only got a few hours to live, let's have some fun."

They hurried into the Sunshine Cafe to find ten or twelve people huddled around a blank television screen. Then the picture flickered on and a frightened newscaster yelled, "Look folks, we have our remote crew at the White House to take pictures of the ship, but for some reason we can't get any clear feeds! Something, or *someone*, is interfering with our transmission!" Then the picture went dark again.

"What's going on," Jeff asked one of the cafe regulars.

"Looks like we've been invaded. There's a giant spaceship hovering over Washington and...and they sent a smaller one down to the White House lawn. They showed pictures and then the damn TV went out!"

Jeff was skeptical. "Invaded? You sure?"

"Hey bro, we saw it!" the man next to Jeff yelled.

"Are they peaceful?" Alana asked.

"They haven't nuked the White House," someone answered seriously.

"At least not yet," another added jokingly.

"Too bad," a third chimed in.

The transmission returned, catching the newscaster in mid sentence: "...apparently meeting with President Storr now. We saw the Alien walk into the White House. Well, *I* didn't see it...or I mean him...or whatever the hell it is. Personally I mean. Oh hell, I don't know what I'm talking about...except it looks like we've finally made contact with creatures from out there...or rather *they* have made contact with us." He stopped and listened to someone speaking to him on his headset. "Okay, we have a good feed now from the White House. We'll turn you over to Leslie Abramson. Leslie, you there? You there?"

The picture switched to the front lawn of the White House. Pandemonium. Security forces scurrying around, some carrying weapons. Ordinary citizens running along the street, some screaming.

Leslie Abramson, the White House Bureau Chief for the CNC Broadcasting Corporation, stood outside the fence surrounding the White House; behind her, a huge crowd of milling spectators. The camera focused briefly on Abramson, then zoomed in getting a close-up of the small saucer-shaped ship hovering a foot or so over the White House lawn. "I guess we're sending you the picture, folks," Leslie Abramson said hopefully. "Are we transmitting? We are? Okay, great. There it is folks, there's the smaller of the two craft. You can see the three other...other Aliens I guess we'll call them, standing by their ship."

Everyone in the cafe crowded closer around the television.

"Oh Jesus, I think I saw one of them move!" a woman in back of Alana screamed. "They're alive!"

"Those guys must be ten feet tall," another said.

A voice from the crowd asked, "How can you tell?"

"I've been to the White House. Just looks like it to me...looks like they're about ten feet tall."

The three "visitors," dressed in some kind of shimmering, close fitting uniform, stood calmly by their ship.

The man on Alana's left moved closer and peered at the television and said, "They look *kinda* human...except they don't. Look at the heads! Huge! Oh my God, they're *not* human! Oh my God," he muttered.

Leslie Abramson broke in. "We're going to aim one of our cameras over the White House to let you see the other ship, the mother ship. It's a mile above Washington. You won't believe this folks." The picture jiggled, then stabilized, and the giant mother ship came into view, eliciting gasps from those watching.

"How big *is* it?"

"It's a mile up there? Shit! That thing's gotta be a couple of miles across. Gotta be at *least* that big!"

"Unh-unh, couldn't be."

Alana agreed, the ship *did* look that big. And like something straight out of *Star Wars*: a giant disc two miles in diameter, colored lights flashing everywhere, strange spidery-shaped protuberances sticking out at odd angles.

Leslie Abramson continued, "No other ship has emerged from the mother ship, only the one you see on the lawn. I believe..." she paused, then yelled, "Oh oh, I wouldn't do that if I were you!" The camera showed a man scrambling over the fence. Eluding the attempts of two Park Police to tackle him, he ran towards the three Aliens, his arms outstretched, yelling, "We welcome you bothers! We love you! Let me..."

One of the Aliens raised his arm slightly and the man dropped to the ground and did not move.

"Oh Jesus," Leslie Abramson murmured.

Many in the crowd outside the gates began screaming and running. The Alien made no further movement. "We're staying here," Leslie Abramson stated firmly. "This is the news story of the century and I am not going to miss it. But I'll tell you what, I'm staying on *this* side of the fence," she said. She tried to continue but was drowned out by the yelling and screaming of the crowd behind her. Then *she* yelled, "Okay, here's the moment we've been waiting for! We have word that the President and the other Alien will be coming out of the White House and that they will give us a statement!"

The picture on the television flickered, threatening to quit. "No, no you don't!" someone in the back of the cafe yelled. "Stay on, dammit!" As if obeying his command, the picture flickered one more time, then stabilized.

"There they are!" Leslie Abramson screamed. "Get in tight!" she yelled to her cameraman.

The President and the other Alien came down the steps.

Now, as the two of them walked side by side, it was quite clear how large the Alien was—President Storr stood over six feet tall and the Alien towered over him by at least three feet!

"Jesus, look how big it is," the woman in back of Alana exclaimed.

The President began speaking, his voice amplified without the aid of any visible sound equipment. "My fellow Americans, we are...we are..." He threw his hands up in the air. "What can I possibly say? They're here...and...and everything is okay my friends! Everything is okay! Everything is okay!" he yelled for the third time.

Before the President could continue, the Alien spoke, his voice also mysteriously amplified and sounding oddly metallic and synthetic, like the synthesized voice on a computer chip. "I am Ancon and I come from a star system you have not yet discovered, and so it has no name, not one that is easily translatable into your language," he said. Glancing at the three other Aliens guarding the small space ship, he continued, "My companions and I come in peace and we greet you my Earth brothers and sisters!"

A man standing next to Leslie Abramson yelled through the White House fence, "What do you want? Why have you come here!"

"I wouldn't do that if I were you," Leslie Abramson whispered.

"Yeah, you see what they did to the other guy?" someone else warned.

Ancon turned in the direction of the questioner and said, "It is alright, I will respond."

"You *heard* that?" Leslie Abramson asked incredulously.

Ancon nodded almost imperceptibly and replied, "Yes, our hearing is extraordinarily acute. Much more so than yours." He paused to watch as the man lying on the ground was helped to his feet by the Park Police, then he went on, "Let me assure you, the human is only stunned and will recover. But he is a warning not to approach our ship unless we authorize you to do so. Now to your question. We are a member of the Galactic Federation, although not *your* galaxy, but another, far away. We have come to tell you that it is time for your planet to leave its barbaric ways and to learn new, peaceful ways of living. When you accomplish this, when you begin to live peacefully, you will earn admission into the Federation and you will thereby usher in a glorious era of peace and prosperity. We have come to assist you in this transformation. Have I answered your question?"

The man thought for a moment, then yelled, "But what if we don't *want* you here! What if we want to take care of *ourselves*!"

"Why would you not want us here?" Ancon responded. "We bring you incredible gifts—technologies and inventions to make your life easier and safer. Why would you not accept these offerings?"

"No offense, but maybe we don't *want* you here!"

"No rational being would refuse the gifts we bring."

"Like what?" another called out.

President Storr interrupted by saying, "Wait! Let's wait! It's not the time for this discussion. We will address these issues at our upcoming national press conference. That is, if you agree," he said, craning his neck to look up at Ancon.

Ancon ignored the President. The camera moved in close. Ancon's face filled the screen—a humanoid face...except for his eyes. They were slightly hooded and seemed flat, almost devoid of expression. Reptilian was the word that came to Alana.

She was about to ask Jeff if he was seeing the same thing when Ancon resumed, "I will respond now. I realize that many of you have questions and that you must be anxious. After all, not everyday do beings from another galaxy drop in on you to interrupt your life, so I will respond to the question. I speak to you," he said, facing the man across the fence, "and I speak to the world you call Earth. We bring you many gifts, and among the gifts we bring is a cure for a disease infecting many upon your planet. There is here upon your planet a dreaded diseasement you call AIDS. An ailment that ravages many, does it not? And you live in great fear of this disease. I tell you now, we have a cure that we will gladly share with you. This is no trick. We will give the cure to your Earth scientists to test and they will tell you the good news. This is a gift, is it not?"

The questioner from the crowd was silent.

"Yes, it *is* a gift, Ancon, a *great* gift," President Storr said fervently. "And on behalf of all Americans and for all those who suffer from this horrible disease, I thank you." President Storr waved his arms as if to head off any further questions and said, "We must now let Ancon depart. But he will return, and we will hear more about these great gifts he has brought." He shook Ancon's hand. "Thank you for coming. We need you. Thank you."

As the world watched, Ancon strolled to the waiting ship and disappeared inside. His three companions followed. Without a sound, the small craft rose a few feet into the air and instantly vanished, eliciting many Ohs! and Ahs! from those watching at the White House and from those in the Sunshine Cafe.

Everyone in the cafe began talking at once.

"Wow, you see that? One minute it was there and then proof! How'd they *do* that?"

"A cure for AIDS. Wouldn't *that* be great. Wonder what else they can cure?"

"Peace and prosperity, how are they going to pull that one off? How are they going to stop all the fighting?"

Alana listened to the questions and to the buzz of small, excited conversations going on around her. She read the energy, and what she got was a mixture of fear and excitement.

Alana had the same feelings. Beings from another galaxy! Here upon Earth! And speaking to humankind! Her own heart beat faster with the enormity of it! Aliens! What did it mean? How different were they? All of a sudden, she felt protective of her beloved Mother Earth and of those who dwelled upon Her. Perhaps Ancon and the others were friendly and meant well and would indeed make their life easier. But a primitive fear spoke to her—they were obviously technologically superior to Earth, or so it seemed. But just because they were technologically advanced didn't mean they were wiser or kinder. What if they *weren't* here to help? What if they used their superior technology to harm Earth?

Leslie Abramson's face filled the television screen. "It appears we must wait for more news. The information we have is that at ten tomorrow morning Ancon will return to give us further details of...well, I suppose you could say of his plans for Earth. Okay, I guess there's not much more I can say. Maybe we'll give you one more look at the mother ship and then send you back to the studio for some national reaction. Sure to be plenty of that!" The huge mother ship once again came into view, suspended effortlessly above Washington, so gigantic it seemed to fill the entire sky.

The cafe was quiet; then the woman in back of Alana asked, "Did that really happen? I can't believe it. Feels more like a movie."

Many others had the same reaction.

The man next to her shrugged his shoulders and said, "Man, I think it *was* real. I think they're here. And..." He shook his head. "Yeah, it *did* happen."

Someone else asked, "Are these the guys we've been talking about?"

"What do you mean?" someone wanted to know.

"Are these our Space Brothers? The guys we've been counting on to help us? Or...someone else?"

His question was met with silence.

Jeff whispered to Alana, "You want to stay? Might get some more information on the television."

"I want to walk," she said, grabbing his hand and pulling him out the door.

She led him back down the street, then turned up East Castle towards the tiny patch of wetlands, one of her favorite spots in Mount Shasta.

Horns honked in the distance, tires squealed as people drove faster and crazier than usual, people ran into the streets, yelling and shouting, all of it proof that most of the town had heard the news. There was even the distant Pop!

Pop! Pop! of fireworks. They passed a house on Alma where a woman leaned out her window and called, "Hey, you hear? The Martians landed in Washington!"

Alana waved to her and hurried on.

"Hey, slow down," Jeff said.

"Oh, sorry."

"What's going on inside you, sweetie?" he asked.

"I'm not sure. Kind of overwhelming."

Jeff felt the same.

They passed the library and the middle school. Alana led him into the large open space where she sometimes came to sit and to take in the panoramic view. They found a spot facing the Mountain and sat down on the grass.

Alana looked pensive...and a bit worried.

"What are you picking up?" Jeff asked.

"Didn't the whole thing seem, oh, a bit staged to you?"

"Hard to say. Pretty dramatic. You think it was staged?"

"Uh-huh. Something doesn't feel right."

Jeff trusted her intuitive feelings. "Like?"

"Ah...it doesn't feel loving. Not at all loving. Were you watching Ancon?"

"Well, sure. Hard to miss *that* guy."

"Did you sense any love coming from him?"

Jeff looked perplexed. "I didn't check that out," he admitted. He thought for a moment and went on, "Maybe where they come from they don't operate like that; I mean like we do, with emotions and all that stuff."

"Exactly, and that's what bothers me."

As announced, the White House held a press conference the next morning. Most of the group had gathered at Alana's to watch. Missing only were Andrew, whom Alana couldn't contact, and Nancy, who was out of town.

The press conference was held in the familiar White House briefing room...with one change: a hastily erected stage now dominated the far end of the room. On the stage stood Ancon. In back of him sat several government and military personnel. All men. Alana recognized President

Homecoming 175

Storr, the Speaker of the House, General Williams of the ATSF, and the head of the Joint Chiefs of Staff. The rest were unfamiliar to her. Alana knew intuitively that these men were there to listen only and that they would play no part in the news conference. This was Ancon's show. Something else interesting: the military and government people all looked relaxed, while the media people shifted around in their chairs, anxious and ill at ease.

Ancon dwarfed everyone. As was the case the day before, he spoke without the aid of a microphone, and his amplified voice had the same odd digitalized sound.

"Quiet!" he commanded. "I will begin now!" Instantly, all noise and all movement in the room ceased. Ancon went on, "Much fighting is upon your planet. The Galactic Federation demands an end to the violence! Immediately! We have selected three areas of your Earth: one is the city of Las Vegas; one is an area in the state you call Idaho; and one is in the country you call Uganda. These places are no better or no worse than other locales on your planet; we have selected them by random drawing. We have warned the individuals in these areas. You need not understand how. Trust us, we have warned them that *unless they immediately cease their fighting their life force will be terminated.*"

There were murmurs from the media, but no one interrupted Ancon.

"We know this may seem harsh to you," he continued, a slight smile on his face, "and yet it is the only way. We have studied your civilization for some time—for centuries—and we have learned that *you* learn by example, the more powerful the better; and so we have decided to proceed on the assumption that this is the most effective way to bring peace to your planet. We do not judge this trait of yours; this is simply the way you live."

A giant television stood in one corner of the press room. The screen now flickered to life.

Ancon resumed, "Fortunately for us, and for you, we have calculated that more than 90 percent of your planet's population will see the following demonstration and will conclude that to continue the hostilities is useless. We will begin now."

The television picture, taken from a great height, showed a city. The camera zoomed in closer, displaying an area of several square blocks. Rubble and broken glass littered the streets. People—obviously looters—sauntered out of stores, arms full of merchandise. In an alley between two tall buildings, three men mercilessly beat another man. The bodies of other dead or wounded humans lay motionless in the streets. Several buildings were burning.

Ancon continued, "We take this picture from our mother ship. We show you your city of Las Vegas. As I have said, we have warned these beings to cease their unlawful, destructive behavior. They have not heeded our warning. We will now warn them again. Once!"

A voice sounding much like Ancon's and coming from the mother ship warned those on the ground: "We of the Federation demand that you lay down your weapons and cease your hostilities! We have no wish to harm you, but we warn you that unless you obey immediately we will terminate your life force systems."

No one stopped fighting or looting. Several people cursed, raised their guns, and shot at the mother ship.

"What are they going to do?" Anna whispered.

Ten seconds later, as if they had been swatted by some giant unseen hand, all the humans fell to the ground. They did not move. What happened next boggled Alana's mind: in an area of at least one square mile, all signs of life—people, buildings, automobiles, everything—simply vanished. Deleted.

Several media people jumped to their feet as they realized what had happened. But one glance at Ancon and most of them sat slowly back down.

The voice coming from the television continued, "We speak to those of you on Earth who have witnessed this event. Please do not think that we have accomplished this by some electronic trick. It is no trick. The life force of these entities is gone and will not return. Their molecular structure has been disorganized and the atoms scattered."

The voice paused, then a moment later went on, "We will now travel to another selected site, the place you call Idaho. Our ship travels instantly. Here is the picture." On the screen, a heavily wooded area, men running from tree to tree, shooting at each other. The voice from the ship broadcast the same warning, with the same results: no one took the warning seriously. A moment later, they, too, vanished.

"Hey, wait a minute," Brian protested. "Why didn't they give those guys time to see what happened in Las Vegas? That's not fair. Maybe they would have quit fighting."

Alana wondered the same thing. Then she realized that the beings in the ship *knew* that those on the ground would ignore their warnings...and they didn't care, *for the Alien's real purpose was to demonstrate their power, not to have the combatants lay down their weapons.*

Moments later, the same scene was repeated in Uganda.

The voice from the television concluded, "People of Earth, we sincerely hope you take our demonstration seriously. We give you twelve hours to cease your fighting. You who wish to live, take us seriously, change your behavior, and lay down your weapons. If you do not, you will be terminated."

Again, Alana noticed how different were the reactions of those in the room. The men sitting behind Ancon appeared calm, while the faces of those in the media clearly showed their distress. Many appeared outraged. Some were openly crying. Still no one spoke. Alana knew they were silenced by fear.

A woman journalist from a major West coast daily newspaper stood up and sobbed, "Did you really have to do that? Wasn't there a kinder way?"

Alana saw a flicker of something in Ancon's eyes, but she could not identify it. "No kinder way was possible," he responded evenly. "Do you honestly believe had we issued another warning or had we eliminated but a few, that the rest of your world would have listened?"

"Yes, dammit!" the woman reporter yelled. "Yes, they might have! What you did, that's not how we do things here on Earth!"

Ancon was quick to respond. "That is an illusion. You Earthlings understand but one thing: that the being who is stronger and has the superior weapons must be listened to."

"But that's not true of everyone," she protested.

"For most on your planet it is," Ancon replied.

Harry Stapleton of United News Service called out, "Mr. President! Is this the position of the government! Have you given complete control to these...beings?"

President Storr glanced briefly, and, Alana thought, apprehensively, at Ancon, then replied, "I know their way seems harsh, but I have met with these people and many in our government have met with them, and we believe they have the best of intentions. And perhaps they are correct. We tried to stop the fighting...God knows we tried. We tried *everything*! Nothing worked. Perhaps this was the only way. You will see! They have wonderful things to give us. But we need peace on the planet! Otherwise, all the new inventions and all the new technologies will do us no good. Can't you *see* that?"

"No, Mr. President, I can't," Harry Stapleton replied sadly and sat down.

"Well *I* do," another front row reporter said. "You're right, that's the only thing these jerks will listen to! I applaud your courage," he said to President Storr. Then to Ancon, "I welcome you to Earth. You have been needed here for some time." Thunderous applause filled the room, evidence that many agreed with these sentiments. Those, like Harry Stapleton, who did not agree stared dejectedly down at the floor. A few quietly left the room.

Ancon concluded by saying, "Your President is correct, we have many gifts to give you. As I promised you yesterday, we have given your scientists at the Atlanta Center for Disease Control the Aids vaccine and the Aids antidote. They will perform their tests and will see that we have given them what they have been searching for these many years. And we have other gifts to enrich your life. Much is planned for your planet, much that is rational and good. Have faith in us."

With that, the press conference ended.

Chapter Twelve

The people gathered in Alana's living room shifted around uncomfortably as the reality of what they had just witnessed sunk in. Glenn looked around, then commented, "Seems like these guys can do about what they want here. There's no way anyone could stop them... even if they *wanted* to."

Alana glanced at Camille and Jonathan; they seemed much calmer than the adults.

"Anybody else here have the heebie-jeebies?" Evelyn asked.

They laughed.

"Could they really do anything they wanted?" Karen asked. "What if they wanted to exterminate us?"

"They don't want to do that," Alana assured her.

"But *could* they?"

"Probably," Alana replied. "They won't, though. But if you mean do they have the technology, I'd say yes."

"They're so *advanced*," Anna said.

"What *are* they going to do?" Cassandra asked. When no one answered, she went on, "Any ideas at *all*?"

Alana offered her opinion. "They will bring peace and prosperity to the planet," she stated. She did not say what else her intuition told her.

"Well...that wouldn't be so bad, would it?" Vicki asked.

"That is precisely what Hitler said he wanted to do in the beginning," Emil interjected.

"Except these guys are so...so far ahead of us. They have stuff we haven't dreamed about," Brian said. "So maybe they'd be..."

"Different?" someone finished his thought for him.

"Uh-huh."

"Smarter or more loving you mean?" Evelyn added.

"Why not?"

"Possibly, but I don't get that feeling from them," Kate said.

Alana agreed.

"You think they'll really bring peace to the planet?" Connie asked.

"Sure," Alana answered. "Might take awhile, but they'll do it. In fact, I bet they'll do whatever they *say* they'll do."

"What about the people who don't want to quit fighting? Won't they resist?" Vicki asked.

"Not for long," Brian laughed. "You saw what happened. How could anyone resist that kind of technology?"

"I agree," Glenn said. "If you resisted *that* you'd be stupid."

"Suicidal," Jeff added.

"Dead is more like it," Anna commented dryly.

"Why *are* they here?" Jerry wanted to know. "I mean hey, guys, that peace and prosperity stuff, you really buy that?"

"Yes, there's something creepy about these guys," Cassandra said. "Don't you feel like...kinda like we're lab rats and we're being experimented on?"

"*I* do," Vicki answered.

"Me too," Evelyn added. "I'll tell you something else, I sure like the idea of peace and prosperity. Heck, I've wanted that all my life," she said with tears in her eyes. "But I don't want *their* kind of peace and prosperity. Feels wrong."

"Like?" Jeff prompted her.

Evelyn thought for a moment. "Don't know. There's

something fishy here. I want to know what their intentions are."

"They won't tell us," Veda said quietly. Everyone turned to look at her. "They have great secrets. That is their essence—secrecy."

Anna leaned forward in her chair. "Veda, do you suppose Saint Germain..."

Veda smiled and said, "He thought you would never ask. I do believe he has a few choice words to say to all of us. Want me to bring him in?"

"Do ducks quack?" Jeff joked.

Veda looked around the room. "Anyone have any objections? He isn't pushy you know."

Evelyn laughed. "Veda, dear, I do believe you are developing a sense of humor."

"It's from being around all you flaky people," Veda replied, trying not to grin.

"You got that right," Jerry agreed. "Flaky people are *my* kind of people."

"Mine too," Veda said, smiling shyly and sneaking a quick glance at Jerry. "Now, if you would go within and quiet yourselves for a few moments, we will see what Mr. Germain has to say."

Veda inhaled deeply a few times to center herself. She closed her eyes, then quickly—much more quickly than usual—she opened them and Saint Germain's dark and intense eyes lovingly surveyed the room. "Greetings, beloved ones, I am Saint Germain, come to be with you for awhile. And how are you all doing?"

It did not bother him that no one answered his question. "You have guests it seems. Unexpected company perhaps? From out of town?" he asked lightheartedly.

Brian laughed. "You mean the guys from galaxy...wherever it was?"

"Indeed, *those* guests."

"Uninvited guests," Jeff muttered, more to himself than to anyone else.

"*Someone* has called them," Saint Germain gently corrected him.

"Well not me, *I* sure didn't invite them," Jeff declared with conviction.

Saint Germain looked him in the eye but said nothing.

"Did I?" Jeff asked, now sounding not so sure.

"Mm, you had your part in their coming."

Looking embarrassed, Jeff defended himself. "But...but I don't understand. I don't like their energy...or what they did to those people. I don't *want* them here, so how could I have invited them?"

Saint Germain smiled mysteriously and replied, "I did not say you personally sent them an engraved invitation...and yet you had your part. As did all in this room."

"Would you please explain," Jerry demanded.

"Of course. There is upon your planet at this time a pervasive feeling of helplessness and powerlessness."

"And fear," Alana added.

"Yes, beloved one...and fear. These powerful emotional tones comprise a message—a *calling*—broadcast daily in all directions, far out into the Universe. These beings have simply responded to the calling."

Evelyn frowned. "Are you actually saying that these...these whatever they are...are here because we all *called* them? I mean literally *called* them?"

"That is precisely what I am saying."

Evelyn shook her head. "Unh-unh, not me."

"You deny the truth of this because it does not fit the image you have of yourself...for you see yourself as independent and self reliant, do you not?"

"I sure do."

"And indeed you are."

"Saint Germain," Evelyn began, "sometimes you are the most exasperating person I have ever talked to. I declare, sometimes I get so confused when I hear you. Would you please explain how I can be independent *and* helpless at the same time?"

Saint Germain surveyed the room, gazed deep within each of them and asked, "How many here have had feelings of helplessness and powerlessness, of not knowing what to do or how to manage your lives?"

Several tentatively raised their hands.

"Your response is not overwhelming. Why do you find this so difficult to admit?" Saint Germain inquired.

Brian answered, "No one wants to see themselves as powerless."

"I did not ask you to admit that you are powerless, only that you sometimes *feel* this way. There is a difference you know."

"Oh, I get it," Brian replied. "Sure, I get that way lots of times. Especially lately, with the earthquake and the debit card and now these guys from Galaxy X dropping in on us. Sure."

"And how is it with the rest of you?" Saint Germain wanted to know.

"Same way," many answered.

"And when you feel helpless and powerless, do you put out a call for assistance?"

"Yes, I think most of us do," Anna answered for them all.

"And when you put out your call for help, *are you specific about who it is you ask to assist you?*"

"*I* am," Cassandra replied proudly. "I ask *you*. Well, at least some of the time."

"Indeed, and I hear you. And the other times? Who do you call in to assist you?"

"I'm not sure," Cassandra admitted.

Saint Germain continued, "You who are assembled in this room are beings who are coming into the understanding of your own power. You have only to look at what you have accomplished lately: You have a home now, do you not? Free and clear you might say. And dwellings. In other ways, too, you are regaining—*remembering*—the truth of you. *Your* feelings of helplessness and powerlessness are...fleeting, for you quickly return to the knowingness of your power. *Yet even you have these feelings now and again.*" He took several deep breaths, then resumed, "Now, imagine how it is with your brothers and sisters, your brothers and sisters who have *no idea of their power*. They feel, you might say, down on the ground most of the time.

Prostrate. And they cry out for help. And their cries go out to the farthest corners of your Universe and are heard by many. Now these cries have been answered. This is not to judge them; there are many reasons for these feelings and many there are upon your planet who encourage and fan the flames of such emotions."

"Are you saying people feel this way most of the time?" Evelyn asked.

"Indeed, are you surprised?"

"Guess not," Evelyn replied glumly.

Thinking of all those people she had recently met who appeared to yearn for a strong leader and for someone to tell them how to run their lives, Alana wasn't surprised, either. "But not everyone is like that, are they?" she asked.

"Indeed not."

Alana continued, "So, I'm confused. Looks like the Aliens will be here for quite awhile so..."

"They will be here as long as the picture of helplessness is powerfully upon your planet...as it is now," Saint Germain quickly replied.

"Okay, but those of us who *aren't* feeling powerless, what do *we* do? We don't want someone to take over our lives. Except I guess maybe once in awhile," Alana added sheepishly. "But most of the time..."

Saint Germain interrupted her. "It is no sin to feel powerless or to ask for assistance. It would, however, be wise of you to be specific about who it is you ask for help. Intend that your assistance comes from those beings who, let us say, *honor your path and who have your highest good as their focus. And who will respect the limits of your physicality*. Then you will not be surprised—unpleasantly surprised—who shows up at your door."

Silently, they contemplated his advice.

"Saint Germain, what is going to happen to us?" Vicki asked.

"What is it specifically you wish to know?"

"Are these beings going to take over the world?"

"As you know it, yes," he answered cryptically.

"What about our valley? Are they going to...to...." But

she could not finish, did not even want to admit the possibility into her mind.

Saint Germain saw into her heart and read her question. "What do *you* think?" he asked gently.

"I...I'm afraid," Vicki stammered. "They're so...smart. They'll see *everything*. And if they can see everything, then they can control us."

"Mm, they have much advanced technology with which to accomplish these goals... *if they wish*."

"That's what I *mean*," Vicki exclaimed.

"But why would they be interested in *your* valley and *your* dream?" Saint Germain gently inquired.

"Well, I thought...I just thought they would," Vicki whispered. Many in the room shared her conviction and her fears.

Saint Germain went on, "Do not assume *anything*, for as you well know, what you believe will happen, will happen. These beings you call Aliens have indeed come here to serve the planet." His words brought groans from everyone. "But it will help you to know that they have *not* come to serve *you*. Not directly."

Jeff shook his head. "You've lost me."

"These beings have come to serve those who have called them, those who desire someone to take control of their lives. The responsibility of making choices is felt as a burden by many of your brothers and sisters. They have called for someone to come and make these difficult choices for them, and these beings—these Aliens—have answered the call and will do what your brothers and sisters have asked them to do. This is why they are here. They are *not* here to meddle with or to destroy your dream...unless this is what *you* need."

Glenn shook his head. "Saint Germain, nothing personal, but you don't understand. These beings—Ancon and the rest of them—will be *everywhere* on the Earth, and they will have a say in everything that happens here. Right?"

"That is the probable reality as we see it now."

"Well, if they are going to be everywhere on Earth, how will *we* avoid having to deal with them? It's one thing to ignore the county building inspector, but these guys...these guys have supernormal powers, so..."

"Does anyone have an understanding of this?" Saint Germain inquired.

Kate raised her hand. "Glenn's right, these beings are in a different league from the county people or the government or even the Gray Men, so..." she hesitated, unsure what she wanted to say next. Her face brightened. "Oh, *I* see, you mean they won't care about our community, or even that they'll support us in some way. Is that what you mean?" she asked hopefully.

"Supporting a community such as yours goes against everything they believe in," Saint Germain responded evenly.

The smiles on their faces faded as they heard this.

Jerry voiced what many were believing, "So we *will* have to fight...or go underground...or something. Or give up maybe. I mean that's what you're saying, isn't it?"

"Who would you be fighting, beloved one?"

"Me?"

"And do you have clarity about this?"

Jerry took a minute to answer. "I would be fighting the part of me that says I can't have what I want."

"Indeed," Saint Germain began, "you would be believing that you must fight for what you want—for your dreams. You would be believing that your heart's desires cannot come to you easily and effortlessly."

Jerry pounded his fist on the floor. "Oh man, that is so hard for me to get!"

"Most here share your frustration," Saint Germain consoled him.

"You mean they have the same picture?"

"Yes."

Jerry glanced inquiringly at those assembled. "Yeah?"

Several in the room nodded.

"Talk with each other in your group," Saint Germain suggested. "Share your thoughts and your frustrations and your insights."

"We've done that...a little," Alana responded.

"More discussion—more understanding—is needed," Saint Germain counseled. "Understand the gift these beings bring you."

"They're bringing *us* a gift?" Kate asked.

Saint Germain smiled and replied, "These beings—these your visitors—are assisting you to bring more clarity into your lives, are they not?"

"How?" Kate asked.

"Their very presence and their apparently supernormal powers are stimulating deeper layers of doubts and fears to surface. This is a great gift, for now you will be able to clear the way for even deeper understanding to come into your life."

Alana smiled. "Saint Germain, there is something you aren't saying. I can *feel* it. Something you want us to get. Something you are hinting at. Am I correct?"

"Indeed, you have blown my cover."

"Well, are you going to tell us?" Alana asked coyly.

Saint Germain remained silent.

"He wants you to ask him a *question*, silly," Camille chided her.

"A question?"

"Yes, it's a game. You have to ask the right question. Then *he* will tell you the right *answer*," Camille said, looking pleased with herself.

Alana knew Camille spoke the truth. "Hmm, the right question. Let's see, we're all worried how we're going to avoid dealing with these Aliens. How we're going to avoid struggling with them. And Saint Germain is saying that one way is to change our struggle pictures, the pictures that say we have to fight for what we want. That much is clear. So, it's something else. Anyone have any ideas what the right question is?" Alana asked the group.

Glenn raised his hand. "Does the question concern what I was talking about before? I mean about the aliens being everywhere?"

"Indeed."

"And you said..."

"I said I agree they will be everywhere on your Earth,"

Saint Germain replied. "Although this may take some time."

"So, if *they* are on the Earth and *we* are on the Earth, and if they are as powerful as you say, then there is no way to avoid them...yes?" Emil responded.

"Which Earth are we speaking of?" Saint Germain asked.

"Which Earth? *This* Earth!" Glenn said, sounding annoyed.

"Saint Germain, are you playing with us?" Evelyn asked.

"Mm, in a manner of speaking."

"You still haven't asked the right question," Camille scolded them.

"Okay, miss smarty-pants," Cassandra said. "What *is* the right question?"

"Which Earth?" Camille answered matter-of-factly. "There's lots and lots of them. When Jonathan and I go outside to play, sometimes we go to another place. It's..." Camille furrowed her brow, searching for the best words. "It's next door to *this* place. We just say we want to go there and we're *there*! Our mom and dad think we get lost, and one time they *really* thought we were lost, but..."

"So *that's* what happened!" Kate exclaimed. "You weren't lost at all!"

"Nope, not at *all*," Jonathan replied. "We knew where we were all the time."

Kate smiled as she remembered. "Camille is right," she said to the group. "We had the darndest time with these kids. They were always disappearing. One time we even called the police."

With a huge grin on his face, Jonathan said, "But we were *right there.*"

"Well, I guess I won't worry about you then," Kate said, sounding relieved.

Everyone in the room turned their attention back to Saint Germain. He continued, "You have discovered many things about your valley, have you not? That it is different in many ways?"

"That's for darned sure," Evelyn said under her breath.

"And one thing you have discovered is that it is, you might say, halfway between here and there. Here...and yet *not* here. It is somewhat like a magician's trick."

Alana caught on. "You mean we won't have to deal with these Aliens or the Corporation or the Gray Men *because we won't be on the same Earth?*"

"Precisely," Saint Germain replied. "At this time, you are between worlds. You have one foot in this dimension and one foot in another. This is very apparent when you are in your beloved valley, for this magical place is indeed an interdimensional doorway," Saint Germain said, slowly surveying the room. "Have you not noticed that you often feel stretched these days...much as if you were a rubber band?"

Cassandra understood immediately. "Yes, I feel like that most of the time. Like I'm being pulled apart. Yucky feeling."

"You feel discomforted because you are remembering how to be multidimensional beings—to exist in more than one reality at one time," Saint Germain said. "You are stretching your abilities, that is all. Your journey will become easier. Your beloved Mother Earth is going through her own transformation, one that almost perfectly mirrors *your* journey. Her consciousness is expanding, much as yours is. She has decided that the present dramas—of war and greed and the enslavement of souls—will no longer be allowed...*here.* And yet a place must be found for those who desire and need such dramas. So, there will be two Earths, one for them and one for you. You did not come here to do battle with the Darkness. You came here to assist your Mother to transform herself—to co-create a Heaven on Earth—*and then to enjoy the fruits of Her transformation. Is this not true?"

"I've wanted that all my life, and these folks have, too," Evelyn answered tearfully.

"You will have your dream," Saint Germain replied tenderly. "You who dream this dream will move to the other Earth. You came here to co-create this other Earth, this Heaven on Earth, and then to dwell upon Her. And so you shall."

"Saint Germain, when will the transformation happen?" Kate asked.

Saint Germain turned Kate's question around. "How soon can *you* transform *yourself?* How soon can *you* allow peace and prosperity and joy in *your* life? That is when your Heaven will manifest."

For several moments, everyone in the room silently contemplated Saint Germain's words. Then Alana said, "I have another question. Or maybe it's a worry."

"Indeed, you have appointed yourself the group worrier, have you not?"

Alana sighed. "I suppose."

"Do you get paid enough for having shouldered such a heavy burden?"

"No," Alana giggled.

"Learn to play more," Saint Germain suggested.

"I'll work on it," Alana said.

"Indeed, and that is your dilemma, is it not?"

"Okay, I get it. I'll *play* with it."

"The children will assist you," Saint Germain stated.

"I'd like that," Alana replied. "Now, my question is...or my worry is...I don't see how we are going to live together. As a group I mean. Recently, we've had some problems, some conflicts that have come up, and they just aren't getting resolved. Am I just worrying about nothing?"

"Mmm, not exactly," Saint Germain answered. "Others here share your concerns, so I will say a few words about this topic. What is your picture—your expectation—of this community?" he asked Alana.

"That we live together in honesty and openness. *And* love."

"And the picture underlying *this?*"

Alana shrugged her shoulders.

"Is it not your picture that *by simply stepping into this magical place, this valley that is now your home, you and all the others will be instantly transformed, all defects gone, all problems resolved...perfect and divine beings?"*

When Alana didn't answer, Saint Germain resumed, "When you and your wondrous husband first entered into your present relationship, did you come into it as perfect beings, all problems solved?"

"No, of course not. We've worked hard."

"Indeed, and so it will be with your community. It is a *relationship*, and it will unfold as any other relationship does. Of course there will be things to work out."

Alana sighed. "But it feels...overwhelming, like all the personal stuff—the disagreements and the conflicts between people—will shake the community apart."

"This 'personal stuff,' did it shake your marriage to pieces?"

"No," Alana admitted, "but we came close. Okay, okay, I see what you mean. We have to take things as they come, one day at a time, like we did in our marriage."

"Yes. And these children will help you greatly, for they have come into your lives to teach you about honesty and openness. *And above all, about love.*"

"I've seen some of that already."

"There is more they can assist you with. You have but to ask. Their greatest wish is to assist you in these matters. To bring you these gifts is why they have incarnated onto Earth at this time."

"Okay."

Saint Germain glanced around the room. "Beloved ones," he began, "I feel the heaviness in your hearts. Some here have need of personal service, of personal unburdening, and of the Divine Mirror, and this I will gladly offer. But first, I wish to say a few words about these your visitors from outer space.

"Remember," Saint Germain began, "many, many entities inhabit the region you call "space." Some are of high consciousness and great integrity. They love you dearly, and many of them have been assisting you and your Earth for millions of years. Eventually, some of these Beings will also appear on your beloved planet...in their own time. And you will have a grand reunion, a gathering of family and friends as it were.

"Others of these Aliens, as you call them, are not as highly evolved. Many have great lessons to learn. This may surprise you. You may imagine that, given their dazzling technologies and their apparently superhuman gifts, surely they have resolved all their personal issues. *This is not the truth.* The beings who have so unexpectedly dropped in on you, while technically quite advanced and logically brilliant, nevertheless have much to learn. They have great need of the understanding of the heart and of the emotions. The learning of these truths is one reason why they are here, for your Earth is the "Heart Planet" and the perfect school for these lessons. And you, beloved ones, have elected to be their teachers.

"You think of these beings as the "guys in the dark tee shirts," but in truth they are neither bad nor good, they simply have a part to play in the drama now unfolding upon your beloved Earth.

"Remember, *these visitors represent but a small part of those in the nonphysical realms.* You need not fear that all who land here will have these energies, for they will not. And you need not become cynical about those who live on the "other side." You have friends in these realms. They are real and they will show themselves. Worry not," Saint Germain counseled. He remained silent for a full minute, then continued, "Now, are there more questions?...Mmm, more questions of a personal nature that is?"

Tears welled up in Cassandra's eyes. "Saint Germain, could you help me with something?"

"Indeed, and how may I assist you?"

Cassandra took a moment to answer. "Alana's right," she began, "we have lots of problems here. And I'm...I'm about ready to leave the group. I don't *want* to. I love the idea of community, and the valley is so beautiful, it's everything I've always wanted and..." She glanced at Emil through her tears. "And I'm afraid what it would mean for Emil and me if I leave. I know he wants to stay. But I'm going nuts."

"What *exactly* is causing you so much distress?" Saint Germain asked.

Homecoming

"Alana," Cassandra replied angrily. "It's Alana. I know she's really wise...and she brought us all together and..."

Saint Germain corrected her. "This is not the truth. You brought yourselves together."

"Right, but she had a big part in it, and I appreciate what she's done, but damn, I *just can't handle this*! She treats me like I'm a little kid. I'm not! I don't need that energy in my life! I'd rather live someplace else!" she yelled.

"Take a moment to compose yourself," Saint Germain suggested. "Then we will continue."

Cassandra dried her eyes and took a few deep breaths. "Sorry. I'm ready now."

"You have no need to apologize. Many of your brothers and sisters here struggle with these, or similar, issues; it is simply that you have the courage to voice the pain in *your* heart."

Cassandra smiled. "Thanks. I appreciate you saying that."

Saint Germain turned his gaze towards Alana, "And you, what is in your heart, beloved one?"

"I agree, we have a problem," Alana answered. "And I'd like some help." Then, to Cassandra she said, "Thanks for sharing your feelings."

Cassandra looked surprised.

"Come and sit in front of me, the two of you," Saint Germain suggested. When they had seated themselves, he asked Cassandra, "And you, you who love this community so much, you would consider leaving because of this conflict?"

"Yes. Like I said, it's driving me crazy. I can't paint. I can't concentrate. I can't do *anything*. So, yes, I'm thinking of leaving. She's always *mothering* everyone. You can ask anyone here. They'll tell you the same thing."

Saint Germain listened patiently, then asked Cassandra, "The conflict you perceive is between you and this woman, what is *your* part?"

"It's *her* problem," Cassandra replied defiantly.

"And you wish to pursue this no further?"

"You mean work on it with her? No, no way, it's *her* problem."

"And when you and your beloved have a similar disagreement, do you view things in the same way? That it is *his* problem and you, let us say, wash your hands of it?"

"Oh God, I knew you'd say something like that," Cassandra moaned. "See, uh, it's not the same. Emil's my lover. Who knows, we may even get married. So we *need* to work things out. But Alana *isn't* my lover. I don't have to work things out with her. *I don't have to do anything about this!*"

Saint Germain's reply was gentle and loving, but firm. "Indeed, you do if you wish to live in this community."

"You mean I have to change and she doesn't?"

"Of course not. She is involved as well."

"Then ask *her* about what's going on!" Cassandra yelled at Saint Germain.

Saint Germain's expression did not change. He regarded Cassandra with eyes that expressed only love and compassion. There was no anger and no sarcasm in his voice when he said, "Very well, I will speak with her for a time." Turning his gaze toward Alana, he inquired, "Beloved one, how is it that you view this woman?"

"Honestly? I'd say that most of the time she's rather childish."

Cassandra's face darkened and her body tensed.

Saint Germain replied, "Indeed, this woman has within her a wondrous and free child. It is what allows her to bring forth her art. And you appreciate her art, do you not?"

"Sure, but that's not what I mean," Alana argued, sensing a trap and trying to elude it. "By childish I mean she's always...always..." She hesitated, obviously frustrated. "She never takes things seriously."

"Excuse me, I most certainly do!" Cassandra barked.

"And you," Saint Germain asked Alana, "how is the state of *your* child?"

"Mm, pretty good," she answered glibly. She met Saint Germain's loving eyes, then looked away. "Oh, okay, I still don't know how to play very well," she admitted.

"Indeed, you do not allow much of this inner freedom. And this woman you call childish indulges her child daily, revels in this aspect of herself."

"Yeah, that's what drives me crazy about her," Alana said, as the understanding began to dawn.

"What drives you crazy is that *you* cannot give free reign to your own child. And since you cannot do this for yourself, you judge those who can."

Alana knew Saint Germain spoke the truth. "You're right," she said, sighing deeply. "I *know* the whole conflict is in me. I just forget it sometimes."

Saint Germain asked Cassandra, "And you, how is it with the mother who lives inside *you*?"

"My mother is dead. She died two years ago in a car crash," Cassandra replied, anger and sadness in her voice.

"Indeed, she has departed her physical life and yet she still lives inside you, does she not?"

Cassandra did not hear Saint Germain's words; in an almost trancelike voice she continued, "She was hard to live with. Always nagging at me. I just wanted to draw and paint and have fun and she...she had a problem with that."

Saint Germain went on, "If this woman who was your mother was still physically alive, how old would she be? Would she be about the same age as the woman who sits next to you?"

"About. Maybe a couple of years older."

"And when you gaze upon this woman and you hear her speak, who is it you see and hear?"

"I know what you want me to say, but it's not that simple," Cassandra argued.

Vicki raised her hand. "May I say something?"

"Of course," Saint Germain replied.

Looking at Cassandra and Alana, Vicki said, "I love both of you, so I don't think I'm taking sides. Sure, Alana has a problem dealing with you, Cassandra, and she has things to work out. But I want to tell you something. You may not like this, but...sometimes when Alana talks to you, it really doesn't seem like you hear *her*. It seems like, well, like you're hearing your mother. Is that possible?"

Cassandra was quiet for a long time. No one hurried her. "I don't get why it's so hard to admit this," she said softly. She rested her head on her knees, staring off into space, then said to Alana, "Okay, I can see what Vicki is saying, because I remember one time when you said something to me. I forget what. I knew you were just giving me some advice, or your opinion, but I swear I wanted to fight and to argue with you. It made me kind of crazy. I knew it was you talking to me, but I could also hear mom."

Vicki followed her intuition. "Are you angry at your mom for dying?"

"Sure, we were just beginning to be friends. It wasn't fair!" Cassandra replied bitterly.

Vicki came over, put her arms around Cassandra, and held her while she cried.

Saint Germain waited; then he said, "There are many here who will assist the two of you. Is this not true?"

"Yes," several murmured.

Saint Germain resumed, "Remember, the community you are birthing is a *relationship*, just as you might have with a mate or a friend. No different. And, as in any relationship, you must be willing to examine *everything*. And you must be willing to see yourself in the other. Always. Understand, beloved ones, I use this word literally—*always*. When you begin to have the attitude that it is the *other* who has the problem, know that you are indeed in the midst of a grand illusion—a grand self-deception. You must commit yourselves to this community in the same way—*the exact same way*—that you would to a marriage or some similar relationship. I will say good-bye for now. We will meet again, for I am always here to assist you. Have the courage to follow your dream...*and* to allow yourselves to have it."

Veda opened her eyes. One by one, slowly, people stretched and began to move around.

"Wow, pretty intense," Jerry said. "I sure admire the two of you," he said to Cassandra and Alana. "I couldn't do that yet, spill my guts like you guys did, but I'm sure glad it happened. I'll be in your shoes one day and the way Saint

Germain helped you, it gives me a...uh...what's the word?"

"A model of how to resolve conflicts," Kate suggested.

"Yeah, a model. I want to remember that. Did we get it on tape?" he asked Veda.

Veda nodded.

"Can I have a copy?" Jerry asked.

"Sure."

"I'd like one also," Glenn said.

"Tell you what," Veda said. "I'll go ahead and make copies for everyone. In fact, if you will pay for the cost of the tapes, I'll make copies of all of Saint Germain's sessions."

Veda had been channeling for over two hours. They all needed a break. One by one they left for home or to run errands or to have lunch in town. The good-bye's were easy, for they knew they would see each other again soon.

Chapter Thirteen

December 1998:

Events moved swiftly in the next few days.

Alana and Jeff decided that their yurt was livable, so the next day, with Anna and Evelyn and Brian helping, they moved two truckloads of their belongings to their new home.

Coming over the crest of the hill, they spotted Andrew's tent pitched under some trees at the far end of the valley.

Alana hugged Andrew. "So this is where you've been hanging out," she said. She told him of the channeling the day before.

"Sure sorry I missed hearing brother Germain. Guess I shoulda told you folks what I was planning to do."

"No problem," Jeff said. "Pretty soon we'll all be living out here. Then, no more missed messages."

Andrew whistled. "Want you to meet my dog, Mollie."

At the sound of Andrew's whistle, Mollie picked up her ears and came bounding over the meadow to join them. Sam ran to meet her.

"Andrew, she's a golden retriever like Sam," Alana exclaimed as Mollie approached.

"Yup. I've had her six years now. She's my best friend," Andrew replied with love in his voice.

"They could be brother and sister," Evelyn remarked.

Mollie sat down in front of Alana. "She's beautiful, Andrew," Alana said as she reached down and ran her fingers through Mollie's thick golden hair.

Her hello's done, Mollie nudged Sam and they took off racing side by side towards the creek. Alana's heart filled with joy as she saw her beloved Sam happily playing with Mollie.

They worked hard that day and the next moving Jeff and Alana. The following afternoon, with the rest of the community helping, they moved Glenn and Vicki into their dome and Evelyn into the other yurt.

That evening, they ate dinner in Glenn and Vicki's new home.

"Still a little primitive I'm afraid," Glenn joked, lighting some kerosene lamps.

"But it's *happening*," Anna exclaimed happily. She was planning to move in a few days. By the end of the week, more than half of them would be living in the valley.

"By the way," Jeff began, "did we tell you, Alana and I found a spring about halfway up the hill. A big one. As long as the water checks out okay, all we have to do is build a spring box and lay some pipe and we have our water. And the spring's high enough up the hill so we should have plenty of pressure. Much better than using the creek. Anyone into digging ditches?"

Five days after his press conference at the White House, just as Evelyn was putting the last of her things away and just as Jeff and Emil were about to begin work on the solar panels, Ancon held another press conference, this one at the United Nations.

"You want to watch the Mr. Ancon show?" Jeff asked those gathered in the living room.

"Yes and no. But I guess yes," Alana replied.

Jeff brought the little television set out of its "hiding"

place and adjusted the antenna. "I'm amazed at the reception we get here with only the rabbit ears," he said. "Something else that's peculiar about our valley. We're at least seventy miles from any station and the reception is almost as good as with a satellite dish."

Not entirely good news in Alana's opinion. Now that they were in the valley and off the power grid, she looked forward to being away from the television and other such electronic equipment. Sure that they generated signals that interfered with normal functioning, she wanted these devices out of her life as much as possible. But she had consented to having the television—for occasional use—and she had to admit an almost overwhelming curiosity about Ancon's plan for the planet.

In the six days since Ancon's spectacular, and rather grim, "demonstration" in Las Vegas, Idaho, and Uganda, most of the fighting had stopped. Stunned by what they saw, most of the combatants simply laid down their weapons. Even the crazed city dwellers quieted down: the mobs dispersed, the looting ended, people returned to their homes to wait and see what Ancon would do. As Jeff had joked to Alana, "I guess those people weren't suicidal after all. They saw the light. At least they saw what happened to those poor guys in Las Vegas and the other places."

Those who did not heed Ancon's warning met the same fate as those in the "demonstration" zones—they were eliminated. Ancon called this "the cleansing."

The Middle East had been the most resistant area. Despite the graphic demonstrations of what awaited those who continued their violence, most of the combatants refused to stop fighting, obeying, instead, some deeply implanted picture that drove them to continue their violence, even if it meant their own sure death. Ancon did not wait for them to "see the light." He gave the warring parties in the Middle East one brief warning; when they ignored it, they were "vaporized." Much of the Middle East was now a barren wasteland, devoid of people or buildings or life of any kind, turned into a dead zone in one brief instant.

At first there was an outpouring of grief and anger from

around the world. But surprisingly, this outcry quickly subsided, due in part perhaps to Ancon's quick reaction. Immediately after the Middle East "cleansing," he spoke to the people of Earth via a global television hook-up, explaining the necessity for his actions. "We regret taking these drastic measures," he began, "and we regret the loss of life, but if we are to bring peace to your beautiful planet there was no other way." He spoke for another fifteen minutes. Those who watched and listened—even the ones who vehemently opposed Ancon—reported feeling calmer... *and* in complete agreement with his decision: of course millions had died, but Ancon was right, these people would never have agreed to peace. The "cleansing" was the only way.

The sophisticated opinion polls taken in the days following these "cleansings" showed overwhelming worldwide support for Ancon's actions.

The Middle East was the most public of the "holdout" areas. The others were in remote parts of the world, and when they were "cleansed" few people were aware that millions of others had perished.

For the most part, then, the citizens of Earth cheered as the fighting ceased. Peace at last! Could it really be possible? Many had never known peace in their entire lives—not for one single moment—and now...Peace!

On the whole, Ancon's arrival appeared to be a boon to humankind.

True, millions of Earth's citizens had reacted with fear and panic in the first few days following the Alien's landing, and some of these had to receive treatment—usually medication—to resume normal functioning. But amazingly, most of the panic had subsided as people watched the news stories and the replays of Ancon's two public appearances. Like Ancon's speech to the world, these replays had a curiously calming effect on Earth's inhabitants.

Most calming of all, however, was channel "F." The "F" was for "friendship." A joint project of all of Earth's governments, this television channel—broadcasting a picture of the mother ship, nothing more—was beamed around the world twenty-four hours a day. Many people scoffed at first, but when they gave in and watched the picture of the giant silver ship, they reported an almost euphoric sense of calmness and well-being. And in as little as ten minutes! Most people had made it a habit to watch at least once a day.

And what about Ancon's promise to bring fabulous gifts to the planet?

Three days after his dramatic landing on the White House lawn, the Center for Disease Control in Atlanta reported that Ancon had indeed given them the cure for AIDS, a cure that was easily replicable...and "safe." The Center announced a crash program to manufacture this drug, but Ancon was one step ahead of them. In a worldwide television broadcast, he'd said, "We know the ravages the disease called AIDS has inflicted upon your planet, and we have brought with us millions of injections of the antidote." Two hours after his announcement, several of the smaller space ships flew the medicine to every major city in the world. The next morning, hundreds of thousands of people lined up at specially designated centers to receive the injections; millions more would receive them in the days to come.

As for the vaccine, the CDC promised to make it available, free of charge, within two weeks. The method of inoculation, according to the CDC, would be unique and would employ advanced technology brought by the Aliens. An almost microscopically small computer chip would be injected just under the skin. This chip would carry the AIDS vaccine...*and* would also protect the recipient against a host of other diseases. In addition, the Center proudly announced, the chip could be programmed with the individual's complete health history. And other information, if appropriate.

Could there be any doubt about the kindness and the generosity of these beings from outer space? Was there anything—any disease, any problem—they could not cure or fix? Most on the planet thought not, and they opened their hearts to receive the Aliens.

Homecoming

"Okay gang, here we go," Jeff said as he turned on the television.

The scene was the United Nations in New York. The hall was packed, people of all nationalities jammed into every corner. Ancon rose to speak. Instead of his body-hugging silver suit of a few days ago, he was now clad in a looser fitting garment of a soft blue material.

Ancon began, "Greetings to you my Earth brothers and sisters! We of the Federation greet you and we welcome you into our family. First, we must apologize for any fear we may have caused you. Our abrupt appearance must have surprised you, and perhaps upset you, but there was no other way. We also realize that you may have doubted our good intentions; you may have even feared that we were here to harm you. We are sorry. But we understand from talking with your scientists and your doctors that the initial worry has ceased for most of you. We are glad. And we are glad you are beginning to comprehend what we have brought to you. Already your Earth is a more humane place—the fighting has ceased and many are now receiving the medical help we promised. And we have more to give you. We have brought advanced technology with us, technology that will rebuild your factories and revitalize your farms. Soon, no one on your planet will go to bed hungry, and no one will be without a job." The audience reacted with thunderous applause and wild cheering. Ancon smiled and waited patiently, gazing upon them with obvious approval, much as a proud parent might gaze upon a child who was demonstrating a newly mastered skill.

"You notice a difference in him?" Evelyn asked.

Alana went deep within herself and asked for the understanding. "Yes, he feels... *softer.*"

"Hey, yeah, you got it," Jerry exclaimed, propping himself up on his pillow. "And I kinda trust him more now."

"Didn't you before?" Jeff asked.

Jerry scratched his head. "I don't know... I just kind of like him more now."

Yes, Alana decided, Ancon had definitely changed. He had learned how to talk to human beings, how to garner their trust and how to win their hearts. Whereas before he had seemed distant and cold, now he projected the image of the wise, kindly, all-powerful father. She giggled. Next he would be out on the campaign trail, shaking hands, eating apple pie, and kissing babies.

As the cheering died down, Ancon resumed, "And now, as to why I am here in your United Nations, this place where so many men and women of goodwill have gathered to bring into manifestation their dreams for a better world. I have chosen this revered place for a specific reason: The United Nations began as a dream many decades ago. It is now a *reality!* Yes, a *reality!* I am here to announce that your world governments have decided to gather together in true brotherhood and to institute a World Federation Council to be based here in this city you call New York." The rustlings and stirrings and murmurs that greeted Ancon's announcement gradually subsided, and the audience waited for him to continue.

"Some of you may view this development with a certain apprehension. Fear not, you of Planet Earth! We come in peace! You have seen what we have accomplished in these few brief days. Fear not. We wish only to bring you into the family of the Galactic Federation. Our Federation is a peaceful place; war has been unknown for centuries. Think of the progress possible with extended peace! But to quiet any remaining fears, let me tell you what we have done. In these past few days, we have personally met with all of your world leaders and all of your governing bodies. And we have made them a promise: *those citizens who do not wish to join the new world community will not be coerced into doing so.* We have given our word and we will honor the decision each of you makes. But we are confident that once you see the benefits of joining our family, you will gladly do so.

"We begin this new era of true brotherhood by making these following proclamations: Beginning today, all borders between nations are open! Beginning today, all goods and services may be freely exchanged anywhere on the planet! Beginning today, all symbols of divisiveness and separation between the peoples of Earth are eliminated! The pitting of nation against nation, of race against race, of brother against brother, is not the destiny of your beautiful planet and *will not be tolerated*!" he thundered. And with these stirring words, the hall erupted in wild jubilation. Instantly, people were on their feet yelling and shouting, embracing one another, and dancing in the aisles. Ancon raised his hands like a cheerleader asking for more.

"Oh boy," Glenn said. "Is he moving fast or what."

"He's talking about one world government, isn't he?" Nancy asked.

"Sure sounds like it," Jeff answered.

"But people won't go for it. They didn't before, why would they now?" Nancy continued.

Alana took a deep breath and said, "Yes, I think they will. There may be some resistance at first, but it won't last."

"Why not?" Evelyn asked.

"Because anyone who says no will be dead," Jerry said dramatically.

Alana appreciated Jerry's sense of humor. She laughed and said, "Ah...no, that's not quite it. Close, but not quite. People will go for it because they are tired and very disillusioned. What's happened lately—the earthquake, the Market crash, the takeover by the Corporation, and now the civil war, it's shattered their dreams. They have nothing to believe in, nothing to hope for. Doesn't this remind you of what happened in Nazi Germany?" she asked Emil.

Emil nodded. "Yes. Germany was in terrible shape in the twenties and the thirties, much as this country is now. And Hitler promised resurrection and a shinning, bountiful new world, the same as Ancon is promising."

"Except Hitler wasn't able to pull it off," Alana said. "But you see, the thing is, Ancon and the others who came with him can deliver the goods. They *can* pull it off. It's as simple as that," she added, smiling ruefully.

"You mean like jobs and health care?" Evelyn asked.

"Yes, and lots more we don't know about yet," Alana added. "And that's why people will follow him. Even if they know, deep inside, that much of what he says is a lie, they'll follow him. They'll follow him because he promises them they can have their dream back—the American dream of material abundance and retirement plans and lots of leisure time. And they know he can deliver."

"But those kinds of things, they were an illusion to begin with. You can't find happiness in things outside yourself," Evelyn protested.

"Doesn't matter," Alana said firmly. "It's what gave meaning and structure to their lives and they want it back. At any cost."

"Ancon seems like he's promising something else, too," Brian added. "He's saying everyone will have the basic necessities, like food and shelter. Don't get me wrong, I don't much like the feeling I get from these guys, but there sure are lots of hungry and homeless people in the world, and my guess is that in a few weeks you won't be able to find one single hungry or homeless person anywhere on the planet."

"Yes, he'll deliver on that, too," Alana admitted.

"Maybe his program is not so bad then," Karen said hopefully.

"It's not a matter of good or bad," Alana replied. "It's more like...welfare. Anyone here ever been on welfare?"

Karen and Anna said they had.

"What was it like?" Alana wanted to know.

Anna thought for a minute. "I sure got used to it fast. Gave me lots of time to do the things I wanted."

"And?" Alana pressed her.

Anna sighed. "It was so easy. All I had to do was to show up for an interview every once in awhile."

"I never knew you were on welfare," Evelyn said. "What was going on?"

"I didn't have a job. Heck, in those days I didn't *want* to work. And I felt like...I guess I felt like the world *owed* me."

"I didn't like welfare," Karen said. "Made me feel kind of dirty. I remember I used to get up in the morning and wonder what I would do all day. Lots of freedom, like

Homecoming

Anna says. But the problem was, I didn't have any reason to do *anything*, and I didn't like the feeling," she said and shivered.

They turned their attention back to the television to listen to Ancon's final words. "Where I come from," he began, "we live for a long time as counted in your Earth years...centuries as you would calculate. We have been to many planets such as yours, planets walking the line between life and death. And make no mistake, my brothers and sisters, you came close to falling into the darkness. And you may still choose this if you wish. You may reject our wisdom and the technologies we offer and you may go back to your insane killing. But we are sure you will not. However, for any of you who still doubt our intentions, I make you a promise: When we have assisted your World Federation Council to bring the nations of Earth together into one loving family, and when we have imparted all our wisdom to you, we will leave. I have nothing more to say for now," he said and smiled.

Alana unplugged the television, and once again they were aware of the valley sounds: the creek tumbling and splashing over rocks, the raucous cawing of a crow, Mollie and Sam barking playfully.

Kate had a question. "Do they mean what they say about not forcing people to join their...their whatever they call it?"

"The World Federation Council," Glenn reminded her.

"Yes. What do you think? Will they make us join?" Kate wondered.

"They're pretty sure almost everyone will accept their plan, so my guess is they won't pressure people to go along," Alana replied.

"What about people like us? People who...who want to go and live in their own communities?" Karen wanted to know.

"Remember what Saint Germain said about the two Earths?" Alana asked her.

Karen nodded.

"That's the answer."

"You mean we'll be one place and they'll be somewhere else?" Karen asked.

"Uh-huh," Alana replied. "Might not happen overnight, but eventually there will be two Earths. And in the meantime, we let them do what they need to do. We stay focused on our path. We don't resist. We deal with our fears by asking for the truth. Nothing to it, right?" she joked.

"Sure, piece of cake," Jerry quipped. "God, I wish I really, really believed that."

That evening, after dinner, Jeff and Alana strolled down to the creek, found a comfortable place on the mossy bank, and sat and listened to the night sounds; and although there were other people only a few yards away, they felt completely alone. Jeff was right, the valley was shaped in a way that allowed for maximum privacy. But there was also something about the valley that *honored* this privacy.

Alana remembered something she had learned in a college anthropology class about a tribe of Indians who lived in the Amazon rain forest. They lived in close quarters, many people in each dwelling. Difficult to have privacy in such circumstances. They solved their dilemma in an elegant way: when they wanted to be alone, they simply turned around and faced the wall, and everyone treated them as if they had gone into another room and closed the door. A beautiful, dignified solution to a difficult living situation. And the valley had the same energy. The valley said: intend that you have privacy and it is yours.

The memory of the Amazon tribe triggered an even earlier memory, a memory of her life in Lemuria as the woman Alana. She had experienced the same honoring of privacy there. She remembered walking down beautiful jungle paths, fragrant flowers and sparkling streams everywhere. Often, she would stop to commune with the beautiful Earth, to smell a flower or visit with an animal. Others on the path would read her intention to be alone and would go on their way without disturbing her, *treating her as if she was invisible*. She sighed. Why did people today have such a difficult time honoring each other's privacy? Why were they always intruding? This valley, though, was different, more like Lemuria.

She returned from her remembering to find Jeff talking to her.

"We could put a bench down there," Jeff said. "Maybe one of these days, when everything *else* gets done..."

Although Alana had missed many of his words, she immediately caught his emotional tone. "You feeling overwhelmed, sweetie?" she asked. Jeff was doing much of the building, either by himself or supervising the others, and he looked tired.

"There's just so much to do."

She squeezed his hand affectionately. Then she drew her legs up, rested her chin on her knees, and stared at the water.

"And you? *You* feeling overwhelmed?" Jeff asked.

"I'm not sure."

A year ago, not wanting to intrude, Jeff would have let the matter drop. But he had discovered that while he *thought* he was giving Alana space by not pursuing these issues, in reality often he was running from himself. "Well, *something's* going on inside you," he said gently.

Alana silently watched the water tumbling over rocks. "You know what it is? Just about everyone on the planet is going to join the new world Ancon is building. They *are* you know."

"I agree. So?"

She sighed.

"You feeling lonely?"

She reached over and tweaked his cheek. "You are so smart," she said, smiling. "Maybe that's it, maybe I *am* feeling lonely. There won't be many of us who don't follow him. A small and select group you might say. Not many."

"There never have been many of *us* anyway."

She laughed and said, "You mean the ones who never felt they fit in this world? The ones who felt like "strangers in a strange land"? Those ones?"

"Uh-huh, *those* ones. People who could walk into a

valley, a valley that's there and not there, and revel in the magic of the place. People who are getting ready to walk into another Earth...and not even look back. Well, that's a bit of an exaggeration. I guess I'm looking back some."

"So am I," she admitted.

Jeff glanced up at the stars just beginning to show themselves in the deep blue evening sky and remarked, "So much has changed. I remember a few months ago when you were in that Marin County channeling group. I felt like you were really weirding out on me. I mean with all we had going for us, I asked myself, who needs to be talking to disembodied spirits? And what if the neighbors find out? After all, I was an upstanding member of the Marin County community. Almost joined Rotary. I had a reputation to protect." He reached down and picked up a creek stone, felt its smoothness, unconsciously read its ancient energy, then gently replaced it and went on, "And now look at me—living in a mysterious valley that's not quite here...and loving it. Such a funny thing, to feel like you have to fit in. Fit in? Fit in to what? But the thing is, until a few months ago I felt I *did* fit in. Now I have serious doubts. Now I think I may be as wacky as you are. Definitely an unnerving experience."

"I'm a bad influence on you, huh?"

Jeff squeezed her hand playfully. "Absolutely. But now stop avoiding the issue and tell me why you're feeling so down."

Tears instantly filled her eyes. "It's silly."

"Nope, it's what you're feeling."

"Uh-huh," she agreed. "You bring anything I can blow my nose with? Oh wait, I have something."

"You're stalling."

"But it's *silly*. Oh, okay, okay. The thing is, I want them all to come with us." And saying that brought a fresh flood of tears.

"You mean all the ones who will be choosing the other Earth?"

She nodded.

"Yeah, I understand," Jeff said. "It's kind of like...well,

almost like a family that's splitting up. Maybe not the best family in the world—lots of arguments and lots of heartaches—but at least it was *your* family."

"Yes. And I don't see why everyone can't wake up and *get* it," she said angrily. "Then we can all go together. Wouldn't that be wonderful?"

"Yes," he agreed. "But this way is wonderful, too."

"Doesn't feel wonderful."

"That's because you want so much for everyone to see what *you* see."

"I don't get why..."

He interrupted her. "You've taught me a lot in these months, and one of the best things you've taught me is that everyone has their own path and that it's exactly right for them. Most people on the planet aren't ready to allow Heaven on Earth. They need another kind of experience first. It's not better or worse, just different from the one people like us are calling into our lives."

"My kid doesn't believe you," she said morosely.

"Yeah, your kid wants everyone to be happy."

"Uh-huh. Guess I need to talk with her, see if I can get her to accept that everyone has their own way of doing things and that maybe some people need to be unhappy for awhile."

Jeff held her; then, arm in arm, they walked back to their new home.

One week later:

"Jerry, that's a brilliant idea!" Alana exclaimed.

"Well, actually, it's Veda's idea," Jerry said, putting down his cup of coffee.

Alana and Jeff exchanged meaningful glances. Alana said, "Hmm. We haven't seen much of Veda in the past few days. Come to think of it, we haven't seen much of *you* either."

Jerry blushed. "Well, that's because...well, shoot, you guys know, don't you?"

"Know what?" Jeff asked, feigning ignorance.

"About Veda and me."

"Oh, you mean about you being *friends*," Alana said.

"Ah, no, actually, see, it's more than that. We're...living together."

Alana laughed. "So *that's* why we haven't seen you," she said. "Well, you going to tell us about it?"

Jerry beamed. "Hey, I'm in love. Totally. And it's awesome. She's absolutely the most wonderful woman I've ever met. Kind and gentle...and wise and beautiful."

"Are you saying you like her?" Jeff teased.

Catching on to his teasing, Jerry nodded happily. "You might say that."

Alana hugged him and said, "We're happy for you. You guys are so cute."

"So, it's Veda's idea about the trailers?" Jeff asked.

"Yup," Jerry replied. "We were talking the other day about how in the heck we're going to live out here. We don't have the money to build, so Veda suggested moving her trailer out here."

"She has one?" Jeff asked.

Jerry nodded. "Not very big, but big enough for us for awhile."

"Great idea," Alana said. "With one or two more trailers everyone could be out here."

Jeff agreed. "We'll start looking around. Shouldn't be too hard to find a couple of good used trailers," he said. Then he asked Jerry, "By the way, Jerry, you keeping up on Ancon and friends? What's the latest?"

"Well, a couple of days ago the Congress and the President passed a law: We are now officially in the World Federation and subject to its laws and jurisdiction," Jerry answered.

Jeff looked puzzled. "What does that mean?"

"Beats me. Feels kinda like the UN—the UN with teeth. Nothing really new...except I guess now when these guys talk everyone will listen. I'd listen, too, if I was the President of some country and the World Federation Council told me to do something and I looked up and saw that mother ship hovering over the capital of my country."

Jerry paused and sipped his coffee. "Something else I was going to tell you. Oh yeah, now I remember, Ancon wants to go to a worldwide debit card system. One huge data bank. He's got this awesome computer he's going to let us use."

"Of course," Alana said sarcastically.

"Oh hey, hey, dig *this*!" Jerry exclaimed. "There's going to be something called...oh shoot, what *is* it called? Something funny." He scratched his head. "Yeah, regional living units. Ancon says our system of cities and states isn't efficient, so he, or someone, is going to create lots of these regional living units. Then things like police and fire protection can be done more efficiently. That's the plan anyway."

Although Alana had never liked the Gray Men and their secret world government, she had admired their intelligence and their organizational skills. They were master planners and they accomplished their plans swiftly. Ancon and friends also had plans for the Earth—the worldwide debit card and the regional living units were just the beginning. But the Aliens brought a super intelligence to the planet far surpassing anything the Gray Men could ever hope to match. These beings would be many, many steps ahead of everyone. Many *years* ahead. They would accomplish their goals with dazzling, dizzying speed.

"What's the reaction been?" Alana wanted to know.

"Far as I can tell, no problem," Jerry replied. "But hey, who's going to tell that big guy they don't like his ideas? I don't know if *I* would."

Alana had another question. "Jerry, you used to listen to those radio talk shows. You know, the ones where people call in with their opinions."

"Still do. I got myself a beautiful new AM radio. Shortwave too. Picks up *everything*," he said proudly.

"So, what are people saying?" Alana asked.

"Ah, mostly I'd say they're real positive. Excited. They think Ancon is wonderful. Kind of makes you want to puke after awhile, the way they go on about him and how great he is. Anyway, they have all kinds of ideas, things they want him to do. And they think he can do *anything*...like he's Santa Claus."

Alana smiled knowingly and said, "And Ancon isn't discouraging that kind of reaction, is he?"

Jerry shook his head.

"Anything negative?" Jeff wanted to know.

"Not really. But maybe they aren't letting those dudes on the air."

"Or maybe there aren't many of them," Alana suggested.

"Yeah, maybe not. Or maybe..."

"Maybe what Jerry?" Alana asked.

"Maybe nobody's thinking about anything, except how good everything's going to be. So they don't ask any embarrassing questions, like the ones *we'd* ask. You know, like where's all this good stuff coming from? And what's the price tag? Nobody seems to *care*. Feels like...this is going to sound crazy...but it almost feels like everyone I'm listening to is hypnotized. But that's too weird."

"Are you and Veda watching television?" Alana asked, trying to keep the worry out of her voice.

"Nope. Veda made me give it up."

"Good," Alana said. "I have a feeling we need to be careful about the television. Watch it only when we absolutely have to. And figure out some way to protect ourselves when we *do* watch. Might be good to talk about this when we meet. Which is...when? I guess we need to plan another get-together. Jerry, will you help us get in touch with everyone?"

"Sure."

Jerry stayed for awhile and helped Jeff install some solar panels on the roof of the yurt; then he left for Veda's to make some calls to set up their next meeting.

Chapter Fourteen

"Hon!"

Unaware that someone was calling her, Alana kept on walking. She was about to turn down the brick path to Evelyn's bookstore when someone grabbed the arm of her coat.

"Hon! Wait a sec!"

Alana turned around to find a middle-aged woman smiling at her. "What? You talking to me?" Alana asked.

"Well sure. Remember me?"

Alana shook her head.

"Edna! Edna from the cafe! Remember? You came in a few weeks ago for a cup of tea. We had a real nice conversation, you and me and Mel and Haley. Remember?"

Alana pulled herself back from her daydreaming, focused on the woman's face, and said, "Oh sure. Hello Edna. I didn't recognize you at first."

"Heck, nobody does when I'm out of uniform. How've you been?"

"Good. Fine," Alana stammered.

"You going in *that* store?" Edna asked, pointing to Evelyn's bookstore.

"Yes," Alana answered.

"Huh. Never could find anything interesting to read in there. But what the heck, as my late husband always used to say, it takes all kinds."

Knowing Edna wanted something, Alana waited.

"Oh, by the way," Edna went on, "you remember Haley? The young one?"

"Uh-huh."

"Well, she went and got herself knocked up. I tried to tell her about those men she was hanging out with, but she wouldn't listen. Men! We know what they want, don't we?"

Alana smiled even though she didn't share Edna's picture of men.

"Anyhow, hon, don't mean to keep you; what I wanted was to invite you to join our church."

Alana now felt on familiar ground—people were always wanting her to join their churches. "Oh, thanks, no, I don't..."

"Now, now, wait a minute. This is no ordinary church. This is the Church of the Federation," Edna announced proudly.

"The Federation? You mean the place Ancon comes from? Is that what you're talking about?"

"Yep. Isn't he just the greatest thing. So what if he's nine feet tall and comes from outer space and probably has green skin, he's just what the country needs."

"Okay," Alana said noncommittally.

"Well, you heard about the Church of the Federation I expect. It's spreading like wildfire all across the country."

"No, I don't think..."

"Hon! Where've you *been*? You *must* have heard about our church. There's been programs about it every night on all the channels."

"Oh, that explains it, we don't watch television."

"Oh, *really?*" Edna replied, sounding disappointed. "You don't watch the *F* channel? I thought *everybody* did."

"The what?"

"The *F* channel. The *Friendship* channel. The one where they show the picture of the big ship and play the music. I admit I had to get used to the music at first. Kinda weird when you first hear it. Kinda spooky. Not what you'd call regular music. But now, I swear I get the nicest feeling when I watch and listen. Puts me in the best mood, no matter what else is happening."

"So you think what Ancon's done is okay?"

"*Okay!* Hey, listen to you. What a card you are. He's *saved* us."

Alana nodded.

"I sure hope you reconsider about our church. You're such a nice girl. I could tell from the minute you walked in the cafe. I get to see all types in my business and I could tell right away you had class. We need people like you. Why don't I give you a call? Or I could even come out with some of the brothers and sisters and we could tell you about it. Where do you live anyhow?"

Alana felt a momentary stab of fear. Pushing it down, she replied, "Oh, out in the country." She could hear the evasiveness in her voice.

Edna didn't seem to notice Alana's fear. She smiled and said, "Oh, okay, no problem, just tell me where and we'll come out and visit with you."

"No thanks, Edna. Nothing personal, but I'm not interested. Nice meeting you again." She put her hand on Edna's shoulder, then turned and walked briskly down the path to Evelyn's store.

"Well hello there," Evelyn said and beamed at her. "Come here so I can give you a big hug."

"Evelyn, I love you. You are so *sane*," Alana said.

"I have my doubts sometimes."

Alana took Evelyn's hand. "Come over by the window for a minute and let's see if she's still there."

Edna was standing on the sidewalk, looking at the store as if deciding whether to come in.

"Oh sure, you mean her?" Evelyn asked.

"Yes, her name is Edna. She works..."

"Down the street at Harry's. Yup, known Edna for years," Evelyn said. "She trying to convert you?"

"Yes, I had a narrow escape."

"She's been after me a couple of times. She's okay, just got hooked on this church thing."

"First I've heard of it," Alana said.

"It's big. Seems like half of Mount Shasta is signing up," Evelyn said as she continued to watch Edna. "I get people in here all the time wanting me to be part of it. Children of the Federation they call themselves. You know, there's people I never thought would go for something like this. Now I hear they've joined."

"Are you tempted, Evelyn?"

"Oh, heavens no. They all have that look in their eyes."

"What look?" Alana asked, although she was pretty sure she knew what Evelyn was talking about.

Evelyn laughed. "You know the look, like they've suddenly found the one and only "Truth of the Universe," and like *you* are a little lost sheep just asking to be taken into the fold so that you, too, will feel as good as they do. Of *course* you would...you poor little lost lamb. Wouldn't you?"

"Yes, that's the look."

They watched Edna pull her coat tightly around herself and walk away.

"Evelyn, do you tell people where you're living?"

Evelyn hesitated before replying. "Well, no, actually I don't. Funny you should mention that. Anna was in here the other day. Asked *her* the same question."

"And?"

"She said the same thing," Evelyn replied. "And you?"

"I thought I was okay with telling people, but...when Edna asked me, I felt a lot of fear come up."

"Shoot. We're spooked," Evelyn remarked.

"What's going on? Are we actually afraid someone is going to march out there and tell us we can't live there?"

"I expect so."

"We'll have to trust ourselves more, trust that we're really manifesting our dream and that we're protected."

"We will," Evelyn assured her. "By the way, I'm selling the store. Did I tell you?"

"No," Alana answered. "You are? Why?"

"Been asking myself the same thing. But when this woman from Colorado walked in a couple of days ago and asked me if the store was for sale, I sure didn't dilly-dally

Homecoming 219

around. Said yes before she had the question out of her mouth."

"But you don't know why?"

"Oh, I expect I do," Evelyn replied, straightening a few books. "I've owned this store almost eighteen years and I'm kind of tired running around these aisles searching for books. The new owner—name's Wendy—said she'd like me to work here one or two days a week. I told her I'd consider it, but I already know I probably will." She pulled a book off the shelf and wiped the dust on her green jump suit. "I've enjoyed myself mind you...but...it's time to do something else."

"You aren't going to leave the community, are you?" Alana asked, worried.

"Oh no, wouldn't *think* of it. No sir. The valley's my home. Knew it the first minute I laid eyes on that place," Evelyn answered. She grinned. "And those two lovely children? Kate's children?"

Alana nodded.

"Well, they've kind of adopted me. Call me grandma. Rubbed me the wrong way at first, but it kinda grew on me. I'd like to help bring them up. Unusual children."

Alana wondered if Evelyn knew just *how* unusual.

"And I'm going to build a little place there with the money I get from the store. Going to ask Anna if she wants to share it with me. But I haven't told her yet, so don't spill the beans."

"Okay."

"Think she will?" Evelyn asked shyly.

"I expect so," Alana said, imitating one of Evelyn's favorite expressions.

"Now, don't go getting any ideas about Anna and me. I mean about any of that hanky-panky business."

"Evelyn, I wouldn't think of it."

"Well, good. Because there's none of that going on."

"You mean you're not a lesbian."

"Darn right! You better believe it!"

"Evelyn, I'd love you no matter *what* you told me about yourself."

"I know you would, sweetie. You're one of the most loving people I've ever met."

Alana asked, "Evelyn, dear, do you have a problem with gay people?"

"Well, no, of course not!" Evelyn snapped. She straightened a few more books. "Well heck, who knows, maybe I do. I was brought up differently than you were, Alana. When you grow up on a farm in North Dakota in the twenties and the thirties, you learn that nice people don't do those things. Boys are supposed to like girls and...well, heck, you know."

"But you've been in California for many years."

"Yup. And I've changed some. And I like Connie."

"Connie? You mean Connie's gay?"

Looking guilty, Evelyn said, "Guess I shouldn't have let the cat out of the bag. Oh what the heck, why not, she never kept it a secret. Used to tell people if they asked. That was before you folks came to Mount Shasta. Everyone knew about her and Rose. Rose lived with her for years and then a few months ago she just up and left. Never did understand why. Connie took it hard. We didn't see her in town for the longest time, and when she did show her face, she didn't look so good. You suppose that's why she got sick? A broken heart?"

"Possibly."

"Like I said, she didn't care who knew about Rose. One time I even saw them walking down the street holding hands. They looked real cute. Folks around here didn't much like it, though. Didn't bother Connie. Can't figure out why she hasn't said anything to you folks about...about Rose and all."

"And how is Connie doing these days?"

"Have you seen her recently?"

"No."

"Why don't you," was all Evelyn said.

Alana realized that she'd been putting off seeing Connie, afraid of what she might find out. "Okay, I will," she promised.

"You suppose maybe Nancy is, uh..." Evelyn began.

"Is what?"

"You know, like Connie?"

"Evelyn, it's time you learned to say the word gay. Can you say it?"

"Of course," Evelyn answered indignantly.

"Well, I'm waiting."

"Oh alright! *Gay*!"

"Now, what did you want to ask me?"

Looking at Alana in mock exasperation, Evelyn asked, "Do you believe Nancy is *gay*?" She seemed very pleased with herself for having said the forbidden word.

"She could be. You mean because she's sharing a house with Connie?"

"Yes, and well, she seems sort of...mannish."

"Lots of women have a strong masculine side. Doesn't mean they're gay."

"Just wondered," Evelyn said, obviously not wanting to pursue the matter further.

Alana bought two books, reminded Evelyn of the upcoming meeting day after next, said good-bye, and left for home.

They held the meeting in Alana and Jeff's yurt. Even full of furniture, piles of unopened boxes, and a forest of plants yet to find a resting place, the spacious dwelling held them all comfortably.

The topic of conversation quickly came around to one important question: How were they all going to afford to live in the valley?

"You mean we could move out here *now*?" Kate asked, sounding pleased and surprised and a little doubtful.

"Sure, we just need to find you and the kids a trailer," Jeff said. "Wouldn't exactly be deluxe accommodations, but..."

"No, no, that'd be fine."

"*We* are going to sleep in a tent, like Andrew," Camille announced. "Maybe we'll have two tents, one for me and one for Jonathan. Will you help us, Andrew?"

"Sure. I know lots about tents," Andrew replied.

Vicki had been watching Kate; she now asked, "Kate, what's the matter? You don't seem happy about this plan."

Looking embarrassed, Kate replied, "No, it's not that. I want to be here. The kids do, too. It's all they can talk about," Kate said. She sighed. "It's the same old thing: money. Ted's...well, he's cut us off. Says if I'm going to live with a bunch of weirdo hippies, I'll have to pay my own way. And I can't."

Jeff nodded. "Hmm. Let's figure out where everyone else is going to live and then we'll come back to Kate. There's a way. Not to worry."

"Sure...okay," Kate replied, not sounding at all reassured.

Jeff went on, "Now, Cassandra, you and Emil are moving into the other dome. Right?"

"In a couple of days," Cassandra replied.

"Evelyn and Anna are already in the other yurt," he said more to himself than to anyone else. "And Andrew, you're happy in your tent? You and Mollie?"

"Yup. Real nice down at the other end. Best place I've ever lived. Mighty obliged to you kind folks."

"Andrew, you don't have to thank us. You *found* this place. Remember?" Kate reminded him.

"Well, sure, I guess so, but I still appreciate living here."

"Now let's see, who's left?" Jeff asked.

Brian raised his hand. "I'm going to put up my own yurt."

"Hey, great," Jeff said, surprised. "So we have another one coming from the coast?"

Brian shook his head. "No, this is a tent, a tent shaped like a yurt. You put it up on a wooden platform. Ever see one?"

"No," Jeff answered.

"They're beautiful. I've always wanted one, but they aren't practical in Mount Shasta. Too much snow. But here...perfect!"

"They really are beautiful," Karen attested. "I went with Brian to Oregon to pick one out. They had one already set up. They let in so much light you feel like you're living outdoors. I want one, too, but with the baby coming..."

Alana wondered about Brian and Karen. They'd been up to Oregon a couple of times. And she'd seen them in Mount Shasta on several occasions. She wondered if the community had another budding romance in the offing. Possibly.

"Speaking of snow," Jeff began, "how's Mount Shasta doing?"

"Still coming down. They've had about eighteen inches," Nancy replied.

"And we've had a couple of sprinkles or two," Alana said smugly.

"Still a tad cold, though," Jeff said. "Got down to 45 last night. Sure you're warm enough, Andrew?"

"I'm fine. Been in lots colder weather."

"But next year would you consider having a little house or a cabin?" Alana asked.

"Sure. That'd be nice, too. But I'm okay. Honest."

"Now," Jeff began, "that leaves Karen and Nancy and Jerry and Veda."

Jerry shook his head.

Oh yeah, I forgot," Jeff said, "You guys are moving Veda's trailer out here."

"We're all taken care of," Jerry said, reaching for Veda's hand.

Nancy said, "I'm going to stay in town for awhile with Connie. She needs someone now. And she's been so kind to me. I want to repay her if I can."

"And how is she?" Kate asked for all of them.

Nancy hesitated before answering. "She's holding her own. Taking her herbs and doing guided imagery. But I'm still going to stay with her. That okay with everyone? Would you save a place for me out here if I don't move out right away?"

"Oh sure," Anna replied. And the others also nodded their approval.

"Now," Jeff began, we're down to Karen and Kate and the two kids."

Kate turned to Karen and asked, "Karen, would you like to come and live with us?" Then, remembering that she as yet had no home of her own, she added hastily, "I mean if we can find a trailer?"

Karen clapped her hands together. "Oh, I'd love to! Is that okay with you, Camille? And you, Jonathan?"

"We have our tents, remember?" Jonathan reminded her.

Glenn had been watching carefully. He said, "So, we need a trailer for these guys. Correct? I bet that Vicki and I can come up with enough money for a nice trailer. What do you think?" he asked Vicki.

Vicki threw her arms around Glenn's neck and kissed him. "Oh, you sweetie!" she exclaimed.

Looking embarrassed, Glenn stammered, "Hey, come on, it's only money."

"Unh-unh, it's *not* the money at all. It's *you*," Vicki said.

"Yes, *you*," Alana said, picking up for Vicki. "You've changed. Your defenses are coming down. Fast."

"*I* had defenses?" Glenn asked, surprised.

Several people laughed. Anna said, "Glenn, we always liked you, but you were a bit, oh, how shall I say it, a bit unapproachable. The big Wall Street banker..."

"Broker," Glenn corrected her, bringing more laughter.

"...who always seemed a little above all of us. But now look at you, part of the gang," Anna said happily.

"I assume you're referring to my suggestion to buy Kate a trailer," Glenn replied. "But Kate is, well she's part of the...family," he added, making a valiant but unsuccessful attempt to hide the tears in his eyes.

Someone handed Glenn the community box of tissues. He took one and wiped away his tears. "Well, she is," he said almost defiantly.

Looking at her husband with much love in her eyes, Vicki asked, "Mind if I tell them what else you're doing?"

"Ah, no, let's not."

"Oh come on Glenn!" Emil shouted. "What have you been up to?"

"Yeah, come on. No secrets in *this* family!" Jerry yelled.

When it was obvious Glenn could not answer, Vicki spoke for him, "He's paying for all of Connie's treatments."

Now Nancy had tears in *her* eyes. "Thanks, Glenn. That's really swell of you."

Glenn shrugged his shoulders and said, "No problem, I like her."

Hearts opened, and a current of love passed through each of them, bonding them ever tighter.

"So, that's everyone," Alana said. "We're all here. Home. And you and Connie will join us when she gets better. Right?" she asked Nancy.

"Yes," Nancy replied simply.

"Okay, good," Jeff said. "Now what else..."

"Oh boy, almost forgot to tell you guys!" Glenn exclaimed. "The President is going to give a special announcement in a couple of minutes. My friends back on the Street say it's going to be a real blockbuster."

Although no one in the room appeared too excited about watching another news conference, they plugged in Alana's small set and gathered around. They were early. The gleaming facade of the United Nations building—now called the World Federation Building—filled the screen. The newscaster said, "We'll be back here in a couple of minutes, folks, but first we want to show you a gathering in Central Park. It's one of the most beautiful things I've ever seen. But here, we'll let you see for yourself."

The camera showed a huge throng of people, dressed in white, heads bowed, standing in absolute silence.

"Lord, there must be twenty thousand people there!" Glenn exclaimed.

"Bet you anything they're protesters," Jerry said hopefully. "Probably protesting the news conference and this whole idea of a one world government."

Alana didn't think so. And she was correct.

As the camera panned the silent throng, the newscaster cut in and announced, "Folks, I want to introduce you to

Reverend Williams of the Church of the Federation. He'll explain what's going on."

The television now showed a middle-aged black man, dressed in white, with a green and blue Earth logo over his left breast—the uniform of the Church of the Federation. He shook his head and smiled. "No need to call me Reverend," he said. "That's ancient history. I'm a Child of the Federation now, like you, brother, and like all these beautiful brothers and sisters you see gathered together in prayer and in devotion." And the camera again panned the huge, silent crowd.

The newscaster continued, "Rev...I mean..."

"Brother, I am your brother now. We have dropped all the other titles." He smiled and the light shone forth from his eyes.

Alana went deep within herself and asked the question she always asked when her eyes and her mind were dazzled by what *looked* like love and good will. And that was: is this being's heart open? Really open? And the answer she received was...no.

"Oh, sure. I forgot," the newscaster apologized. "I just joined the church myself. My wife did, too. Haven't quite got used to calling everyone brother and sister."

Brother William's smile widened. "You will, and you will learn to love it."

The newscaster nodded and continued, "But tell me, brother Wiliams, until recently you were a rather militant black clergyman from, uh, Chicago if I recall."

"Yes."

"You have apparently given all that up."

"We all have. There's no need for militancy any more. We're all united now, black and white and brown and yellow, brothers and sisters, one world. No hatred. Brother Ancon has brought us that beautiful gift and we have opened our hearts to receive his wondrous teaching."

"And this scene we're witnessing," the newscaster continued, "I'm told that just a few short days ago these brothers and sisters all called themselves Baptists and Catholics and Jews. And now..."

Homecoming

"Now they have given up all vestiges of division," brother Williams explained. "They are Children of the Federation now, and isn't it the most beautiful thing you've ever seen?"

"Mighty impressive," the newscaster replied. "And now I believe President Storr and the others are ready to speak to us. Thank you for coming, brother Williams."

The scene shifted to the Great Hall of the World Federation Building where President Storr was about to speak.

"Oh my God, he's got one on, too!" Nancy shrieked.

Alana didn't know whether to laugh or cry, for standing on the stage was the President of the United States, dressed in a flowing white robe emblazoned with the logo of the Church of the Federation. In fact, everyone on the stage, even Ancon, was similarly dressed.

"Something else," Jerry said. "There's no American flag. Just the UN flag."

"No, it's the World Federation flag," Emil corrected him. "Looks the same, though."

The President began speaking, "I usually begin these news conferences by greeting you as my fellow Americans. After all, Presidents for many years have followed the same custom. But today all that is changed, and I now greet you as my brothers and sisters. Yes! My brothers and sisters!" The camera moved in close and revealed tears in the President's eyes. He continued, "So much has changed in these past weeks. A few months ago, if anyone had suggested I would be speaking to you dressed in these garments, I would have said they were crazy. But now I wear them proudly, for I have joined the Church of the Federation, as have most of you. Yes, much has changed. I speak to you now as your brother. I am no longer the President of the United States, for that office has been abolished," he said. The audience in the Great Hall was silent. If any of them were surprised or upset at this announcement, they kept still. "There is no President, for there is no longer a United States. Nor a Congress. Nor a Constitution. These forms—these antiquated, outdated, divisive forms—have been dissolved. We are now one united world!"

The camera panned the audience. Four people got up quietly and left. The rest silently waited.

The ex-President went on, "We know there are a *few* of you who do not agree with what we have done. That is alright. We still love you. We wish you well and hope you will understand and that one day you will embrace the truth and the bounty of our beautiful church and of our one united world. When that day comes, we will welcome you with open arms and with open hearts. I will say good-bye for now, and I will turn you over to a brother who has a wonderful message of peace and forgiveness. Brother Stockman, will you come forward please?"

"Holy shit!" Jerry yelled. "It's Aaron Stockman!"

"You mean the militia guy the Feds were after?" Brian asked.

"Yeah, one and the same," Jerry said. "Now what the heck is going on here?"

Aaron Stockman, quite striking in his white robe, strode confidently up to the microphone. "Greetings my brothers and sisters," he intoned.

"I swear," Jerry began, "if one more of them says brother or sister or flashes me one of those big toothy smiles, I'm going to puke."

Aaron Stockman continued, "Many of you know me, but for those who don't, my name is Aaron Stockman. Until a few days ago, I was wanted by the FBI and the ATSF and the IRS...and just about everyone else, too," he said and laughed. "But after watching the events of the past few days, I turned myself in...and here I am. My message to you is a short one. I know some of you are holding out against the new way of life brother Ancon has brought to the planet. I did for awhile. But I have seen the light! I have seen that resistance is not only futile, but unnecessary! Everything I believed in and everything I fought for has happened! *Everything*! Peace! Prosperity! Brotherhood! Brother Ancon has brought us these gifts! Everything we've ever wanted! And more is coming! There is no reason for conflict or resistance now, so please, please those of you who have not yet understood the beauty of this message, I implore you to give it a try." With that, he walked off the stage and sat back down. Ex-President Storr resumed speaking, offering more testimonials to the advantages of joining the Federation Church. They tuned him out.

Evelyn grinned. "Anyone have the feeling brother Stockman was talking to folks like us?"

Jerry was staring at the television, incredulity and amazement on his face. "How'd they get him to do that? A couple of months ago he would have died before saying what he just said. How did they *do* that?"

Veda gently touched Jerry's arm. "Remember what Saint Germain said about those who oppose each other and who fight each other?"

"No, tell me again," Jerry asked.

"He said they are very similar, like two sides of the same coin. So it's not surprising they could appear to change sides so easily. It is not really a change, only a turning over of the coin to show the other side."

"Oh, sure. I remember," Jerry said. "Okay...except, something weird about him, almost like he wasn't actually saying the words. No, that's not what I mean. He was..."

"Robotic?" Alana suggested.

"Yeah! Robotic!" Jerry exclaimed. "Is that possible?"

"I believe so," Alana replied. Then she shared something she had been sensing for some time now when watching public figures. "I believe there are ways to alter human beings that we aren't aware of. So we have no way of knowing whether the people they show us are really the people we think they are."

"Robots? Seriously?" Karen asked.

"Sure," Alana answered. "That would be one way. But there's probably lots of ways. Clones maybe. Or holograms. I'm not sure it matters. What matters is, we're being tricked."

Kate raised a quizzical eyebrow. "Anyone else have the feeling these people are on a different planet than we're on?"

The television was now showing the F channel and the

picture of the mother ship. And a soothing female voice crooned, "For this special occasion, we are bringing you the latest in meditation music. Please leave your television on, sit back, and relax."

Alana stared at the picture and listened to the sounds. Her heart beat faster as she realized what was happening. "Anyone else feeling sleepy?"

Several people answered yes.

"We need to turn it off. There's a powerful frequency control coming through," Alana warned.

"Yes, I can feel something," Cassandra said. "I think if I watched much longer I'd consider joining their church."

"And I'd be calling you sister," Jerry quipped.

Jeff turned off the television.

"Let's do a toning," Vicki suggested. "And maybe our intention could be that the valley remain clear of any such disruptive and unloving influences."

"A toning sounds wonderful," Brian said.

Camille took hold of Alana and Evelyn's hands and asked, "Can we get into a circle?"

They formed a circle and toned for nearly twenty minutes; the sounds wafted out of the door and through the valley, mixing with the wind until it was difficult to say which was wind and which was toning.

They held hands for awhile.

Karen looked around at the circle of faces and asked, "How did this happen so fast? Seems like yesterday we had a President and a country. I guess I don't really miss that stuff, but gosh it feels like..."

"The changes have been happening for quite some time," Alana said. "We just haven't been focusing on the outside world. I bet if we lived in town instead of this magical place we wouldn't be so surprised." And she related her story of Edna's attempt to convert her.

"It does seem like we're on a different Earth," Glenn said. "And like we're traveling further away from these other guys...like two ships going in different directions."

"We couldn't be the only ones on *this* planet, could we?" a worried Anna asked.

"Oh no, for sure not," Kate replied. "I just can't believe that."

"But how can we be certain?" Anna persisted.

"We can't I guess," Kate answered. "But..."

"Rama says there are other people like us," Camille announced.

"Who's Rama, sweetie?" Kate asked.

"You can't see him. Only Jonathan and I can see him. Rama tells us things."

Alana understood immediately. "He's like your friend and your guide. Right?"

Camille nodded happily.

Alana continued, "Camille, what does Rama say about the other people?"

Camille listened for a minute. "He says there are other places like this place, with people like us; he says we will find out about them after awhile. He says the time isn't right yet. He says don't worry."

"What else, Camille?" Vicki asked.

"Well, Jonathan and I can talk to some of the children who live there, if we want to."

"You mean Rama will tell you about them?" Alana asked.

Camille shook her head. "No, we can *talk* to them. In our minds. Can't we Jonathan?"

Her brother nodded. "We just learned how. Rama showed us. But we haven't done it much yet."

"Will you tell us what you find out when you talk with the children?" Nancy asked.

"Sure," Camille replied.

"How about if we take a break?" Alana suggested. "I need to take a walk and stretch my legs."

They reassembled an hour later. Jeff and Emil gave an update on the wind generators, and they briefly discussed how and when to build a central meeting place. Then, a little before six everyone left for home.

Alana invited Camille and Jonathan to stay for dinner. She was eager to ask the children more about their friend Rama.

Chapter Fifteen

One week later:

The entity that had been the United States no longer existed, dissolved by the World Federation Council. Surprisingly few mourned her passing. In fact, this historic action was met with almost unanimous acceptance across the country—an overwhelming 98 percent agreed this was the best thing to do. When asked why, they replied that brother Ancon had convinced them. They had listened to his television "specials" as he patiently explained how dividing the world into separate countries was an outmoded idea, an idea that had caused strife and competition and inequality. They had also "learned" that the Federation was taking care of things much better than the United States ever had: everyone had a job now; AIDS and other diseases would soon be a thing of the past; the fighting had stopped. Yes, the World Federation was a good idea. A *great* idea!

The other 2 percent? They were either too confused or too afraid to speak out.

In the former United States, the World Federation Council went ahead with its plans to create regional living units...causing some worry in the valley.

"You think they'll send someone out here, like they do the census takers?" Vicki had wondered.

Homecoming

No one had an answer. Jeff suggested they wait to see what would happen; and what happened was that one week later the World Federation Council gave everyone in Mount Shasta a questionnaire to complete, the first step in the assignment of the new living units.

But no one came down the dirt road to their valley and Alana doubted they would.

Jeff and Alana walked hand in hand up the hill to a spot they had discovered on their second day in the valley. They sat down on a large bench-shaped rock and listened to the creek singing to them from the valley floor.

"I'm amazed what we've done these past two weeks," Jeff said. "Been easy, too, most of it."

"Everyone feels this," Alana replied. "Easy and effortless."

"Yes, easy and effortless," he repeated. "What's going on?"

"We're following Spirit."

"Hmm. Simple as that?"

"Yup."

They moved closer together, put their arms around each other, and took in the scene unfolding in the valley below: Camille and Jonathan running along the creek, splashing in the water, occasionally disappearing into the thick stands of willows and alders, Sam and Mollie close behind; Veda and Jerry sitting in their new lawn chairs in front of their trailer talking with Andrew about something; Emil working on the solar panels on top of his dome.

"Looks like Glenn and Vicki got their wood stove going," Alana said, pointing to the thin column of blue smoke coming from their dome.

"Yup, we did it this afternoon," Jeff said. "We'll do ours tomorrow."

"Good," Alana responded absentmindedly.

"We got the test results back on the water," Jeff reported. "A few minerals. No problem, really. Emil still wants to purify our drinking water, though. Probably a good idea. Let's see what the others think."

Alana hadn't been listening. "I'm going out to see Connie tomorrow," she said.

"I figured you would."

"Evelyn says she's doing pretty good...but I want to see for myself."

"Want some company?"

"I need to go alone, at least this time. I might take the children, though. I don't know yet."

"I can see why you'd want to take them. Being around them is...what's the word? Grounding. Sort of like hugging a tree."

"Yes, they've been sent to us for many reasons."

"Still hard to get used to their blue skin."

Kate had been confused about what to do about the children's skin; she had asked Alana's advice. "I know Camille told you. What do you think I should do?"

"Do what the children want," Alana had suggested.

"Sure...except I feel so *protective* of them," Kate had replied.

Alana had reassured her. "I wouldn't worry about the children, Kate. We're going to home-school them here in the valley, so they won't be around any other kids. And everyone here loves them. And in a couple of years, who knows, there may be more acceptance in the outside world, at least by some people."

So Kate stopped their tanning sessions and they were again a light shade of blue. And very happy.

"When are you going to see Connie?" Jeff asked.

"Tomorrow morning."

"Let me know how things are."

"Sure."

Alana did take the children, but only after checking with Connie first.

Connie's house, an old Mount Shasta farm house, was dark inside as Alana let herself in.

"Connie?" she called.

"Back here!" Connie yelled.

Connie's bedroom was even darker than the rest of the

house, and smelled stale. Two trays of half-eaten food stood next to her bed.

Connie was propped up on pillows; she smiled and waved weakly when she saw Alana and the children. "Hi you guys. I'm sure glad to see you."

Alana was startled by Connie's appearance: she'd lost twenty pounds, her eyes were ringed by huge dark circles, and she looked exhausted.

"How about if I open a window?" Alana suggested. "Or at least let in some light?"

"Sure, if you want. I keep it dark so I can sleep. That's about all I'm doing these days."

"You need to get up and move around. You'd feel better," Alana suggested.

"You're probably right," Connie replied as she swung her legs over the side of the bed. "Let's go out to the kitchen and have some tea."

Connie hobbled out of the bedroom, obviously in pain.

"Where's Nancy?" Alana asked.

"She's shopping," Connie replied. "You kids want something to eat?"

Jonathan and Camille shook their heads no.

"When are you coming to live with us?" Jonathan asked.

Connie busied herself with fixing the tea. "I guess when I'm better."

"Why not come now?" Camille suggested. "We'll take care of you."

"Oh no, I couldn't."

"Why not?" Alana asked.

Connie took a long time answering. "Maybe because I don't want to be a burden. And I would be. Some days I can hardly do anything for myself. No, you don't want me around."

Alana grinned at the two children and said, "It's called feeling sorry for yourself."

Connie laughed weakly, but didn't say anything. She served the tea.

"Mind if I say something?" Alana asked.

"No, go ahead," Connie replied.
"I'm going to be real honest."
"Okay."
"This house is depressing. Gives me the creeps."
"*Me, too*," Jonathan agreed.
"I don't believe you'll get well in this house. There is...depressing energy here," Alana asserted.

Sighing, Connie looked around the kitchen. "My grandfather built this house in the 1880s. I was born here. Only place I've ever lived."

"Where are your parents?" Camille wanted to know.

"Oh, they died a ...a few years ago."

"Didn't you ever get married?" Jonathan asked.

Connie shook her head no.

"How are your treatments with Kathleen coming?" Alana asked.

Connie's face brightened, "Oh, she's wonderful. And the herbs she gives me, I can feel them working. Only..."

"Only what?"

"Only I guess I'm not as much behind the program as I should be."

"Meaning?"

Connie stared into her tea cup. She wiped the tears from her eyes with the back of her hand and said, "I don't know. I'm tired."

Camille looked very concerned. "Are you tired of being alive?"

"Maybe."

"Do you really want to live here all by yourself?" Alana asked.

"No, but it's my home."

"No. This is *nobody's* home," Alana said. "Just a house with bad memories and lots of ghosts."

"There really *is* a ghost here," Camille whispered. "He's over in the corner. He's mad."

Connie turned white. "What does he look like?"

"He's real thin and old, with white hair, and his face looks mean."

"Does he have three fingers missing from one hand?"

"Yes."

"Jesus, it's my father. He still won't leave me alone," Connie said and broke down sobbing. "Go away you dirty old man! Go away and leave me alone! Let me die in peace!" she yelled.

"He's laughing," Camille said. "He's *not* a very nice man."

"He molested me when I was a child. Kept after me all the way up to when I was a teenager. I hated him. I still do," Connie said bitterly.

"Why not just leave?" Alana suggested. "Let him have the house. You're not happy here anyway."

"I know I'm not. But where would I live? Nancy says all the places out there have people in them. She says you have things all worked out. Where would I live?" she asked, sounding like a frightened, sad, unwanted child.

Alana explained about the trailers. "We found a trailer for Kate and Karen. Moved it out there a couple of days ago. Emil and Jeff are looking for another one. We'll find a place for you."

"But..." Connie started to protest.

"You *belong* out there," Alana replied emphatically. "You're part of the family."

"Doesn't feel like it. I haven't done anything to help you guys."

"That's because you've been sick," Alana replied. "You would've helped if you'd been feeling better. Right?"

"Yes, I want to be part of the community," she said. "I had a dream about all of you. Mind if I tell you?"

"I'd love to hear it," Alana answered.

"Well," she began, wiping her eyes, "we were all walking down a path. All of us. You were there, too," she said to the children. "Then the sun started to go down. You, Alana, you said you'd go with me for awhile, but that you'd have to go back home before it got too dark to see. And the children would have to go with you. Boy, did *that* ever scare me! But I knew I'd have to on by myself. And I did. What do you make of my dream?"

"I'm not sure," Alana replied evasively, at that moment

not wanting to say what she thought the dream signified. Instead, she said simply, "How about if we pack a few things and just go. Lock the house and let your father have it?"

"Yes," Connie began, "let's do that." Then, looking doubtful, she asked, "You *sure*?"

Alana took Connie's hand, pulling her to her feet. "Where are your suitcases?"

They packed a few things, left a note for Nancy telling her that Connie had moved out to the valley, and closed up the house.

Later that afternoon, the community got together to celebrate Connie's arrival. Vicki brought in a lounge chair for Connie; Evelyn donated her favorite afghan; Nancy brought some pillows.

Anna plumped up the pillows and straightened the afghan. "You comfy?" she asked Connie.

"Uh-huh," Connie answered. "I feel like I'm home. Heck, I *am* home. Thanks everyone." Turning to Kate and Karen she asked, "You sure it won't be any trouble for you, me staying with you?"

Kate shook her head. "Nope. Not at all. The kids love being outside in their tents, so that frees up the other bedroom. Nope, no problem. You're welcome to stay as long as you want."

Jeff had been watching. He asked Connie, "We'll have the other trailer in a few days. I assume you and Nancy will share it. Is that the plan?"

"Sounds perfect to me," Connie responded.

"And I'm fine sleeping in my tent for awhile," Nancy said.

"Why not move your tent over close to us?" Camille suggested.

"Well..."

"Oh yes, please do!" Jonathan pleaded.

"You two are hard to resist," Nancy said and laughed. "Okay, I'll do it."

Evelyn came and sat next to Connie. "I talked with

Homecoming

Kathleen, gave her directions how to get out here. She says she'll visit in a day or two with more herbs."

Connie nodded. "Thanks."

"You think *I* could talk to her when she's here?" Karen asked. "With the baby due in a couple of months, I'd like her opinion on some things, like the right foods...and herbs and..."

"Sure," Evelyn replied. "Kathleen knows lots about nutrition. And lots about herbs. She said she'd teach us about herbs if we want."

"Great," Alana said. "I met her a couple of months ago in Mount Shasta. She has wonderful, loving, healing energy."

Andrew had a question. "Does she know about wild crafting?"

Evelyn looked blank for a minute, then said, "Wild crafting? Oh, you mean finding herbs in nature?"

Andrew nodded. "I can spot some, but there's lots more. I'd sure be obliged if she could show us where they grow and when to pick them. And about drying them and all."

"I'll ask her next time I see her, Andrew," Evelyn promised.

Alana glanced around at the beautiful, shining faces gazing back at her. "Sweetie," she said to Jeff, "hand me the box of tissues will you, I'm going to need them." She yanked a couple out of the box and wiped her eyes. "We're all here now. We're home."

They nodded. And many of them had tears in *their* eyes.

Alana continued, "I guess there's no way of telling what will happen. Some of you may leave and others may come. That's the way the Universe is—everything changes. But for now we're all home. We're home," she repeated simply.

They opened their hearts to receive the beautiful truth of Alana's words.

After a couple of minutes of silence, Connie lifted herself up and made an announcement: "I guess you all know how sick I am. I don't look so good and I feel even worse. But..." She was momentarily unable to continue. No one hurried her. "But like Alana said, this *is* home. *My* home. I've been doing lots of thinking about the place I *thought* was my home...and it isn't. So, I've decided to sell the house and also the pasture in back. I've had somebody after me for years to sell it. He'll pay me in gold, too."

"Are people still using gold?" Karen asked. "I thought..."

"There've been some stories about people being arrested," Jeff replied. "But I'm not sure I believe it. Propaganda more than likely. Scare stories."

Connie continued, "I want to use some of the money to build a yurt. Guess I'm a round-house person, too," she said to Jeff and Alana. Then she looked over at Nancy and said, "It's your home, too, if you want."

"Yes, Connie, I'd like that. But I don't have any money, so..."

Connie shook her head. "No problem, there's plenty of *that*." She closed her eyes and appeared to go deep within herself, then opened them again and went on, "The other thing I want to do is to buy a building for our community."

Jeff looked surprised. "You mean the meeting place we've been talking about?"

"Yes," Connie answered. "The meeting place. A place where we can all get together and cook dinner if we want. Or watch movies."

"Or listen to Kathleen give us classes about herbs," Evelyn added.

"Or have dances," Cassandra said.

"Or put on plays," Kate added.

Alana knew that Connie had given them a special gift. Kneeling in front of her, Alana silently embraced her, feeling Connie's heart open. She also felt the frightened child within this woman. Alana went back to her seat and others came and held Connie. No words were spoken, or if they were, they were whispered, heard only by Connie and the one who spoke them.

The group sat silently. Fifteen minutes passed and the

Homecoming

only sounds were those coming through the open window: the wind sighing through the trees, a ground squirrel chittering in the distance, a bird singing.

Vicki was the first to speak. "I can't stand it any longer," she said, looking at Jerry. "There's something happening here. Right, Jerry?"

"Well..." Jerry began, looking embarrassed.

"I'm looking at you and Veda and there's something different about you two. You going to let us in on it?" Vicki asked.

Jerry glanced at Veda. She nodded. "We got married yesterday," Jerry answered.

"So *that's* where you were!" Anna said. "I wondered where you two were going in such a hurry."

More hugs and kisses as people congratulated Veda and Jerry.

"How come you didn't say anything?" Brian asked.

"They're shy," Andrew answered for them.

Jerry nodded at Andrew and smiled. Then he looked at Veda, the love obvious in his eyes, and said, "Yeah, shy. But...gotta be more to it than that. So, why didn't we?"

"I believe we were...afraid to say anything," Veda replied.

"Boy, you got that right!" Jerry exclaimed. "I was *really* afraid. Hey guys, I never ever thought I'd get married, especially to someone I've only known for a couple of months. I mean, wow! Can you *believe* this!"

"What were *you* afraid of?" Cassandra asked Veda.

"Maybe that if we started thinking about what Spirit was asking us to do we would back out. Following Spirit is sometimes...well sometimes it's best not to think too much. Just *do* it," she said, her face reddening with embarrassment. "I'm afraid I'm not explaining myself very well."

Alana reached for Veda's hand and said, "No, you're doing fine. Maybe later, when you two are ready, you could tell us more about how this happened. You know, about following Spirit."

"Certainly," Veda answered. "Now, I would like to tell you something," she said in her quiet voice. Most of them assumed she was going to speak about her marriage to Jerry, but instead she announced, "In honor of all of us being home, as Alana has so beautifully stated, Saint Germain has a few words to say to us. Everyone agreeable?"

They didn't say anything, just closed their eyes, went within, and welcomed Saint Germain.

"Greetings, beloved ones," came Saint Germain's hearty, loving voice. "And how is everyone on this auspicious afternoon?"

"Fine," many murmured.

"Indeed you are," he said, surveying the audience, love shining forth from his eyes. "Much swirls around you these days, does it not? Those in what you would call the outside world—the *other* world, the other *Earth*—have careened crazily off in another direction, a direction you understand yet do not resonate with. They have donned other costumes—and a quick costume change at that—and are acting in a drama you have not auditioned for and have no desire to play a part in. But, although the outside world is swirling and stormy, you are calm and peaceful, much as you might be if you were in the eye of a hurricane. Is this not so?"

They agreed with him.

"You have allowed much for yourselves, much joy and much expansiveness. And yet, in a real sense, your work has just begun, for many forces will try to pull apart what you have created here," Saint Germain warned.

"You mean those in the outside world who are threatened by what we've done?" Jeff asked. "Like the Gray Men and Ancon and the World Federation Council?"

"Yes," Saint Germain responded. "And yet, we have spoken of these forces many times and you are in the understanding of this, are you not?" he asked Jeff.

"Well, yes, I think so," Jeff replied. "So, are you saying there are other forces, ones we don't know about?"

Before Saint Germain could respond, Evelyn asked, "Do you mean we need to watch our pictures. Not watch them, that's not what I meant. Saying it that way sounds like we're all at the movies," she said, laughing at herself.

Homecoming 243

"Indeed, you *are*," Saint Germain responded humorously.

"Right," Evelyn replied, "but what I meant was, we have to change our pictures of reality, the struggle pictures, our "us against them" pictures. Is that what you meant?"

"Indeed, this is also a great truth."

"But you're meaning something else, aren't you?" Cassandra asked.

Saint Germain took a moment before answering. "How is it that you see the task ahead of you, this bringing into manifestation of your dream of community?"

"To me the task is to *allow* the dream," Brian replied.

"Indeed. And what would be in the way of this allowing?"

"I know the answer is *us*," Nancy said. "But I'm not sure what that means exactly."

Saint Germain went on, "The forces, the pressures that will act to tear down your beloved community will come not from the outside. They will come from *within*, from the aspect of your inner self that sees your dream of community—of brotherhood and sisterhood—as *dangerous*."

"*Dangerous?*" Jerry asked, sounding as if he didn't believe what Saint Germain had said. "I don't understand. We *want* this community."

Saint Germain responded quickly, "Indeed, that is *not* the case, not entirely. Let me tell you a story, beloved ones, a story to help you understand what I have said." He gave them a few moments to stretch out on the floor, to get some water, to go to the bathroom. Then he told them his story. "Once, long ago, an expedition from a distant star system came to Earth to explore and map the planet. They decided the best way to accomplish this was to set out on foot, so each of them chose a different direction and began walking. They were not afraid of becoming lost, for these beings were highly telepathic and were in constant communication with each other. One member volunteered to stay in the base camp to guide his brothers and sisters back home when the time came for them to reassemble.

"These beings were a family, like an Earth family, only

closer. They functioned as a unit, although each was also an individual in his or her own right.

"I will tell you the story of one of these beings, of Mishra, a male; but understand, I could as easily tell the story of a woman. It would be the same.

"Mishra's journey led him into the jungle. Saying good-bye to the others, he set out, full of love for his brothers and sisters and full of love and excitement for their mission.

"The jungle fascinated him, and he stopped every few feet to admire some new plant or bird or animal. Never had he seen such a profusion of form and color, for on his home planet there was none such as this. He telepathed his discoveries to the rest of the group. They shared his excitement and the joy of his journey, and he shared theirs.

"Selecting a huge tree that seemed to reach to the stars, he bedded down for the night, feeling warm and comfortable and safe.

"The next morning, he discovered that the communication from the others was occasionally interrupted by some annoying static. Such things had happened before on other of their explorations, so he didn't worry. Besides, he was enjoying himself and he didn't want to think about what might be causing the interference.

"Next day, the static worsened, and he had to stop for minutes at a time to wait for the transmission to clear up. When he telepathed his concern, his comrades told him not to worry, that he might simply be in a magnetic field that was making transmission temporarily difficult. Mishra wanted to believe them, and mostly he did, but he also felt the first small, dark tendrils of fear creep into his heart. He did not understand at first, for fear was an almost unheard of emotion for these beings. They were a family—part of a *whole*—and they knew they could rely on each other at any time. Even more important, they knew who they were: *They were Divine Beings*. This they knew beyond any doubt. Reminding himself of these things, Mishra felt better. Nevertheless, the fear soon returned and he did not like the feeling.

"For the next two days, he sat under a tree pondering his dilemma. After much inner deliberation, he decided to continue. But his almost constant fear dimmed his vision and dampened his joy of discovery.

"He proceeded carefully now, pausing often to peer nervously into the thick jungle. Was something following him? That night as he stopped to rest, his worst fears materialized: he could no longer receive *any* transmission from the others. He decided to sleep, hoping things would be better in the morning.

"But they weren't. Still unable to receive the others, he panicked, running wildly through the jungle, hoping desperately he was headed in the right direction. Hours later, he fell to the jungle floor, exhausted. A tear ran down his cheek as he realized that he might never again see his brothers and sisters. This emotion—this sadness—was also a new feeling for him.

"For days he wandered aimlessly, hoping he would find his way back to the base camp. But he did not. He now spent more and more time foraging for food and making sure he found a safe place to sleep at night. A few short days ago he would have made his bed anywhere in the jungle, but now, it seemed to him, danger lurked behind every tree. He slept poorly.

"The days turned into months and then into years, *and he forgot the original mission, forgot he was part of a wondrous family, forgot everything except that the world suddenly seemed very hostile...and that he must survive at all costs.* He felt alone and naked and frightened. At night, huddled in the branch of a tree, listening to the ominous sounds of the jungle, he sometimes looked longingly up at the stars; he felt something tug at his consciousness, felt something call to him from deep within his being. What? Why did his eyes return repeatedly to the stars? Why did they fascinate him so? He didn't know, and anyway, he had better not waste any energy in such frivolous musings; after all, tomorrow would come all too soon and he would need his wits about him to survive.

"Beloved ones," Saint Germain began, "Mishra is

within each of you. He is your Separated Self, and *he whispers in your ear that your community is dangerous.*"

"Saint Germain, why does Separated Self believe this?" Vicki wanted to know.

"Because Separated Self believes that you are in a struggle for survival. *Always*. Thus, to join together with others, to open one's heart, to truly become a community and a family, to dissolve the walls separating you from others, is foolish and dangerous."

Kate nodded in understanding. "So is it Separated Self that keeps us feeling that others are against us...or *could* be against us?"

"Indeed, to Separated Self *everyone* is a potential enemy, even those you love, those you would never ordinarily view as the enemy," Saint Germain replied.

Looking discouraged, Nancy said, sadness in her voice, "So it's really hopeless. After all, human beings have been believing this for thousands of years, or maybe even millions of years, so what makes us think *we* will be able to live differently?"

Saint Germain surveyed those who sat before him and said, "There are no enemies. Those you call the Gray Men, the being Ancon, the Corporation, and the World Federation Council, these are not your enemies and they never have been. Neither is your Separated Self. Thus, there is nothing to fear and no one to battle with. Give up the battle. Give up the struggle. Bring true peace and harmony and upliftment to every aspect of self."

Andrew also looked puzzled. "Saint Germain, brother, how can we have peace within ourselves? I know the voice of this Separated Self of which you speak. His is an angry voice. He speaks to me every day. He is telling me right now that I am not to trust what you are saying. How can we be free of this?"

"I agree with Andrew," Brian began, "Separated Self is such a *part* of us. He's our ego, isn't he?"

Saint Germain took his time answering. "He is a *part* of your ego, a part that has been taught to mistrust and to see enemies everywhere."

"Sure, but he's still our ego," Brian countered. "And we have to have an ego to get along in the world, don't we? So we can't just toss this Separated Self out. Right? We need it. But, if it's always working against us..."

"Indeed, this aspect of you *is* important, crucial to your functioning in physicality," Saint Germain replied.

"So it *is* hopeless," Evelyn said.

"Indeed not," Saint Germain said. "Remember Mishra? He *volunteered* to go into the jungle, did he not?"

"Okay, so he volunteered," Connie said from her lounge chair. "What difference does *that* make?"

Saint Germain's eyes never lost their humor. "Let us go on with our story. Now gone many years—perhaps hundreds of years measured in your Earth time—Mishra is one day picking some wild berries when he sees in front of him others who look like himself. He is startled, frightened! He sees danger and he prepares to defend himself! But they smile and call his name, telling him he has been lost and now is found! He does not believe them! They are trying to trick him to get his weapons and his food! But they are patient and kind with him, knowing what he has been through and knowing he needs tender loving care and time to trust them. Little by little, he *does* trust them. Why? Remember, he was once a part of a beloved family and knew the joys of union and connection. This understanding has not been permanently eradicated from his soul memory—for truly nothing ever is—*and deep in his soul he longs for reunion, for remembering, for community*. And so it is done.

"It is the same with your Separated Self. This aspect of you wants to remember, wants to put down its burden and be reunited with the larger Self of which it is a part. *Separated Self desires true community*—community with *you*—just as you desire community with others. It needs to be talked to is all, talked to and loved. Patience, beloved ones. Separated self is *not* your enemy. *It is a part of you that has volunteered to be "lost" and now is "found."*

Jerry looked confused. "What's the point? Why would our Separated Self have volunteered to be lost and then found?" he asked.

"That is the subject for another day," Saint Germain answered. "I will tell you this: To be lost and then to be found is an aspect of this you call the human experience, *and you have all agreed to be human...for now.*" Saint Germain smiled. "Something of a puzzle, is it not? I will leave you to ponder it for awhile."

They were all used to his "tricks" and so this did not bother them.

"Is it truly as simple as you say?" Emil wondered. "Can our healing—our reunion with our larger Self—be done with talking and with love?"

"Of course," Saint Germain replied. "But you must *do* it. Thinking about it will not accomplish this integration—this *homecoming. You must do the inner work.* I will be with you to assist you, as will many others. We will speak of this again, for it is not an easy thing at first to comprehend. But for now I will say good-bye. Do not forget—you are the dreamers. And remember, your Separated Self has temporarily forgotten how to dream these dreams...these dreams *you* dream. It is no more complicated than that. Good-bye for now, beloved ones."

They stretched and yawned and talked among themselves; but it was small talk, for Saint Germain was still with them, much as when two lovers physically part only to know that the other has not really left. Saint Germain's words sang in their hearts for many hours after the channeling. His message and his love uplifted them! They could do this! It would take some work, possibly some very difficult work, but they could do it!

After they had eaten a simple dinner, Alana and Jeff walked up the hill to their favorite spot. Alana could smell Spring coming, and with it the beautiful renewal of Mother Earth. And she felt the love and the joy in her heart. She reached for Jeff's hand.

They sat on their "bench" and surveyed the valley.

"This valley, this dream—all we've done—feels so *fragile* sometimes," Jeff said.

"Best to take things one day at a time," Alana answered. "Stay in the moment. But for today, we're doing it, we're really *doing* it."

Suddenly, a small flying saucer appeared over the rim of the valley, hovered, lights blinking.

"Oh my God," Jeff exclaimed. "It's one of the saucers from Ancon's mother ship. See, near the top, the World Federation logo? What's it doing here?"

"Watching us. Checking us out," Alana answered.

"So, they know about us?"

"Oh sure. These beings...they're so intelligent...they've known about us all along."

"Boy, that makes me uneasy."

"Why?"

"I guess I don't like being watched," Jeff answered. "And I guess I don't like the feeling that these guys may be smarter than I am. Makes me nervous."

"Vulnerable?"

"Yeah."

"Kind of naked?"

"Right again."

Alana looked at him and grinned. "I have some of the same feelings. But...but it has nothing to do with intelligence. Just because they're more intelligent and just because they can flit around the world in seconds doesn't mean they're wise in the ways of the heart. And just because they're intelligent—even super intelligent—doesn't mean they can stop us from having our dream."

"Maybe they can't stop us, but they can make things more difficult," Jeff argued.

"No, not even that. Everything depends on us. On us and on Spirit. That's why this path we're on is so exciting...*and* so scary at times. The outcome doesn't depend on anything, or anyone, but *us*. Isn't that the greatest thought you could ever hope to have? That everything depends on *us*?"

Jeff caught her energy. "Yes. I forget sometimes."

The spacecraft departed as quickly as it came, and in the place where it had been, the first evening star twinkled in the deepening blue sky. Alana giggled and said, "Star light, star bright, first star I see tonight, I wish I may...I wish I might...have this wish I wish tonight."

"And what did you wish for, sweetie," Jeff wanted to know.

"To remember I am one."

Looking puzzled, Jeff asked, "You mean a star?"

"Yes," she answered and looked up at the sky. "A star and a daffodil and a dolphin and the bird's sweet song and the wind and a human being, and more, much more. *Everything*." She laughed softly at the thought of this, and the sound of her laughter drifted down to the valley floor. A deer lifted her head and listened. Alana's laughter was a familiar sound, a comforting sound, a valley sound, and she put her head back down and slept.

To be concluded in: *Let There Be Light*,
the third volume in the Family of Light Trilogy.

About the Author

Michael Colin Macpherson

Like many of the characters in this story, I, too, was pulled to Mount Shasta...by Spirit.

I live a few miles from the Mountain, with my two cats, Mr. Squeaks and Sasha. I write, I putter in the garden, and I occasionally offer my services as a spiritual guide. This keeps my brain busy, so that, hopefully, it does not get in the way of my *real* work...which is to follow Spirit without hesitation.

ORDER FORM
All prices include tax, shipping, and handling*

PLEASE SEND ME:

Homecoming $13.00 ea. Quantity___ $____

Remembering $12.00 ea. Quantity___ $____

Checks payable to:
Michael Macpherson TOTAL ENCLOSED: $___

*Books shipped special fourth class "book rate." Please allow 2-3 weeks for delivery. For Priority Mail, add $2.00 for 1st book and $.50 for each additional book.

_____

Name(please print)

_____

Street address or P.O. Box

_____

City   State   Zip

_____

Phone
Checks must be U.S. funds drawn on U.S. Bank

Green Duck Press
P.O. Box 651
Mount Shasta, CA 96067
To order direct by phone : (916) 926-6261